SONS OF THE CRYSTAL MIND

BOOK ONE
OF
DIAMOND ROADS

Andrew Wallace

AC Experiments

Diamond Roads: Sons of the Crystal Mind
First Edition (2014)

Copyright © 2014 Andrew Wallace

All rights reserved. This book or any portion thereof may not be reproduced or used in any manner whatsoever without the express written permission of the publisher except for the use of brief quotations in a book review.

ISBN: 1508512817
EAN: 978-1508512813

Published by AC Experiments
info@acexperiments.com

Cover design by Deborah Joyce

Units #23#1106*737123*1 to #23#2507*737123*44 [edited]
From the Accumulated Experience Realm Account
of CHARITY FREESTONE
Diamond City
2401

1

Darkness ripens to a honey glow as day lights come on over Centria. It reflects off delicate clouds, the part-hidden ceiling above them and shines finally into the apartment, where my breathing returns to normal after this morning's immersive workout.

It was a tough one. In the shared two-hour simulation, various Centrian colleagues and I fought off a MidZone incursion by orange-clad New Form Enterprise soldiers. They had modern weapons. We used Old World projectile rifles that were much tougher to use, although that didn't stop me shooting five of the NFE.

I still clutch the rifle although I've deposited the simulator, whose built-in armour, paddles and restraints gave the workout its bruising physicality. Each muscle is a cluster of dull pain as I place the weapon on the floor. I ignore the discomfort and click DEPOSIT in my ifarm. The floor absorbs the rifle and it lies encased in clear, unfaceted diamond. After a second the rifle vanishes as the Basis breaks it down into its constituent molecules and transfers them back to my account, which rises by 187 kilos.

"Charity."

I stand with effort and turn to see the holo of a kindly middle-aged woman with shoulder-length grey hair.

"Doctor?" I say, surprised.

"Your heart rate activated the ifarm's emergency medical interface."

I clap my hand over my heart angrily, as if it has betrayed me.

"Oh," I say and then become conscious of over-reacting.

"That's... annoying."

"It happens."

"Yes but my performance must be exceptional if I'm ever going to get promoted."

"Your performance was exceptional."

"It wasn't. Some NFE woman giffed a twenty-metre tower right under me and then blew it up so I fell to my 'death'."

I shudder, remembering. I will do anything to avoid a repeat of that experience, which I suppose is the point.

"Charity, even for a fit twenty-three year old girl-"

"I need to do better. Imagine if I messed up a workout and got demoted..."

"That's not very likely is it? Your sister is doing amazingly well. I'm sure that's got something to do with you."

"It's nothing to do with me."

"Aren't you her secretary?"

"No! I mean, I'm more of an executive... er..."

There's an awkward pause as my rudeness taints the air even more odiously than the sodden singlet I'm wearing. It was white when I giffed it but is now grey and streaked with red.

"You need to let the Basis heal you," the doctor says tactfully.

"Right, yes. How much?"

"43 kilos."

The medical package appears as a purchase option on the transparent screens over my eyes. I pull off the singlet and throw it into a corner, where it lands with a slap and is absorbed. Blood trickles from injuries in my sides and legs; my jaw feels odd and the left shoulder is numb where I 'landed'.

I swig water from a glass by the bed and then carefully lie down on my back. The surface beneath me is neither hot nor cold, as if it has matched itself to my body temperature. I click BUY on the medical package and sink quickly into the floor. There is no bowing or concavity; I simply pass through the horizontal plane, which closes over me. The edge tickles where it meets my skin.

In a few moments I come to rest with the soles of the doctor's shoes visible about a metre to the left of my face. The silence is total.

No vibrations are transmitted from elsewhere in the tower or the city at large. I can breathe although my chest is motionless, while my weight has not displaced any part of the floor. I don't know how the Basis does this; I don't think anyone does anymore.

Internal and external wounds begin to itch as the healing begins. I'm used to the sensation and can work without being distracted, so I access the ifarm to arrange another of Ursula's pre-wedding parties. After a while the doctor appears in the lower left of my vision.

"Do you mind if I ask how things are going?" she says.

I enter a clean white virtual space so we can speak.

"They're going very well," I reply, warily.

"You seem to be under pressure."

"Nothing I can't cope with."

I would like to tell her more; however, I don't know who else is listening or which files my replies will end up in. I have to be perfect or I risk losing everything.

"I love Centria you see," I tell her.

"We all do," she replies.

"No, but I really do," I say with a surge of pride. "It's amazing here at the heart of Diamond City, where it's safe, where anything that matters happens. I mean look at it!"

"Yes, it's the most beautiful part of the city."

We reflect on the glory of our home, encased in its gleaming sphere.

"So how are plans for Ursula's wedding?" she asks.

"On track."

"Really? When I organised mine it was chaos."

I grunt as something knits together in my rib cage.

"She must love him very much," the doctor says.

The wedding is an advertising opportunity for the corporate merger between Centria and VIA Holdings.

"Yes," I say.

"How do you feel about the man who's stealing your big sister away?"

I hate him.

"Balatar is a fine man," I say. "Plus, what a catch! Son of the Chief of VIA Holdings…"

"It's the nearest we'll get to a royal wedding."

VIA Holdings are a bunch of subs. However, they possess an enormous quantity of liquid capital, which Centria wants in order to fix its position as the most powerful company in Diamond City.

"I hope so," I say. "The weather will be astonishing – I hope!"

I'm repeating myself because I'm nervous. I'd like her to go. Her role is to keep me company rather than do the actual healing but I was abrupt to her earlier so guilt prevents a swift end to the conversation.

"It will be," the doctor says. "There hasn't been this much excitement since the end of the Ruby War a year ago."

"Now that was a party," I say as if I had something to do with organising it which, regrettably, I didn't.

Our virtual space becomes the view in the apartment floor again, which shifts as the Basis expels me back to the surface. I get up unsteadily and check myself in a holo. Wounds have closed into red streaks and the jaw swelling is reduced. My thick blonde hair hangs in sweaty clumps and I push it aside to check the impact abrasion, which is now just a ripple in the skin. By this afternoon it will be gone, along with most of the pain.

I continue to stare at the holo as if it will give me answers. Instead all I see is an athletic girl of average height whose breasts could be a bit bigger, especially compared to those of her voluptuous sister. I can get my chest enlarged of course but physical alterations might hide some essential truth about me, as if obscuring a clue…

"You're quite lovely you know," the doctor says.

"I've got nice hair," I concede automatically, "but Ursula is the beautiful one."

I squint at the holo, suddenly confused. The holo squints back.

"Are you all right?" the doctor asks.

The holo and I turn to face her at the same time.

"Y-" I start.

I turn to the holo again. Eyes whose colour is hard to determine stare back at me. Are they blue, green, aqua or grey? Each iris is surrounded by a barely visible ring of gold that darkens at the outer edge. Whose genetic heritage is that? I click off the holo and feel oddly alone without its bothersome familiarity.

"I'm fine," I say. "Thank you for this morning, for your help."

"Take care Charity," the doctor says and fades away.

I look around my apartment. I like to think of the broad, kidney-shaped room as minimally styled although the bed used to be Ursula's so that's too big and ornate. The only decoration is a large picture of her on the far wall and a smaller framed one of Mum and Dad beside it. I can never decide on any other home ornamentation so I don't bother. For the first time the apartment strikes me as sparse.

I gif a bath, which rises out of the floor in one corner and fills itself with steaming, foamy water. I climb in and sink all the way under. The foam scrubs dirt off me and heat resonates through my jangling muscles like pleasure. Being underwater is nothing like being in the Basis. Water is a simple element. The Basis is not simple. Rumour has it the Sons of the Crystal Mind worship it as a god.

Mum calls. I don't accept; she will want to discuss the argument we had last night when she asked why I was still single. I told her I wasn't very good at relationships because I don't know who I am. She patiently explained yet again that I had been given to Dad and her as a baby to bring up from somewhere in Centria. She doesn't know where. For once I pushed it and said with her job she should be able to find out. She got angry and said to even talk about abusing her position was to risk becoming an ex.

I thought that was a bit much. Not only is Ursula the Face of Centria and People's Princess, but Mum and Dad are former solders and loyal agents in the Centrian Security Service. Dad risks his life for Centria on a daily basis. He has been on some mysterious mission out in Diamond City for nearly a month. Out there! Among subs, Blanks and the kind of entrepreneurs who will drug you into leaving your kilos to them and then cut your throat.

Thankfully, Dad has got Mum as his Operator. She monitors the mission and supplies him with 'intel' as she calls it to keep him alive. Mum is her usual secretive self about their work although she has been uncharacteristically preoccupied lately.

She calls again. Later Mum!

She calls a third time with an urgent tag, which is strange.

Surfacing, I take the call. Mum looks wild-eyed and panicky. I've never seen her panic before.

"Charity, log out of the ifarm and use your Aerac to call me direct. Do it now."

"But-"

She's gone.

Log out of the ifarm? That's a company offence. The Aer network is free for everyone in Diamond City and can't be intercepted any more than transactions with the Basis can. However, in Centria we enjoy the status of an ifarm interface between us and the Aer.

Admittedly, an ifarm does the same job as an Aer account; both facilities handle communication, ID and personal finance. Everyone in Diamond City has an Aerac but no one in Centria uses theirs; without an ifarm they won't get paid and the enclave's doors will literally not open.

Mum obviously doesn't want Security to hear what she has to say. What is so wrong that she wants me to break her precious rules?

Nervous, I climb stiffly out of the bath and deposit it. I click on the option of my usual blue suit, which flows out of the floor straight onto me like a liquid and blooms into the final design in three seconds. Once finished, the suit sucks off the bathwater and it pools on the floor to be absorbed. I pull a sleeve over my face and hair to dry them and then close my eyes.

I take a deep breath and log off the ifarm. As the familiar visual overlay fades I tense in expectation of the door shattering to admit Anton Jelka and his security guards or, worse, Gethen Karkarridan.

Nothing happens.

I call Mum on the Aerac. She answers at once, her image on my right eye screen.

"Charity, listen to me," she says. "There's something wrong with Centria."

She shakes her head as if to clear it.

"We're finding out such strange things and they don't make sense. But I can tell you there is a threat, a terrible threat to us.

"I don't even know if the wedding is a good idea now, whether or not it will keep you both safe. VIA Holdings… What does the VIA stand for? And the New Form Enterprise… Darling, they may not be what we think they are."

For a moment she is so distracted she actually seems mad. Her eyes focus again. Her gaze is frightening.

"And Charity, please, whatever happens, stay away from the Sons of the Crystal Mind-"

She looks to the left suddenly and the connection is cut.

I call her back but there's no reply. I call Ursula. No reply. I call Dad. Nothing. A terrible dread like sickness creeps up from the soles of my feet to the top of my head.

There's something wrong with Centria.

But what?

2

Centria's crystalline architecture changes regularly. Somehow, the Basis is able to calculate the layout without crushing anyone or removing allocated space and each morning the view is slightly different, as if Centria needs a million different ways of admiring itself. My apartment for instance is in a slim, elegant thirty-storey tower which hangs like a spindle between six walkways that radiate out from the middle to connect with other chambers and platforms. Yesterday, the walkways were at the bottom.

The ifarm lets me know Security is here by opening a little window in the bottom right of my vision that shows four armed guards outside. I cross the room and open the door. There's a momentary dislocation as I look at both the ifarm window and the guards themselves, then the window closes and I stare fixedly at the nearest guard in a way that seems odd even to me.

"Please come with us Miss Freestone," the guard says.

I follow them, giddy with fear as we walk down the short corridor to an opening onto a docking platform. We walk through and I see myself reflected in the mirrored exterior of a spherical Centrian Security cruiser. The hatch between two of the vehicle's four pyramidal Basis interaction pads slides open and I step on board. From inside I can see out in every direction except down through the flat, opaque floor.

Ursula sits by the door in one of the six inward-facing seats. Her physical similarity to Mum, always a reminder of my difference to them, is even harder to cope with today. Both have very dark hair, slightly absurd long legs and improbable but real curves. They share an offbeat beauty: part dominatrix, part girl next door.

As Ursula gets up I can tell she has been crying. I throw myself at her, she catches me and we hold each other so tightly neither can breathe. Finally, we let go and I look up at her.

"It's Mum and Dad," she says.

I'm out of breath with apprehension. Ursula sits, pulls me down next to her and grips my hand. As the soldiers settle into their seats the ship takes off.

"Mum's in a coma," she says finally. "They don't know how it happened. And Dad…" A strange guttural sound escapes her throat. Fresh tears run down her cheeks although she still manages to speak. "Dad has gone missing." She seems to writhe with grief and I fight an urge to do the same. "He isn't dead though."

"Y-you can't be sure of that," I say.

"I would know if he was."

I just nod, suddenly remembering a long-ago Harvest Day when Ursula and I were quite small, about seven and five respectively. It was evening and most of the decorations were up. Mum took our hands and led us into the big bedroom, where she got a box from a cupboard and carefully lifted out two plastic gold stars on frayed pieces of string. We knew immediately they were precious objects even though they were quite battered even then. 'These', Mum said, 'are from the Old World.'

Ursula and I stood open mouthed. Objects from the Old World are almost priceless. The Basis cannot make them because they are not constructed from kilos so Old World items are in short supply and there will never be any more. Mum handed one star to Ursula and the other to me so we could put them up, trusting us with the most valuable things she had…

Ursula watches me.

"We're going to see Mum," she says.

I don't want to see Mum; I want to remember her as she was although something in Ursula's voice stops me saying so. The cruiser lands but the guards stay where they are as Ursula gets off and I follow.

Mum and Dad live in a large two-storey house that stands alone on a promontory overlooking Centria. The garden around it is a simple arrangement of pools and plants in different shades of green. There are no flowers, which keeps the incongruous patch of land steady and soothing.

A little floating island hangs in the air nearby like a piece that has broken away. When we were small we would grow bridges across and run over to play there. The stream running around the island spirals down from steep grassy sides into a central pool with a transparent base so the enclave floor can be seen far below. I realise with a little shock that although the rest of Centria changes daily, the house and its surroundings have always stayed the same.

I push open the door and walk in to the main family room. It feels uncomfortably still. The sofa is the same tatty cloth one that's always been there, as if waiting for someone to come and jump on it or slouch across it or spill something on it. There are pictures of Ursula and me everywhere. The ones of Ursula are glamorous and provocative, all odd angles, red lips and outrageous poses. In the ones of me I look thoughtful and intense.

Between the pictures are cupboards full of objects Mum and Dad could gif on a daily basis but don't, preferring to re-use their possessions so they accrue in value. It's the same smart, sentimental oddness that compels Mum to grow actual ingredients like vegetables and cook with those instead of the stuff Ursula and I eat straight out of the Basis. My mouth waters at the memory of Mum's dinners.

I follow Ursula upstairs, feeling strangely formal. We pass my old room and then Ursula's, both kept as they were in case we come and stay which, I realise sadly, we never do. As Ursula enters Mum and Dad's room my nervousness turns to dread. Ursula stops. I move past her and stop as well.

Anton Jelka turns towards us and I stare at him. It's not just the Head of Security's unexpected presence. I cannot get on with a man so tense his face looks like it's being strangled by his expression, while he can't get on with a girl he regards as chaotic but who has sufficient influence to ensure her chaos becomes his problem. Ursula shifts impatiently beside me and I turn to the bed.

Mum looks asleep. Her chest rises and falls. I hesitate as I reach for her as if whatever it is might be contagious and then touch her forehead anyway. She feels the same; no warmer or cooler than normal. One of her arms is outside the cover and a tiny tube from the floor goes into it. There's a small crease between her eyes, as if she is frozen at the point of pretending she's not in pain.

"It's some kind of artificially induced coma," Anton Jelka says.

"Induced how?" Ursula says.

"We don't know," Anton says.

He seems defensive.

"Via the ifarm," Ursula says.

I look at her in surprise.

"That's not possible," Anton says. "It could just as easily have been a beam or a projectile."

"Did you see anyone fire a beam or a projectile?" I ask.

"No," he says.

"You watch our every move," I say. "What's the point of that if someone can knock out one of your best agents without you knowing?"

Anton shakes his head in exasperation.

"What about Dad?" Ursula says.

"We last heard from Connor at the same time... this happened."

"It happened at exactly the same time?" I ask, astonished.

"Yes. It's as if whatever hit her affected him as well."

"Is he in the same state as Mum?" I say.

"If he was we would probably have found him," Anton says.

"Probably?" Ursula says.

"He may have been taken."

"By-?" I say.

"I don't want to speculate Charity," Anton says. "It won't help."

Ursula starts to cry; I put my arms around her and she bends her head down so her face rests on my shoulder.

"What...?" I try to think of the right words but my mind has become infuriatingly slow. "What is Centria doing for Dad now?"

"We sent ships to his last known location," Anton says, "but there was nothing."

"Where was that?"

"MidZone."

"Yes but what coordinates?"

"You're not going out there Charity."

I glare at him. Ursula stops crying and looks up. Anton shakes his head. His lack of officiousness is disarming; he looks like he is considering what to tell us and what to leave out.

"We sent our best troops," he says finally. "They scoured the surrounding area and utilised our contacts there. And then…" He looks away. "They were attacked. We don't know who by. We nearly lost two soldiers. Investigations will continue of course but… It doesn't look good for Connor. I'm sorry."

"Oh are you-?" Ursula starts.

"Yes Ursula, I am," Anton says. "I admired both of your parents, more I think than…" He stops himself. "Will either of you be staying here?"

The question is unexpected. Ursula and I look at each other.

"I thought not," Anton says.

I stare at Mum without really seeing her.

"Julie will be monitored by the ifarm's medical facility and if there is any change in her condition the three of us will know about it immediately. Security Control will seal the house. Only the three of us and Connor will be able to enter. We should leave now."

I don't want to go but I don't want to stay either. My mind is a jumble of confusion, rage and icy calm.

Ursula leans over Mum and cuddles her. Anton watches as I wait behind Ursula, conscious of being second in line. Ursula finally lets go and moves aside. I look down at Mum. I have never felt closer to her, or so far away.

A small, cold voice tells me that if Mum dies I won't find out who I am. Sick with guilt, I quickly kiss her on the forehead and pick up her familiar smell; slightly spicy and with remnants of the perfume she wears to complement it. Ursula smells the same. Again I am utterly different; I smell sweet like biscuits, or so I'm told.

I straighten, turn and walk quickly out of the bedroom. Ursula follows me downstairs with Anton behind us both.

"She called you," Anton says.

I pause by the front door, relieved my back is to Anton so he doesn't see me swallow nervously.

"She told you to log out of the ifarm," Anton says, "which you did. Why?"

I turn to him.

"She said she was worried about Dad," I say.

He watches me. I look back at him evenly. Ursula stares at us both.

"Is that it?" Anton says.

"Yes," I say.

"It is an offence to log out of the ifarm Charity. Under the circumstances I will let the matter go but don't do it again."

I nod as we step out of the front door. Anton walks past, glances back and I turn to see diamond flow up over the family home. As the shield hardens so does part of me: a violent, dread purpose I can feel in my limbs like a quiet hum. Anton looks at me closely as if he can see this change but leaves without another word.

"Company," Ursula says thickly.

I turn back to see four cruisers fly over the little island. The cruisers are much larger versions of the one that brought me and Ursula here and they reflect four distorted sliding realities as they descend past the front of the house. Once each cruiser has come to rest on its mirrored underside a hatch opens in the nearest and Ellery Quinn steps out.

Centria's Communications Director is a well-built woman who would not look out of place in the army. Her arms, which are proudly exposed as usual, are strong but retain their total femininity. Her walk is an unapologetic heavy-hipped waddle, as if she carries the richness of the world between her legs. In a place where beauty is easily affordable there is something endearingly true about Ellery's lined face and long, thick, crazy red hair. However, despite her dense physicality Ellery seems removed, like a watcher above the world. I imagine her real self is in another dimension with the body I see a grudging emanation into our crude universe.

I don't recognise her expression as she walks up and seizes me. I'm so astonished I go rigid. Ellery tightens her grip until I have no choice but to relax. When she turns her face to kiss the side of my head her lips touch my temple.

"Hn. Sorry," she says.

That's a lot of words for Ellery. The so-called Voice of Centria is the most taciturn person I've ever met. Most of her communication takes place on levels unimaginable to the rest of us. She will be juggling twenty conversations even now and her eyes are hard to meet. They seem to vibrate in a blur of bright green as she reads and processes a document every second.

I put my palms on her sides. I think this is the first time I have ever touched Ellery in four years of working for her. I wait for her to say something else but instead she lets go and extends her arm to Ursula, who slots herself into an embrace. Ellery strokes Ursula's hair. They seem far more comfortable with each other.

I sigh, turn and see who waits patiently beside the furthest ship. I am so astonished my mouth drops open. For a moment I forget everything that has happened.

Keris Veitch stands with her hands in the pockets of a richly embroidered long green dress. She wears Old World light brown boots with wooden heels and there are bangles with unfamiliar designs around her wrists. Her hair is a thick yellow braid with emeralds and flowers woven into it. Bright and lush, it coils over her shoulder and down between her breasts to her waist. She is tall, as tall as Ursula. However, Ursula, who until now I had thought the most beautiful and charismatic person I knew, is a wisp compared to Keris. Keris is like the lost sun.

Five warships hover behind her as if conjured from her sleeves. Roughly triangular with the flat plane uppermost, the warships are huge airborne fortresses capable of disgorging a hundred troops or a terrifying array of heavy-duty weapons. Each is dull red, presumably to signify danger although it's not necessary.

Somehow I know it's all right to stare at Keris even though as Chief of Centria she pretty much rules the world, what's left of it. She's got a mouth that always smiles, its corners turned up, with an ironic touch to her delicate lips. We sell thousands of patents to women who want the same effect although with Keris it is natural. The depth in her violet eyes speaks of tension between a terrible far away realm and this place, this moment. *I have seen such things*, she seems to say, *and no one can understand them except perhaps you.*

Like everyone, I've heard the legends. Some are quantifiably real, like when she led the Centrian army from the front against the New Form Enterprise during her victory in the Ruby War. I've seen footage of her flying her cruiser right into the throat of battle as cannons blasted ships apart either side. Other stories seem more suspect. One tells how she founded the Centria we know from the broken empire of Titan, the original dictator of Diamond City, using a single patent for dancing place mats. Still others, like the fact she personally created the first Blanks, may be true but probably aren't.

As I quietly dither she walks towards me. Feeling important yet absurd I look around self-consciously but Ursula and Ellery have gone. I turn back to find Keris there. She doesn't look much older than I am although there is a gravity to her that suggests she has always existed, like an element.

"Charity," she says.

Her voice is higher than I expected and there seem to be other voices hidden inside it, one for each person she will ever talk to. Keris extends a hand, expression calm as if every moment is a triumph for her.

"I'm Keris Veitch," she says. "It's lovely to meet you at last."

I take her hand. Her grip is delicate but strong, like the filigree cables that hang gigantic assemblies over Centria.

"Hello Keris. Thank you. For coming."

Her expression hardens as she looks over my head at Mum and Dad's house.

"I'm sorry to hear what happened to Connor and Julie. I'm very, very angry about it. I want you to know that we will… deal with those responsible."

I gaze up at the warships hanging in the sky outside our family home. Keris and I look back at each other at the same time.

"Good," I say.

She smiles.

"Walk with me," she says.

So I walk down the path I played on as a little girl with the ruler of the world.

"How are arrangements for the wedding?" Keris asks.

"Good," I say again, "very good."

"I hear you're doing well," Keris says.

Feeling dizzy I go to say something about arrangements but what comes out is:

"What was the mission Mum and Dad were on?"

Keris turns to me as if the question was entirely reasonable rather than an outrageous demand to breach security.

"They found the New Form Enterprise," she says.

I stare at her.

"Connor was tracking them through the Outer Spheres," Keris says. "One man with his skills was less conspicuous than a whole squad. It would seem the NFE found out and attacked Connor and Julie. I'm afraid that's all I know."

"What do I do?"

"What you're doing; the merger with VIA Holdings will make Centria even stronger. In the meantime, we are using all our resources to save Connor and Julie."

"Thank you Keris."

"Thank me when they're back with you."

Keris smiles almost shyly and then leans over to kiss my cheek. She turns and walks back to her cruiser while my face tingles where her smiling lips touched it. A moment later she's gone and the space over Mum and Dad's is as empty as it was when I was young.

3

I look at Ursula's naked body, aware that most people would pay a lot of kilos to see what I'm seeing now. It would be worth it. Somehow, she is perfect without following any of the rules. Her skin is the colour of cream and there is no mottling anywhere. Her breasts and her bottom seem disproportionately large, to the extent that she should have a body like Ellery's to handle them but she hasn't. Instead, she's got these long legs that taper to slender ankles and tiny feet that successfully defy balance, gravity and other minor considerations. Her stomach is flat without being very muscular and her waist is narrow although not grotesquely so. Dark hair forms a soft, inviting shadow between the sweet curves of her hips.

Holographic Ursulas wearing a range of dresses walk across my room past us. The colour and design of each denotes the length of time it will last; the greater the length, the higher the associated status. Some dresses even depict their lifespans, either woven in or stamped on the front. Each dress winks into nothing as Ursula dismisses it. She gets the selection down to three, none of which suit her so I quietly find a better alternative that costs 132 kilos.

"This grey one," I say.

Ursula scrunches her face slightly.

"Grey," she says. "Really?"

If I'm going to get that outfit on her I will have to buy it myself. My ifarm account contains 21,300 kilos. I pass my hand through the grey dress hologram and all the others vanish. As my account goes down to 21,168 kilos, the dress grows out of the floor straight onto Ursula. She looks down at it, unconvinced.

"Don't worry," I say.

My salon seat grows behind Ursula; she sits and her head sinks into the bulb so it looks like she's wearing an old-fashioned space helmet. I decide on her makeup; the seed picks up my instructions and sends them to the ifarm, which relays them to the salon. Soon the bulb melts away to reveal its dizzying enhancement of my sister's beauty: her hair its trademark gleaming dark curtain with an asymmetric fringe and her makeup a series of subtle shades that complement the dress. Ursula gets up and then sways.

Two days have passed since the mysterious attack on Mum and Dad. There has been no change in the situation and no answers have been forthcoming. Ursula and I rely on routines and engagements to get by; tonight for example is another pre-wedding party. We don't want to go but at least it will pass the time, distracting us from silence and restless, bleak rage. I put my hand on Ursula's arm. She turns and embraces me tightly.

Suddenly, I want to stay here with her forever. Everyone in Diamond City thinks they love Ursula but none of them love her like I do. We've got kilos so the Basis will supply us with food, air and water. We will have each other for company and we will be safe.

Inevitably Ursula lets go and reluctantly so do I. She straightens and becomes the People's Princess.

"Come on," she says and walks out.

I look at the salon longingly but there isn't time for me to use it. Instead I put my chin into the crook of the suit elbow and draw the smart cloth up over my face, which emerges made up in its usual way. Shading modulates my inexplicable light tan, shadow with a subtle green design surrounds my eyes to make the best of them and a pale sheen covers my lips to detract from their fullness and avoid looking tarty.

I head through the door after Ursula. As I hurry along the corridor I clench my hair between my upper and lower right arm and pull it between them. The hair emerges clean and conditioned to rustle down my back in a wavy golden fall.

I run onto the walkway and see Ursula stride ahead of me, the grey dress rippling out behind her. The walkway is thankfully deserted, not that Ursula needs an audience for her seductive swagger. I run to catch up before anyone else appears but just as I reach my sister, Ruben Toro hurries out of a side corridor with the fixed look of someone pretending this is a coincidence.

A respected analyst in Gethen Karkarridan's feared Centrian

Business Division, Ruben used to be a small man. He was proud of his naturally occurring baldness and slightly wonky face, which were endearingly original features amid Centria's many perfections.

Now, however, he is tall like Ursula. His hair is thick, dark and cut in a style that Ursula might sport if she was male. Ursula's unconventional beauty is notoriously hard to replicate, especially in men. The most effective option, which is the one Ruben has chosen, is not an exact match but a variation on a theme. Ursula's jaw is slightly masculine anyway and Ruben has had this feature emphasised. Ursula's eyes are striking because of the humour in them as much as their rich hazel colour; again this can't be copied so instead Ruben has enhanced the slight upturn at the outer edges. His mouth is wantonly kissable and his teeth when he smiles are slightly, maddeningly uneven, like Ursula's. The unnerving result of Ruben's surgery is that he looks more like Ursula's brother than I do her sister.

"Woh!" Ruben says. "Hello Ursula!"

"Hello you scruff," Ursula says.

She doesn't break her stride. Ruben is put off-balance but rights himself like an automatic toy and hurries after Ursula. He ignores me but I'm used to that.

"I saw your chat show the other night," Ruben says.

"Of course you did," Ursula says. "I was amazing."

"That chap who supported the Sons of the Crystal Mind; you absolutely tore him a new one. Um," Ruben swallows nervously. "Do you support the Blanks then?"

If Ursula says yes then Ruben will support the Blanks. If Ursula says no then Ruben will probably join the Sons himself. He is not quite a stalker; he would soon be an ex-employee if he was. Instead, he thinks he's got a unique link to Ursula, a belief he has in common with most of Diamond City.

"The Blanks are the Blanks," Ursula says.

She manages to make it sound like an opinion.

"Ah, yes," Ruben says.

He tries to mull Ursula's statement over but the glare of her presence has burned away rational thought like a pleasure drug.

"It's amazing really," Ruben says, "the Basis I mean. You take how amazing it is for granted; well I do anyway, sometimes. Do you?"

"Yes," Ursula says.

"I mean you get used to it being able to grow anything but growing *people* out of the floor? That's a miracle."

"Not everyone would agree," I say.

"No," Ruben says, looking nervously around, "not everyone. I feel sorry for the Blanks. That's not patronising is it? I realise some of them did terrible things but that was a long time ago. Maybe it's because of how they're, er, made?"

"Being born out of the floor isn't that different from a natural birth," I say.

Ruben, pleased to be involved in any sort of conversation with Ursula, is clearly thinking of ways to extend this one.

"I don't know why everyone isn't 'made' like that," he says after a moment.

"For a while a lot of people were," I say. "Armies needed to be created; loyal workers bred. Blanks are no different to anyone else."

"Apart from not needing a belly button," Ursula says.

"Yes!" Ruben says.

"Hence 'Blank'," I say, "which I always thought was a bit harsh."

Ursula clears her throat.

"Where are you going?" Ruben says hurriedly.

"Pre-wed party," Ursula says.

She stops and turns the full force of her charisma on Ruben, who goes so still it's as if there is no movement in his body at all.

"You do know I'm getting married don't you?" Ursula says. "We discussed this."

It's as if she is asking his permission. She is a kind of genius really.

"Yes," Ruben says, dazed. "I hope you'll be… Well, you will be… very… er… you know…"

"Yes I do," Ursula says. "Take care Ruben."

We leave him there, as if on a little island of unrequited love.

At the end of the walkway we pass through an arch and emerge onto a wide skywalk suspended over the fourth edge sector. Hanging gardens and audio sculptures send currents of bright energy through the enclave, while huge diamond buildings refract a thousand coloured points and turn the skywalk into a jewelled ribbon that winds into the distance. Assemblies drift above and etch complex silhouettes against the view, which resembles a great silver-backed undulation of scattered light.

The skywalk is full of people, focussed on multiple ifarm demands as they hurry about their business. Ursula's presence disrupts this controlled flow, which breaks into interesting confusion the moment she appears. Decorum forgotten, the people around us scan Ursula to see if it's really her; there is then a palpable rise in energy as everyone tries to decide how to react. Some people stare at Ursula, some stand and smile while others pretend she isn't there, perhaps in the hope that by not bothering her she will notice them out of gratitude.

The People's Princess absorbs the attention like the professional she is and takes a deep, appreciative breath. A little smile dimples her cheeks. She puts a relaxed arm round my shoulders and looks off into the distance, as if gazing into the future of her astonishing career.

"Let's fly," she says.

For the first time today I feel a flicker of excitement. I go in-Aer, which manifests itself as a slight brightening of my vision. Images of flybikes slide from right to left across my view although as we're in public only I can see them. I choose a smaller flybike than usual so it won't detract from Ursula. It costs 8,050 kilos; I click BUY. My account reels down to 13,118 and the skeletal frame of the flybike emerges joystick first as if surfacing from a still pool. I climb on and the vehicle starts at my touch.

The flybike has a single long seat and Ursula eases onto it behind me. She rides side-saddle because of the dress, a lovely idea. Almost invisible restraints wrap themselves around our legs to secure us in flight but Ursula still slides her left arm around my waist and squeezes. I think everyone on the skywalk would like to be me at this moment. I key up and we rise from the centre of the crowd to a little cheer. Ursula laughs and waves to the people below. They wave back but are soon out of sight.

We soar through Centria, where gloating parks and gardens tumble bright emerald foliage from one to another. The backbone of Centria rises through the airborne architecture like a huge crystal crown, its vertiginous, ornate spires anchoring barely visible cables that suspend assemblies like pendants in a dazzling sweep. Around the perimeter leap huge fountains, which foam into soft, sweet mist to mask the smooth finality of the diamond ceiling.

The exit from Centria is through a large open chamber that can fill itself with solid diamond in the event of attack. Through the thick wall beyond is a broad, high tunnel; we flit through far above the heads of pedestrians and I angle us up to fly over the top of the enclave.

Centria is like Diamond City in miniature: a diamond sphere that contains many levels and chambers. However, the underground city is encased in solid rock, while Centria is surrounded by another spherical chamber linked to it by eight equidistant diamond roads. They connect to a single broad walkway around Centria's circumference that makes the enclave look like a smooth diamond version of one of the old ringed planets.

During the Ruby War, the Centrian ring road glowed blindingly under cannon fire from the terror army of the New Form Enterprise. However, the ring road is part of Diamond City's superstructure, withstanding Earth's pressure fifty kilometres underground. Unlike buildings and assemblies, no weapon grown by the Basis will work against it although that didn't stop the NFE from trying.

I grip the joystick tighter as we pass between two support columns and Centria falls away beneath us. Soon we pass into another spherical chamber that encloses Centria like the next layer of an onion, where enormous train tubes linking floor to ceiling fan into blue distance. I weave through them towards a circular exit and glance behind.

Four armed ships follow discretely. They are far enough away to give the impression the People's Princess is free to do what she wants but close enough to wipe out anyone who tries to cause her trouble.

Ursula moves forward slightly so she can talk directly into my ear.

"What did Keris Veitch want the other day?" she says.

I slow down so I don't have to shout.

"She didn't want anything," I say. "She told me Mum and Dad found the NFE."

"So the NFE did this?"

"Possibly."

"Is that what Mum said when she called you?"

"No," I say. "She said there was something wrong with Centria."

"What?"

"She didn't know."

"Anything else?"

"She said the NFE were not what we thought and to avoid the Sons of the Crystal Mind."

We fly into the next chamber, where VIA Holdings begins to make its presence felt in a series of blocky buildings and assemblies with none of Centria's glamour.

"We need a plan," Ursula says.

"We've got one," I say. "You marry Bal."

"But-"

"As a result, you and I get much more powerful; then we go after the people who hurt Mum and Dad and mess them up."

"The New Form Enterprise?"

She is hungry for a fight but I hesitate. The NFE are just too convenient an enemy.

"We don't know enough yet," I say. "What about Mum and Dad's mission files?"

"Anton won't give you those," Ursula says.

I feel Keris's energy inspire me.

"What's Bal going to do after the merger?" I say.

"He doesn't know. He's actually worried he'll be seen as a mummy's boy with no real power."

"What if we were to give him a job now?" I say. "As Director of Security."

"So Anton reports to Bal," Ursula says.

"And Bal will do what you say."

"And I will tell Bal to give you the mission files."

"Make sure Bal knows his new job was my idea," I say.

"I will," Ursula says, "although I don't know why we don't just go after the NFE and nuke the little orange fucks."

"Because there's something else, something that doesn't make sense."

"What?" Ursula says.

"Mum and Dad were hit at the same time, right?"

"Yes."

"I can believe the NFE might have noticed Dad following them but how the hell did they find out about Mum?"

4

The party venue is a huge golden saucer spinning slowly between the floor and ceiling of a great dark chamber whose walls are studded with multicoloured lights. The venue is spectacular more for its size than anything else but that's VIA Holdings for you. The saucer has several ways in; Ursula's ifarm opens one of the upper entrances and we fly through.

Beneath us the assembled party guests are arranged in casual lines of influence. Someone shouts; the tops of heads morph into upturned faces which register Ursula's arrival and homogenise at once into appropriate expressions of delight. Although the saucer shell spins, the floor remains stationary so I bring the flybike down at a steep angle and people step back a little too fast. I deliberately cut the deceleration; we bounce off the floor and then skid to a halt, the flybike's nose turning satisfyingly at the last moment.

"Nicely done," Ursula whispers.

She leaps off the flybike and strides into the crowd. As it closes around her I let go of the joystick and climb off. I click DEPOSIT and watch the floor absorb the flybike. My account goes up by just 7,889 kilos because the patent owner keeps 2% of the transaction. The patent owner is Centria as usual, although if I worked anywhere else the transaction percentage would be 10%.

I need to meet Balatar Descarreaux's people to discuss how tonight's material should be managed. They will have something to say about our entrance but for now I can't face it. Instead I go straight to the bar, where the barman regards me for a moment. A body language expert, he will be able to work out the right drink for the occasion and then back his decision up with access to various files on me, some of which I'll know about and others I won't.

The barman looks at a point on the bar between us. A glass grows there, squat and heavy as if the pale amber liquid now filling it needs a strong container with an inlaid metal design like a spell. The barman nods and moves off. I lift the glass.

"You're not actually going to down that are you?"

There is an immersive recording based on a film from the Old World, in which rocks fall endlessly down a cliff into a deep shaft. The voice beside me sounds rather like that, if the shaft had been lined with velvet. I turn.

For a moment everything goes quiet and still.

His smile gleams above me like an ivory wall and is even more impressive against his very dark brown skin. I sense whether I down the drink or not will make no difference to his amusement; the laughter in his eyes is a trickster's energy rejoicing in its capacity for trouble. Creases in his cheeks parenthesise that smile, which implies he knows me, doesn't mind my faults and even likes them. His tightly kinked hair appears to have just won a fight with itself and hangs in little dreads while a small moustache and chin beard make him look wicked, so wicked. His large hands rest on the bar. They look like they could snap it in two.

White people can easily become black but something in this man's humour tells me he is the real thing. I can also tell his beauty is not the result of surgery. Like Ursula's, there is something slightly ridiculous about it you couldn't make up.

The man's clothes are unlike anything I've seen. Black and slightly worn, they look heavy but clearly don't weigh him down. They creak slightly as he moves and a strange smell comes off them; almost shocking but rich and weirdly familiar. His clothes are Old World! A blue shirt under his jacket hangs freely over a waist that's much slimmer than those brute shoulders. I know if I touch his stomach it will be a hard grid of ebony muscle. I wouldn't just touch it though; I'd jab it, scratch it, bite it…

What's the matter with me? I can't let him think he can tell me what to do. Turning away I pick up the glass but my fingers don't work properly. I concentrate so I won't smack myself in the mouth or fall over and manage to get the drink in. I swallow it and for a moment everything seems okay but then the stuff begins to burn.

I feel enervated and detached.

No! This drink was meant for a different occasion, an occasion that did not involve the man beside me. Things go a bit blurry. I wait for the effects to pass so as not to reveal them; I will then allow myself to look at him again, as a reward. When my eyes regain their focus I gather my composure and turn back.

He's gone. My head snaps around in one direction and then another with involuntary desperation. I don't even know his name! I could have scanned him for it but that would have been rude.

I glare at the crowded room. Soft music pulses and light blooms in different colours over the gorgeously attired crowd. I see Ursula laugh in Balatar Descarreaux's arms as the beautiful couple bask in the smiles and well wishes of everyone around them.

Like Ursula, Balatar is tall and his blond hair is a striking contrast to Ursula's gleaming dark tresses. Bal whispers in Ursula's ear and makes her laugh while seeming to make eye contact with everyone in the room. Unlike Ursula, however, Bal's appearance is clearly the work of a surgery patent. He looks too perfect. His jaw is too square, his eyes too blue. It's a nice effect but my sister outclasses him.

The plan of the recs taking footage of the event was sent to me yesterday and I close my eyes to look at it. Hmm. Expansive rather than imaginative, with fewer vix opportunities than I would have liked. Typical VIA.

A message appears: Ellery wants a key image immediately even though the evening has only just begun. I fret for a second but fortunately Ursula and Bal laughing together right now is exactly what we need. I wonder if Ellery is psychic. She seems to intuit what everyone in Diamond City wants before they do, although I sometimes think she understands people without really caring about them.

"Charity."

The voice is French-accented, sulky and charming. I open my eyes to see Loren Descarreaux. The slim, seemingly ageless Chief of VIA Holdings wears a glittery yellow scallop-fronted gown and her usual expression of a woman glad to have been caught doing something naughty.

"Is Keris Veitch here tonight?" Loren says.

"No, sorry, ah…"

The question is unfair and Loren knows it but she continues to watch me expectantly. There is an uncomfortable pause. Loren absently twiddles one of the dagger tips of her shiny copper bob as it points towards her delicate chin, the movement appreciative rather than nervous. Her fingers are long, the nails sculpted into talons and lacquered orange, purple and gold.

"I thought she would be here, considering," she says.

"I don't – I'm not sure what her… What she's doing tonight," I say.

I wait for Loren to help me out. She is not usually this ungenerous.

"We will soon be like sisters, Keris and I, as you are with Ursula," Loren says eventually.

"What do you mean?"

"Well, you two are so different, as I am from Keris, non? But this merger will bring us all closer together."

Loren smiles and reaches over to stroke my cheek with the tips of her talons. The sensation is unexpectedly soothing.

"Relax!" she says.

"Okay, yes."

"Always working," she says. "You should have some fun."

"Well, it's a great party."

"Of course it is," Loren says.

"No it isn't," Balatar says.

I didn't notice Loren's son walk up to us. He hasn't got his mother's seductive accent; his voice is standard, like everything else about him. He smiles as he looks everywhere but at me, his eyes icy with rage and his voice tense with polite contempt.

"You're supposed to be her secretary," he says to me. "Do something."

"But what is wrong?" Loren says.

"That," Balatar says through clenched teeth.

I turn. In the centre of the crowd, Ursula dances with the man from the bar.

"Charity," Loren says, "think of the weather."

She's right. I am going to be up all night sorting out this mess. The man from the bar twirls Ursula around like a doll. Ursula doesn't laugh the way she did with Bal; instead she's got a hungry look. That's not good.

"What's his name, that black man?" Loren asks.

"I don't know," I say.

"Send Ursula a message," Bal says. "Get her to scan him and let you know who he is."

I should have thought of that. Bal's eyes narrow.

"You like him," he says.

"No I don't," I say, too quickly.

I chew at my lips and swallow. Loren watches me, her expression uncomfortably similar to Bal's. I have to keep their trust, or in Bal's case earn it. I can't let some ruffian mess up my career no matter how handsome he is or how like a god he moves.

Yet I don't send the message. The seed hidden under the skin between Ursula's eyes will scan an identical device on the man from the bar. Ursula will then send me the message, my seed will pick it up and the name will appear on my eye screen.

I don't want to learn his name like that. I want to be told in that beautiful voice. I want him to sweep me away.

I turn to Bal.

"Leave it with me," I say.

I send a message to the Musician, whose six arms cause the music and light to begin fading. I then forward Bal a short speech he was supposed to read later and he grunts to indicate receipt. He walks towards a central podium; when he reaches it and steps up the music disappears completely. Bal begins his speech as I reach Ursula, grab her arm and turn towards the man from the bar. He's disappeared again.

"Stop throttling my elbow," Ursula says.

"Who was that man?" I ask her.

"I don't know."

The crowd cheers something Bal has said.

"What's his name?"

"He didn't say."

The crowd laughs at a joke I wrote for Bal.

"Did you scan him?"

"Charity Freestone! Where are your manners?"

The crowd applauds Bal.

"Why are you such a tart?" I ask Ursula.

"Dunno," she says.

I shove her towards Bal and it takes all my self-control not to kick her arse. Instead, I cross to some unoccupied tables, sit down and watch the scene for a while. Ursula and Bal laugh, the man from the bar is nowhere to be seen and the energy in the room feels correct as once again the event moves through its proper sequence.

I close my eyes and sink into the ifarm. It's immediately clear a lot of people have followed Ursula's antics and want to know about the man from the bar. I activate a series of automated programs with faux personalities of their own that disseminate a message about the man from the bar being a friend of mine from the past, a past I will now have to invent.

Maybe he could help. I could hire him and he could pretend to have been my partner. Of course, if anything actually was to happen between us then, well, I'm not sure what I would do. I send Ellery a message that says I am going to find the man from the bar and get him to do some work for us. She responds with a blank approval note. I open my eyes.

The man from the bar sits on the other side of the table.

"You!" I say.

"Me," he says.

"You caused a lot of trouble tonight."

He stares off into the distance behind me and nods sagely.

"Hmm," he says. "I tend to do that."

"What's your name?" I say.

"Just scan me."

"No."

"Why?" he says.

"It's rude."

He laughs, a big sound that should mock but doesn't.

"So if I've scanned you does that mean I'm rude?" he says.

"Have you?"

"Scan me," he says, "And I'll tell you."

"I will not."

Despite everything I laugh. We look at each other for a while.

"I'm Charity Freestone," I say, finally.

"Charity Freestone," he says, savouring my name in that rich voice.

"Do you know who I am?" I say.

"No. Who are you?"

"I'm Ursula Freestone's sister."

"Ursula," he says, handsomely confused and totally uninterested.

"She's the People's Princess!"

"A princess you say?"

"She's way out of your league, mister."

"Oh, I can get any woman," he says. "I'm like gravity."

"Well you're not getting me!"

There is an awkward pause.

"Right," he says, embarrassed.

Oh no…!

He gets up.

"Nice to meet you Charity."

He walks through the crowd and out of the door. I sit and watch him go as if paralysed.

5

The Column floats high over a park in one of Centria's inner districts. It is the most exclusive bar in Diamond City, a status guaranteed by the means of access. If you can afford to gif a diamond column tall enough to reach it you get in, otherwise forget it. I've never been. The only reason I'm going tonight is because Ellery has invited me and is growing the column I now ride up on.

Around me the purple darkness gathers. I rise past great crystal buildings that spill glowing colour into the night. Light sculptures twirl through the mist above like mysterious airborne creatures and soft music pulses in a dozen harmonies across the enclave as if the structures are calling to each other. The column rises through a bright-rimmed opening in the underside of the assembly, where a spiral of docking bridges caters for ascent columns of different widths. The very rich gif the thickest columns and don't need a docking bridge at all. Ellery's column is one of these.

I'm strangely unimpressed. I think it's because of the two little icons superimposed over the bottom left of everything I see. One shows my continuous call to Dad, which is still unanswered. The other icon shows Mum's condition, which is unchanged.

After the dramatic panorama outside, the large bar seems alarmingly intimate. I step off the column and look around for Ellery. Her message was characteristically terse, just a brief written invitation with time and place. I expect she'll want to discuss Ursula's wedding plans, which have slipped slightly.

The bar is not crowded, which is one of its attractions. Discreet booths and low tables hidden with subtle lighting make it hard to determine who's actually here. I'm sure everyone can see me though and I'm tempted to hunch over and hurry to one side. Keris wouldn't do that though, so neither will I. I stand as I imagine she would, proud but not aggressive, prepared to stay there all night unless someone comes over and offers me something. Sure enough, someone does: a smiling man in a red suit who I immediately feel I've known my whole life.

"Miss Freestone, welcome to the Column. How was the journey up?"

"It was really very special," I say, surprised at how relaxed and confident I sound.

"Ah, good. I'm Martyn. Please let me show you to Ms Quinn."

He leads me across the bar. When we reach a curtained recess near the back he directs me into it.

"Thank you," I say.

Martyn smiles and walks away as I part the curtain and walk through. At the bottom of a short flight of steps is a small circular table with a single cushioned seat. Ellery sits there staring down at an empty glass. It's hardly the exalted position I expect until I realise we are invisible to everyone else in the Column. I look at the top of Ellery's head; the flow of her thick red hair glints softly in the dim light.

"Charity," she says, without looking up.

"Hello Ellery," I say.

Her reticence makes me nervous. Am I in trouble? Or… is Ellery the problem with Centria?

I descend into the dark recess and sit next to Ellery, keeping my face neutral. She doesn't look up.

"Hn," she says. "Not got long."

Her voice doesn't sound quite right. She's drunk!

Out of the table in front of us grow two identical drinks: an orange liquid with a glittery golden swirl that spins and spins. Ellery points at one of the swirls as if to give her the necessary focus.

"Can only get it here," she says. "Just as well."

I take a sip. It's delicious. Ellery presses a finger to the base of my glass as I take it from my lips.

"Drink," she says.

I knock it back and it begins to work at once. I put the glass down. Another grows in its place.

Ellery watches me strangely. I realise her eyes don't seem to vibrate; she is not engrossed in fifty other documents, fifty other conversations. It makes her look completely unfamiliar.

"You're a funny little thing Charity Freestone," Ellery says. "Do you know that?"

"No. Why am I funny?"

"Hn. You've got no idea about yourself. You're like a beautiful country with gold and jewels just lying around because you don't know to pick them up."

I can't think how to respond. I sip the second drink nervously and then sip it again for something to do with my hands. The effect spreads through me. It feels the way it looks, calming but with a streak of power.

"Ellery, I don't understand what you mean."

"You've got questions."

The world shrinks to the bright green of her eyes.

"Who… am I?" I whisper.

"You need to understand the Guidance."

"What guidance? You mean instructions for something?"

Ellery shakes her head. Suddenly, she looks up and to her left. I follow her gaze. There's nothing there.

"She has to know!" Ellery shouts to the empty space.

"Ellery?" I say, scared now.

Ellery looks back at me again.

"Not instructions Charity. You've got to understand the Guidance. What it is. What it means. How it defines you-"

"Ms Quinn."

Martyn stands over us, looking worried as Ellery's breath speeds up.

"Damn it," she says.

Martyn looks close to tears.

"I've been told I have to…" he stutters.

"This girl," Ellery says, "this girl!"

She grips the table as if about to wrench it loose, then looks at me and goes to say something else.

"Please!" Martyn says, his voice high-pitched with nerves.

Suddenly, Ellery is up and out of the recess so fast it's as if she was never here. Martyn follows without another look back.

For a while I sit in stunned silence.

The curtains twitch apart and Anton Jelka walks down the stairs. He stops at the bottom, frowns for a moment and then sits beside me on the cushioned seat.

"What just happened?" I finally ask him.

"Ellery Quinn is, as you know, the Voice of Centria," he says. "But there are limits that need to be observed."

"Who am I Anton?"

"You're Charity Freestone."

"What is the Guidance?"

"No one talks about the Guidance."

"But what is it?"

"What is what?"

I tut and turn from him to scan the Aer. There are numerous references to guidance for specific things but nothing that relates to me.

"Charity," Anton says.

I turn back to him.

"It seems I have a new boss," he says, face still and eyes cold.

"Oh?" I say.

"Yes. Balatar Descarreaux is now 'Director' of Security, at your sister's request."

"Right."

"He has told me to give you the files pertaining to the recent mission carried out by your parents."

"Really?"

He leans over until his face is centimetres from mine.

"Ursula would never have thought of that," he says. "I know you are responsible."

"Let's have the files then."

Anton leans back.

"Have you got any idea what it takes to run a security operation like the one in Centria?" he asks.

"I've never thought about it," I say.

"It would take you a year to begin to learn. I have been doing it for ten. Balatar Descarreaux has been in the job for ninety minutes.

Do you know what that means?"

"Hm. No."

"It means he needs me more than I need him. It means for at least a year, assuming he doesn't get bored before then, I don't have to do anything he says. It means you will not get those files. Not now. Not ever."

He gets up and looks down at me. He doesn't look angry; instead he seems to search my face for something. After a moment, he walks up the stairs and out through the curtains.

6

The man from the bar looks guilty. It suits him. The latest party for Bal and Ursula swirls around us, not in the golden saucer this time but in a great dark ballroom lit with bright patterns that blossom in the walls. The ballroom is part of a building complex overlooking VIA Holdings and is enclosed by a broad corridor full of Centrian and VIA Security. Everyone else here looks like they enjoy themselves professionally and the man from the bar seems completely out of place.

"You weren't invited," I tell him. "I organised this party and know every guest here but I don't know you."

"Ah," he says, "that's clever."

"That's organised is what that is, mister. You never did tell me your name."

"And if I choose not to tell you now?"

"Oh," I say. "Security…"

"Which ones?"

"The ones in the uniforms that say 'SECURITY'."

"Not the undercover ones over there?"

"They aren't-"

"Parties are meant to be fun aren't they? That woman by the wall wouldn't know fun if fun made her naked and she felt fun's hands run over every adorable contour of her willing body so that when fun eventually… Anyway, you get the picture. My name's Harlan Akintan by the way."

"Harrity- um – Charity Freestone-"

"Yes I know."

"Good. Good. What can I do for you? I mean, why are you here?"

"I'm here for the girls, obviously."

"Well then. Good."

"I'll see you around Harrity."

He laughs and moves off. People don't notice Harlan Akintan unless he focuses on them, after which they can't take their eyes off him.

I shake my head. I should have him removed. Everything is at stake; not just my career but also the stalled investigation into what happened to Mum and Dad. Ursula's wedding must be a success if we are to get any answers. Yet I drift and recall dreams of white teeth and black skin...

I nearly bump into Bal, who glares at me as usual.

"You got me a job I can do nothing with," he says.

"You're Director of Security for the most powerful organisation there is. What more do you want?"

"Anton Jelka refuses to do what I tell him."

"I find that unlikely," I say. "Anton has always been very loyal."

"Not to me."

"You're just going to have to find a way aren't you?"

He looks past me.

"That man is here again," he says. "Why did you invite him?"

"I... He's, uh-"

"What's the barman doing?"

The barman has got on top of the bar. He's not the barman from the last party, even though I asked for the same one. He is of medium height and muscular with a wildness about him that suits his long, blue-black hair and wide, grey eyes. The music fades into silence.

The barman looks slowly around the room with that clenched calm of the righteously angry. People at the bar glance at each other, embarrassed at this breach of protocol and unsure what to do. The barman's presence and behaviour are so unusual that conversation begins to die away as more and more people turn to look at him.

Despite manners I scan the barman, whose name is 88 Rabian. I've never heard of him. I'm about to check in-Aer when the wall patterns coalesce into white sheets that transform the ballroom into a harsh bright cube. The Security Chief looks my way and I nod my approval for intervention. As the security team starts towards 88 Rabian he slowly removes his black shirt to reveal-

"BLANK!" someone screams.

All the people who are supposed to be serving drop their trays with a crash and strip to the waist. None of them have got navels.

The nearest Blank to me is a woman with short blonde hair and the wiry, androgynous physique of a dancer. Her expression is solemn, as if she deals with excitement like this every day. She looks at something that forms in the floor in front of her. It's a fuze. As it emerges she squats to wrap her hand lovingly around the grip and then she straightens, her breathing deep as if she is turned on.

I don't understand; VIA Holdings own this facility and no one except them should be able to gif anything in here. I go in-Aer to check the status of the building and discover someone else has bought it.

The other Blanks have grown weapons as well, not all of them as modest as the blonde woman's. The Blanks snatch up their guns and fire over the top of the crowd, which panics. The security guards get into attack position.

"Drop your weapons!" the guards shout almost as one.

The VIA and Centrian guards in the outer corridor rush in. Centria's guards wear dark blue and VIA's are in white. There's a lot of shouting as each group of guards tries to drown out the other with instructions. Taking advantage of this confusion, the Blanks grow thick diamond walls between the guests and the incoming guards, trapping us. The Blanks hold their weapons ready but do not fire.

A VIA guard takes this restraint as provocation. He shoots at the blonde woman but she has already seen him aim and jumps aside so the bolt hits a table, which clatters into some chairs. Tension in the reduced space makes everyone overreact to the noise and suddenly we are in the middle of a gunfight.

A small blue-haired woman in a costume of pink and purple beads spins with unnatural, eerie grace and falls. The beads break away from their fixings and roll in all directions, some adrift in a widening pool of blood. The woman starts to scream.

Horror catches up with me and I freeze. The dread sense of having no idea what I'm doing is never far and rears up with its usual dull power. Someone with the correct knowledge and ability should step in.

"CEASE FIRE!" the barman roars.

His amplified voice drowns out all other sound. Everyone stops and looks at him, even the guards and the woman on the floor.

"We are the Blanks," 88 Rabian says, his voice quieter now. "We have control of this building. We have control of you. You can fight us if you want but a lot of you will die."

His gleaming muscular stomach rises and falls rapidly as he breathes. There is something deeply disturbing about its unbroken flesh, as if 88 Rabian is over-finished.

"You shot that woman," Ursula shouts from the other side of the room.

88 Rabian goes white with a rage so pure I can almost feel its heat from six metres away.

"She was shot by your own incompetent security force!" he shouts. "And you blame us for it as you blame us for everything! It has to stop!"

He gets himself under control and shakes his head, exasperated as much as furious.

"We have tried to be peaceful," he says. "We have tried to be patient. But we are hunted like vermin and we are not vermin; we are human beings just like you. It is not our fault we were born the way we were and we have come here tonight to tell you that we will not take it anymore!"

"We aren't the Sons of the Crystal Mind," a man in the crowd says, I can't see who.

"The Sons are funded by people in VIA Holdings and people in Centria," 88 Rabian says. "How else could they afford to buy every cosmetic patent that would allow us to blend in? By striking here we strike at the Sons and their medieval beliefs."

"Are you going to let that woman die?" Ursula yells.

"No," 88 Rabian says.

The woman begins to sink into the floor and I see her arm move. She is clearly still alive and about to be healed by the Basis, probably at 88 Rabian's expense.

"She's dead!" someone screams. "She's going into the floor!"

"No!" I shout.

Even if anyone hears they ignore me. The VIA security guards rush at the Blanks, clearly in the hope that raging determination will win out. The Centrian guards, better trained and smarter, try to form themselves into a barrier between the guests and the Blanks. The Blanks, presumably used to blind onslaughts fuelled by ignorance and hatred, remain calm. Their positioning is not random. They are spread out in a configuration that is impossible to surround and cannot be attacked without putting guests in danger.

Some of the VIA guards realise; they slow down and the Blanks open fire on them. Two VIA guards are hit immediately and sink quickly into the floor. They lie buried in clear diamond, their positions identical to when they fell with scarlet wounds vivid against the white uniforms. After a few moments the dead guards seem to lose definition. They blur and then vanish as the Basis breaks them down and the kilo worth of their bodies goes to friends, family, idols…

Guests cower behind furniture and run mindlessly to bounce off walls, guards and each other. A few even try to take on the Blanks but the Blanks are better trained and disciplined than a lot of the guards so the guests don't stand a chance. Although the Blanks knock the attacking guests down, they don't kill any.

The guards are not so lucky. Two more are killed, which galvanises the Centrian team. They have arranged themselves so that instead of taking on all the Blanks they just target individuals and now fire three beams of lethal energy. Two Blanks are fatally hit, one with multiple blasts that spray his torso over a number of guests. The Blanks abandon their restraint and go berserk. The guards are no match for them and the fight enters a new pitch of savagery and hysterical panic.

There is less screaming now because some of the guests and a couple of guards appear to have gone into shock. Most people unable to find shelter lie on the floor, either curled up or with their hands covering their heads, perhaps in the hope that shutting out reality will keep them safe.

Two male guests jump the blonde female Blank and overwhelm her with simple weight. She shoots one of them in the stomach and he falls back going "oh oh oh". The other guest pins the woman down and punches her repeatedly in the throat. She twitches underneath him for a while and then goes still. As the dead Blank is absorbed the guest picks up the gun but it melts in his hand. Two other Blanks shoot him dead and the rest begin to kill any guest still standing.

I'm grabbed from behind; I struggle and see Bal's profile. As I try to work out what he's doing I see the Blank in front of me take aim.

Bal is using me as a shield.

I know the Blank is moving fast but he seems to take ages to get his gun level with my head. Faced with actual tedious, disappointing death I'm rewarded with enhanced perception that's useless for anything except a good view. I'm not even scared.

Harlan steps up behind the Blank and points at him. Something flickers out of Harlan's right index finger: a beam of red light, there for an instant and then gone. One end of the red beam touches the Blank, who jerks forward and falls on his face. He is quickly absorbed into the floor and vanishes.

Bal has still got hold of me as if he can't think what else to do. Harlan walks through the fighting, stops and looks over my head. His face has none of its humour now. Bal's grip loosens and he runs off.

Harlan takes my hand and tries to pull me away but I can't move. He puts an arm round me, hoists me without effort and runs to the empty bar. Around us the fighting is a kind of dread-filled inertia punctuated by screams and gunfire. A shot explodes against the front of the bar as Harlan ducks down behind it. He pushes me up against the structure and shields me with his body.

I still can't move. Every shot, scream and crash deafens me. I want to tell them all to shut up but I can't speak. I'm cold, yet not cold. My whole body shakes.

I look at Harlan's lapel as he crouches over me. I can smell his clothes again and I can also smell him; not a scorched nervous smell but a raw musk. I've wanted to be close to him since we first met. Why did it have to happen like this?

An explosion shakes the building and debris crashes onto the bar. I find my voice.

"URSULA! I WANT MY SISTER! WHERE IS MY SISTER?"

Harlan's clothes and Harlan's body muffle my shout. Suddenly he's gone and I just lie there listening to the sounds of grief and terror. I stare numbly at the floor, which is a different colour to the rest of the white ballroom: a calming dark grey.

Something dark-haired and sweary lands next to me followed by Harlan.

"There," he says. "Now shut up."

Ursula is hollow-eyed with shock and we clutch each other.

Harlan peers carefully around the edge of the bar, his movements surprisingly flexible for such a big man. There is another explosion followed by the whine of a large vehicle. Harlan eases back behind the bar. He licks the pad of his thumb and wipes at blood over Ursula's eye.

"Ah," he says to her, "not your blood."

"What's happening?" I ask.

"The Blanks have giffed some sort of tank and are getting away in it."

"How?" Ursula says.

"I blew a hole in the wall so they could escape without letting Security in," says Harlan.

I want to ask him how he blew a hole in anything since he isn't carrying a weapon but it doesn't seem important now.

"You helped them?" Ursula says.

Everything gets quieter, dimmer.

"They could stay but then we'd all kill each other. I think I was right, don't you?"

"Er, yeah," Ursula says.

"Jolly good," Harlan says.

I go to sleep or something.

7

I used to imagine going to Keris's office, perhaps to advise her about some important matter or accept an engagement only I could carry out. I never thought it would be to explain a massacre at a party.

Keris lives and works in an airborne assembly that drifts through Centria. Only a few people know which assembly it is and there are no markings or codes to identify it. Like the rest of the enclave, its shape changes often and currently it is a series of linked opaque globes that glow softly in the mid-morning lights. Like Keris herself it is understated but dazzlingly beautiful. Other assemblies and vehicles in the vicinity are actually warships in disguise; I flew over one to get here and glimpsed a cannon three times longer than I am.

We sit at a round table: Keris, Ellery, me, Anton, Balatar, Loren and Gethen Karkarridan. This is the first time I've seen Ellery since that night at the Column and she has been uncharacteristically quiet on the ifarm. I try to catch her eye but she ignores me. Her focus is Gethen.

It is said of Gethen Karkarridan that if you give him kilos to invest he will make a profit with them before they even hit his account. He thinks in multiples of a billion. His team is the biggest in Centria and a financial empire in itself. He's got more money and power than anyone except Keris and it would be tempting to think it's more than he knows what to do with. However, Gethen will always know what to do with money and power: make more money.

He gets away with it because Ellery turns his exploits into the story of how Centria's success is really that of Diamond City as a whole. The attack on Ursula's party was a disaster because it has substantially undermined this narrative. As a result bad weather engulfs us, which means profits are down.

I watch Gethen. I know him, although not well, because he and Ellery work incredibly closely. They have also been lovers for years and almost seem to blend into one being at times. Their combined presence is an enervating counterpoint to Keris's serenity as they process the city into manageable portions for her so that when she makes a decision it is not only well informed but also apparently prescient.

Gethen is the most streamlined man I've ever seen. He's even taller than Harlan but wiry and rigid instead of muscular. He only ever wears grey. His head is bullet-shaped with hair the colour of metal shaved close to the skull. His movements are methodical; he does not waste one joule of energy and is often very still. There is rarely any emotion in his chilly blue eyes and his teeth, when he does smile, are almost sharp. I worry he will bite off his tongue, not that he says much or even eats anything, as if he subsists on numbers alone.

"The Blanks' attack was a triumph for them," Keris says. "Their popularity has risen in inverse proportion to our own."

Ellery's eyes are a green blur as she processes information to distil the optimum message. Everyone watches her. She seems to ignore us but I know our expressions and body language will be another factor in her calculations.

"Hn," she says eventually. "We had no position on the Blanks. Best get one."

"Will that deflect the bad weather?" Keris says.

"Some," Ellery mutters.

Keris looks at Anton.

"We've traced the people in Centria who support the Sons of the Crystal Mind and dissuaded them from doing so again," Anton says. "Balatar has done something similar in VIA."

"People will want to know why we didn't do that before," Keris says.

"The Sons of the Crystal Mind are customers as well," Gethen says.

His soft voice is imbued with total authority. Just hearing it makes me nervous.

"Well that is all right then Gethen, yes?" Loren says and laughs, her eyes bright.

Not for the first time I detect a touch of madness in Loren. Gethen's gaze clicks over to register her and I realise the strange tension in the room is between these two.

"Anton Jelka," Bal says, seemingly oblivious. "Tell us what went wrong with the Security operation please."

"Nothing went wrong with it," Anton says, unruffled. "Our protocols and yours were aligned. However, if VIA Holdings chooses to sell its assets by the half-hour we can't be expected to second guess who buys them."

"Who bought the building?" Keris says.

"The Blanks," Gethen says. "They didn't even use a front company. Nothing was flagged because they have never been a threat before."

"I think everyone was at the wrong party," I say.

There is an almost physical change in the room. Even Gethen looks surprised. He runs his palms back over his head.

"All the security protocols were set to the building the Blanks bought," I say.

"Not set by the ifarm?" Gethen says.

"No," I say. "Only people from Centria have an ifarm. The rest of the city, including VIA Holdings, does without. So if we'd tagged building access to the ifarm then half the guests wouldn't have got in."

"After the merger, both groups will use the ifarm," Anton says.

Loren and Bal glance at each other. Only I seem to notice.

"The Blanks deposited the building they bought and grew another identical one," I say. "The security codes would have automatically been reset, which is why there was no alert. Buying a building is not in itself a threat VIA sells them all the time."

"That is true," Loren says. "It is a key income stream. Our coordinates in the city are second in status only to Centria's. We will sell an existing building to people who want to trade in close proximity to VIA Holdings and benefit from that status. We then disengage from the area so trade falls away, buy the building back from them at a massively reduced price and keep the difference. Simple, non?"

"We were in the wrong place and never even knew it," I say. "It's how so many people who shouldn't have been there got in."

I wait for someone to mention Harlan.

"Hn," Ellery says.

Everyone gets her document on their eye screens at the same time. It's a set of instructions disguised as a message:

This incident occurred because everyone in Diamond City has the freedom to do, buy and believe what they want.

Centria and VIA Holdings cannot be held responsible for individual choices.

We can, however, learn from them.

Both companies discourage support for the Sons of the Crystal Mind and indeed have never encouraged it.

We digest the words and nobody questions them. They are going to underpin every statement made by both companies whenever the subject of the party comes up, which Ellery will ensure won't be often.

"The Blanks clearly have a range of uniquely marketable skills," Gethen says. "We can get a database together to indicate which ones…"

"…and base any future support for them on that," Keris says. "But not too quickly. We don't want to look like we are reacting positively to an attack on us."

"What about the guests who died?" I ask.

"Yours weren't they?" Ellery asks Loren.

Her voice is uncharacteristically even, with all emotion and nuance removed.

"Yes," Loren says with her little smile. "It is not important."

There's an odd pause, which Balatar takes as a cue.

"What happened reveals another problem: we are seen as being out of touch with the rest of Diamond City," he says.

Ellery glares at him and I'm tempted to join her. After Bal's terrible behaviour I have avoided all contact with him. However, I think his statement is accurate.

"Yes," I say.

Bal looks at me and I sense a connection.

"I've got some ideas about that," I say. "I'll talk to you about them Ellery."

Ellery nods and Keris gets up. Everyone else does the same and there is a murmur of pleasantries and farewells as the table and chairs sink into the floor.

Anton is first out of the door, then Ellery and Gethen. I go to follow and catch Keris's eye. She shakes her head slightly so I stay where I am.

"Balatar," Keris says.

Bal looks at Loren, who twitches an annoyed eyebrow at him and then walks out. Bal reluctantly turns back, regards Keris and tries to ignore me. Keris waits. Bal swallows, glances at me and then back at Keris.

"You used Charity as a shield," Keris says. "A human shield."

Bal stares at Keris. She doesn't seem to do anything other than look at him neutrally but Bal is terrified and I can understand why. With the others you can guess what they might do but not Keris. She could be about to open a door beneath Bal's feet and watch him plummet for a kilometre or she might be about to hug him. Bal gulps.

"Yes," he says.

There is a long pause.

"I don't know what to say," he manages.

It comes out as a literal truth rather than an indication of embarrassment. He turns to me.

"Charity, I am sorry. It was... weak of me. I didn't think. I am— I imagine that I am... important somehow and that you... you wouldn't... mind?"

"She minds," Keris says. "I mind."

"Of course, of course. She has done... such a good job. You should be proud of her Keris and reward her."

Keris appears able to mould the atmosphere at will. Now, for example, the room seems freezing even though I am not cold.

"Never, ever tell me what to do," she says.

"I- of course," says Bal. "I'm sorry. It's just-"

"Get out," Keris says.

Bal seems unable to move. Finally, he backs off, turns and exits like someone remembering how to use their legs.

Keris looks at me, the violet eyes gazing steadily into mine.

"How are you?" she asks.

"Oh, fine," I say.

And at that moment it's true.

"Good," she says.

I know it's time to go but I want to stay. Instead I put out my hand. Keris looks at it for a moment, then spreads her palm theatrically and puts it in mine. We shake firmly. I turn and leave.

I feel like I could do anything.

8

I lie between Mum and Ursula on the bed at Mum and Dad's. We speak in whispers.

"Are you going to call him then?" Ursula says.

"Do you think I should?"

"Yes. It's about time you got laid."

I punch her arm.

"Sexual frustration is making you attempt a pathetic form of violence," Ursula says. "Mum, what do you think? Hm. Hm. Yes. Mum agrees."

"Oh right," I say.

"She does. I can read her mind because I am her real daughter instead of someone else's crappy cast-off."

I scream in mock outrage and climb on top of Ursula.

"How dare you!" Ursula yells, "I am the fucking People's Princess you bint!"

"You are out of order!" I shout.

"We only got you so I could have something to play with and you were cheaper than an autopony."

"But you had an autopony!"

"Because you were rubbish!" Ursula says. "You just sat and thought all the time! Now get off before I give you a proper slapping."

"You being such an accomplished slapper."

"Yeah," she says.

We giggle at the same time and then I get off. Ursula rolls over and looks at Mum. After a moment, she gently pinches Mum's nose, lets go and then pinches it again.

"Silly Mummy," she says.

When she rolls back again there are tears in her eyes.

"You only get one life Charity," she says softly.

"I know."

"Do you? Mum worked like mad and look where it got her."

I feel Mum's silent presence without looking.

"You should do something that isn't career," Ursula says, "which let's face it is easier than having a real life."

"It's not easy!"

"It is for you," she says. "You work directly for Ellery Quinn at what, twenty-three years old?"

"Hmm."

"Then you go to meetings with Keris Veitch who personally whips my beloved on your behalf…"

"That was satisfying."

"You're being groomed for big things my girl."

"I'll call Harlan tomorrow," I say.

"Call him now."

"All right."

"Go out with him now."

"All right!"

She looks at me with one eyebrow raised.

"It will probably be outside Centria," I say.

"And?" Ursula says.

"I'm still shaky from the other night."

"So is he most like. You both need a nice cuddle."

"I feel a bit unwell."

"Call him or I will," Ursula says.

She's got that hungry look.

"Okay," I say hurriedly.

I scan the Aer.

"That's odd."

"What?" Ursula says.

"There's nothing about him, only his name."

"Get on with it."

I smooth my hair nervously and call Harlan. As the ifarm links the call to his Aerac my heart beats louder and harder, louder and harder. I get up dizzily and pace the small area left by the diamond security shroud.

When Harlan doesn't reply I look at Ursula and shrug tightly.

There's no left-message box on so after a couple of minutes I end the call and sit on the bed, relieved and disappointed.

"Aha!" Ursula says.

I stare at her blankly.

"Coordinates for somewhere called New Runcton just popped up next to his name," she says. "And a time."

"What time?"

"7.15pm."

"That's in forty minutes," I say.

"You'd better take the train."

I look down at my blue suit.

"Should I gif another outfit-?"

"No!"

I glance at the door.

"Run Charity!"

"Right," I say.

Ursula gets up and puts her arms around me.

"Not as good as an autopony," I mumble into her shoulder.

"That autopony was a bastard," she says and kisses my forehead.

She lets go and shoves me gently. I turn and run from the room before I change my mind.

**

As I walk through Centria's great doorway I get the familiar prickly sense of being followed. It will be for my protection and I should be used to it but today the Security presence makes me feel like I'm doing something stupid, something wrong. My own desires seem trivial against a backdrop of conspiracy and fear.

I feel myself stop walking. I can't forget Mum just lying there or the unanswered call to Dad. My parents blend in memory and imagination to form a single entity whose features are indistinct but who radiates love like warmth. I remember the Harvest Days and the bubbles and toys and stars and rows and food and hugs and... and...

People and vehicles whirl brightly around me as they would

whether I was there or not. I breathe once, twice, think of Ursula and think of Keris. Unexpectedly, it's the thought of Gethen Karkarridan that gets me moving; his quiet determination, his ruthlessness.

I buy a ticket to New Runcton and start to walk again. My steps increase in speed. They take me along the road from Centria and through a broad, high arch in the wall of the surrounding chamber.

I emerge in the train terminal, which is another hollow sphere whose underside is a few hundred meters or so from the exterior of Centria. The terminal's fifty-six train tubes are spread equidistantly over its surface to reach every part of Diamond City. Each tube has a platform like a shelf beside it and I head for the nearest, where the train seems to wait for me alone. It's a series of spherical carriages, each with its own opening into the carrier tube and two decks connected by small elevators. An indicator flickers over my vision to indicate which carriage is mine; I get on and feel strangely elated.

The lower deck is empty, with four quadrants of seats that face inwards. I choose one on the outside edge and settle into it. A chime sounds; the portals in the carrier tube close themselves with walls that grow automatically out of the floor and the door seals retract. For a moment the train hangs in the vacuum tube and then it starts to move, quickly reaching terrific speed. The opaque carriage walls allow sufficient light through to let me know I'm moving but not enough to make me motion sick.

New Runcton is on a different floor to Centria so after a while the train enters a tube that angles up, although the carriage remains level. My carriage then fires off from the rest of the train into the gentle curve of a circular route.

Now I am underway I feel calm. Is it the fixed nature of the journey that gives me this curious sense of inevitability?

Soon the carriage slows under a vertical connection, through which it immediately rises like an elevator. Light streaks down around me until eventually the train eases to a stop. The doors connect with the carrier tube and I walk through the resulting short corridor out into New Runcton.

The place has got nothing going for it. In an insignificant part of MidZone, it's a crossroads formed by a series of units that are part commerce and part residential. A sign swings on a post even though there is not, never has been and never will be a breeze here. The sign says NEW RUNCTON with misguided civic pride.

The architecture barely qualifies as such and is not so much poor as mean. The determination of the residents to avoid every interesting building patent suggests an utter hatred of beauty.

Cubic or rectangular buildings have been grown along either side of the crossroads. Others overhang or are squeezed in behind them regardless of how absurd the result looks. Instead of utilising space in a sensible or creative way, everyone here has done their own thing to maximise their allocated area. The mess feels oppressive, as if this is where ambition comes to die.

A couple of children play quietly on a patio and an old man stares at me with open hostility from a narrow porch. He wears the remains of a uniform and his left arm is withered. After a moment, he goes inside a dwelling not much broader than he is. Soon the children run into their house too. Although the settlement now looks deserted I know I'm being watched. In Centria the surveillance is functional; here I feel judged.

The ceiling is very high and the dimming day lights reveal New Runcton's only redeeming feature: the sense above me of an actual open night sky. The train's carrier tube glows softly as it rises out of the ground and disappears into the darkness. The doors close and the carriage shoots up silently to leave the area eerily still.

Another carriage arrives in the tube. Two Centrian Security officers, a man and a woman, emerge self-consciously and try to look like they haven't followed me. I know them both vaguely and there isn't anywhere they can hide. The man shrugs. I laugh and give them a little wave.

There is no way Harlan lives here. I start to walk and reach the centre of the crossroads, where I look up at the sign and then at a star. Wait, a *star*? A moving star? It swoops down low behind the two officers so they don't see it until it's almost on top of us.

It isn't a star, it's Harlan on a flybike. I'm used to seeing vast floating assemblies but that flybike is so huge it shouldn't be airborne. The thing is a brutal commingling of black and chrome with an exostructure of dazzling white lights. They pulse over its surface like an energy field holding the entire unlikely mass together.

Harlan approaches too fast to land, like he's going to attack. He is already between me and the guards and blocks them with the flybike's broad underside as he leans over. He flies a metre above the floor and comes straight at me, his left arm outstretched to encircle my waist. I feel his muscles lock and suddenly the soles of my shoes are skimming over the diamond road. I glimpse the two guards, who have produced their guns but can't shoot in case they hit me. The male guard waves his arms frantically while the female speaks, apparently to herself but more likely to Security Control.

The bike rolls back into an upright position and all its lights go off. I look down at my legs as they hang over the rushing dark and sense rather than see movement as the bike rolls to the right. I seize a warm surface that rises and falls and realise I've been swung up behind Harlan. My thighs brush either side of the saddle as if I'm drifting in the air and I clamp them together. The saddle is absurdly wide and my legs don't seem long enough. There are no protective restraints.

Putting both arms around Harlan I press my cheek against his back and breathe him in. His aroma is a fixed point in this wildness and I tighten my grip. The wedge of his upper body tapers down to a narrow waist, where ridges of muscle make it a beautiful landscape of its own.

We have left New Runcton far behind, the way I suspect most people do, and another part of MidZone shines ahead. We could be in outer space as we fly towards a distant galaxy, boiling with the power to change everything.

"Charity!"

Anton Jelka has called me.

"I'm all right Anton," I say without moving my cheek from Harlan's back. "I'm following a lead."

"Charity, we follow leads. You just tell us about them."

"I'll let you know if anything goes wrong," I say. "But… nothing will go wrong. Goodbye now."

I break the connection and look up.

Multi-coloured light silhouettes Harlan and streams off him in all directions. We descend and fly through diamond canyons whose bases vanish into hazy fluorescence kilometres below. The buildings are crude compared to Centria, but what they lack in sophistication they make up for in sheer size. One even has a train tube through it.

Harlan flies down at a steep angle towards a spindle that glows acid green in the distance. I feel our height for the first time and clutch him tighter.

Unlike Centria, all the light here is advertising. Unused to the constant war of blinding images I squeeze my eyes shut but that only enhances the sound, which is like the amplified scream of a million lunatics who each thinks he knows what I want. Just as it reaches a crescendo it stops but the silence feels even more aggressive and penetrating.

The bike tilts beneath me and I open my eyes. The spindle has resolved into a circular platform below and Harlan drops us straight down towards it. The great buildings rise on every side, disappearing into the garish dark above. Their brightness is muted now and I realise a damper has blocked out the advert noise.

The bike lands with a bump that goes from my underneath to the top of my head. Reluctantly I let go of Harlan, who swings his long legs off the flybike to land in a single motion. I jump off too and stand beside him.

"Good club this," he says.

I look up at him and smile. We both start to walk at the same time.

The roof of the building is a circular platform thrust up into the bright chaos of the MidZone night. Shorn of their gruelling racket, the adverts streak and pulse. Some of them literally fight each other, like huge characters made of light. Assemblies and ships, also adverts, crash through them and the whole relentless process begins again. Endlessly evolving illumination floods the platform and the fifty or so vehicles parked there throw odd shadows that stretch and turn like dark fingers pointing at a moving target.

A lot of the adverts feature my sister. Over there she soars on the latest flybike, different from the last one only in the runner design although I must admit the change is an improvement. There's also one for a product called Vingo that cooks itself while you eat it, which holo-Ursula is in the process of doing. The sexuality in her movements and expression is magnified by scale and Harlan's overwhelming presence. I seem to need more and more oxygen, breathing deep, then deeper…

I focus on the most striking advert, which is for Centria itself. Hanging over the others, it is a huge hologram of Ursula's head. Her eyes gaze steadily down, the iris and pupil altered to show Centria's logo: a filled circle surrounded by a thick-bodied C, both elements glowing a soft otherworldly blue. The limbs of the C nearly meet, perhaps to resemble Centria's great door open, perhaps to show the ring road that brings everyone close or perhaps to suggest Centria's grip on Diamond City.

As we continue across the roof there's a sudden deafening clang and a beam of yellow light flashes up from a shadowy area ahead to stand in the night like a golden pillar. Discordant music tumbles out of it and rises along with my hackles. Just as I start to feel actual anger the music resolves so sweetly I can almost taste it.

A woman flies up inside the pillar of light. She laughs and waves her arms as a man follows in a slow somersault. More people rise: a fountain of people. Some move gracefully in the absence of gravity; others bump into each other and the gentle impact sends them flying apart, mouths open in delight as if propelled by laughter.

We reach the light and I look down through a large, circular hole that opens a third of the roof. People fly up at us from a bright disc far below, increasing in size the closer they get and then diminishing once they pass.

The music is beautiful now and follows the movement of everyone in the air. A man flies on the crest of a rising chord while two women, solemn and curious as children, collide with a soft, echoing boom. Even the light has a sound: a low sibilant hiss one moment and the next a thousand voices joined in a single astonishing note…

Harlan picks me up and leaps off the edge.

Weird arse clench sick and lovely-

How can I fall *upward?* Harlan starts to let go and I grab at him. We rise together past happy people who move in the air and smile at us. I breathe deeply and feel better. Although I register the airborne drug my overwhelming focus is Harlan. As he stares up at me my gaze traces the dark contours of his expression, the thrilling whites of his eyes and his curlicues of hair as they begin to float around his head. He gently pushes me away and this time I don't mind.

My hair is a soft cloud as I fly up feet first. I panic as I realise I'm at the high edge of the golden light but there's a buzz and I bounce off the side of the field to head across it in a different direction. I flex my arms and legs in a slow cartwheel, then gyrate, curl and stretch to extend my body into every conceivable position. Sweetly hot inside my clothes, my own smell is an intimate intoxication.

I am free of gravity and self-consciousness, free of guilt and fear, free of confusion and thinking. When I run my hands over myself it's like they leave a trail of sparkles.

There is a slow drain away and the golden glow dims. When I focus on my surroundings again I see I've already dropped past the edge we leapt from. I continue down into a huge room with levels built around the column of light.

Harlan reaches up and pulls me out of the air; I land in his arms and he strides through the dispersing crowd. We head up a spiral ramp to the first level and a table at the back, where Harlan lowers me to the floor. He gestures to a chair and I sink into it as he sits opposite me. Two drinks grow out of the table; we pick them up and sip without breaking eye contact.

"You're a phenomenal dancer," Harlan says.

"Oh stop."

"I imagine you work out a lot."

"Everyone in Centria has to be at battle-ready fitness," I say.

"And are you battle-ready?"

"Did you want to start something then?"

"Yes," he says.

"Why me?"

"You just happened Charity. Do you mind?"

"No. You owe me though."

"Hmm?"

"You messed up my party," I say.

"The one where I saved your life?"

"No, the other one. There's still a load of weather about who you are. You need to pretend to be my boyfriend for publicity purposes."

"We both know I'm not going to pretend to be your boyfriend."

I feel myself blush. I need to say something important, something striking.

"Harlan," I say, "have you ever heard of something called the Guidance?"

He goes still.

"How did you hear about that?" he says.

My heart jumps.

"Someone trusted me with it," I say.

Harlan looks at me for what seems like a very long time.

"I don't know much," he says. "But in my various misadventures I get to hear things."

"What things?"

"Where the real power is. That's always worth knowing."

"Is that what the Guidance is? Power?"

"Yes."

I watch him, poised. Harlan takes a deep breath.

"Everyone accepts that Diamond City is a pure capitalist utopia," he says. "There's no government and there's no one in charge."

"We stand and fall by the market," I say.

"Or do we? Because it seems there is an authority after all and the Guidance is it."

"You say 'it'-?"

"Could be a group or a person or…"

"Something else? What?"

"I don't know Charity."

I'm dizzy; my body hums with mysterious energy and my thoughts seem barely my own. There's a strange, deep itch between my legs and I realise I've been wet since Harlan picked me up and jumped into the light.

"You need to make love to me," I tell him.

9

The room is in a MidZone hotel. There are no windows, which is fine, and low lighting, which is also fine. A round, white bed grows with infuriating slowness out of the floor.

I hurl myself at Harlan, astonished at the violence of it. I grip one of his legs with both of my own and hear myself scream. He claps a hand around the back of my head, uses the other to grip the front of my jacket and yanks me up so I'm almost on tiptoe. He kisses me and as our lips touch I lose the ability to see.

Everything comes back blurred. My eyes ache. I thrust my tongue into his mouth; he tastes of apples and wine. I dig my fingers into his wiry hair and pull it and he gasps. I whip my legs around his waist; the spreading feels so good that my skin shakes and all my muscles jump. Beautiful energy builds uncontrollably in my centre. Too amazed at it to stop, I come in a sweet storm of agony and arch back-

A thousand inexplicable images erupt in my mind, each a fragment of some mysterious whole and gone before I register it. My mouth stretches in a silent scream. Harlan pulls me back and holds me tight as I twitch and shake against him.

"Bad girl," he rumbles in my ear.

Recovering, I start to wind myself around him again and deposit my clothes; they run down us like wax into the floor. Now I'm naked against Harlan my skin feels one molecule thick. I rub my breasts against the coarse material of his jacket and the friction triggers crashing waves of pleasure. I begin to drop out of thought.

I try to kiss every millimetre of his face and his rough moustache makes my lips raw. His hands are huge on my body and he grips my backside so hard I cry out but it's good pain. I writhe with it and try to crush him with my thighs but ecstasy makes me weak. I grit my teeth and try again but each contact is a delectable ache. I make a funny yipping sound as my eyes begin to water. I forget to blink, to breathe.

He wrenches me off and hurls me onto the bed. I bounce and roll over to look at him through my spread legs. He slowly takes off his jacket and deliberately doesn't look at my sex, all beautiful and spread out for him. I snarl. I want his great white teeth to chomp me in half so I can taste the blood as it pours out.

Instead he slowly removes one garment after another. As each one falls he takes a single step closer, his touch the lightness of proximity, air change, pressure. I can see my thighs shake; I will come again any moment but it won't spend me. It's as if I've never come properly before and all those sweet explosions have backed up and need to be released. Harlan slowly sits on the bed beside me. He reaches between my legs, slips two fingers in and…

I'm blind again and scream inside my head. It's like all the beautiful music at the club magnified in intensity by a thousand… soaring, soaring, the golden column, the light… then darkness for a while, a blank moment of total satisfaction.

I rise as if through the Basis only this time it is Harlan's arms that lift me, healed of a wound I never knew I had. He leans back against the headboard and holds me to him so I lie across his chest. He carefully, thoroughly and gently kisses me. I feel precious and unique as his hands stroke my face and plunge into my hair. His strength is so great and so generous it feels like my strength too.

I feel steadier now as he lays me down. My hand finds him and he is hard and impressive. He lowers himself towards me and my mouth waters so much that some runs down my cheek. Generous though he is he enters me easily because I am ready and because I was made for him.

Until now I didn't know how to use my body. I was just a passenger in it, some tinny voice unrelated to the delightful, terrifying complexities that now overwhelm me.

The Old World is suddenly much closer. I am formed of its oceans, land and sky like a living memory. Its madness makes sense to me now as I feel its colossal energy reach the final, cataclysmic-

10

Harlan lands his bike on the circular roof of a disc-shaped building. It is part of a complex formed by a loosely spread stack of similar constructs, wider near the floor and separated by slim columns. The complex is on the border between MidZone and the Outer Spheres, which are visible in the distance as a curious lack of structure.

Harlan wears the same outfit he had on last night. I'm in a red and yellow jumpsuit, which is very easy to move in and follows my figure snugly without being ridiculous. The jumpsuit is made of smart material that cleans and recycles everything and has the added advantage of very lightweight hidden armour. I wear chunky boots made to walk long distances over smooth, unyielding diamond roads and my hair is slicked back into a tight, shiny braid. I run my palms back over it. It feels good.

We get off the flybike and cross the roof, where the view is dominated by the neighbouring assembly. An inverted version of the complex we are on, it's fixed to the huge chamber ceiling. The lowest circular level acts as a dock and three ships are attached to the side of it. One is a sleek dart, another a graceless rectangular transport and the third is cloaked with a holographic dragon. From time to time the dragon looks around and then gnaws furiously at its right inner thigh as if it's got an itch.

"Nice dragon," I say.

"Keeps the neighbours out," Harlan says.

The assembly's base is suspended about thirty metres above a holographic tropical oasis that emerges like an island from the diamond plain. Despite this decoration, the area looks deserted. There are a few generic ads, probably here as part of a citywide scatter rather than because this place is a desirable market. The only one that stands out is an actual old-fashioned paper poster on a wall. 'XPRO: WE KILL ANYONE' it says.

Harlan stops in the centre of the roof. All he has said about our destination is that he wants to get me a gift. I look up at him, unusually calm.

He smiles as a ring of orange light glows in the floor around us. The circular area becomes an elevator platform that descends smoothly and silently into an opaque tube. After a few seconds the elevator stops and its containment slides open to reveal a curved corridor whose walls are inlaid with small glowing green discs. Harlan steps out onto the pearly floor and turns back to me.

"We're going to meet someone," he says. "Please bear with him, he doesn't get out much."

I feel an unfamiliar sense of balance, as if I'm ready for something but don't yet know what it is. I nod and we follow the corridor's curve until Harlan stops at a door made up of four triangles pointing at the centre.

The triangles recess back to reveal a man who seems almost eaten away by nervous energy and rage. His jaw is permanently clenched and his body is a knotty arrangement of near fleshless musculature. He stares at us.

"Morning Dodge," Harlan says.

Dodge grunts. I think the sound is meant to be a word as it struggles for life between the clamp of his teeth. He glares at me, his eyes a watery blue as if all reason has been diluted out of them.

"Charity Freestone eh?" he finally manages.

"Hello," I say.

"Bit nice for you isn't she?" Dodge tells Harlan.

"Harlan," I say, "who is this gentleman?"

"Dodge69," Harlan says. "He's a genius."

"Yes," Dodge69 says.

Dodge steps aside; Harlan strides in and I follow.

The room is unadorned diamond and almost empty other than an odd-looking screen the height of a person in the corner by a table. One wall is completely full of a dazzling image from the Old World, a 'photograph' or a mock-up of one. The image is of a creature long dead; a sort of flying animal, with a small body and big, brightly coloured wings. I can't remember the name of it.

"Butterfly," Dodge says. "Limited image patent."

"It's beautiful," I say.

As I watch, the photograph fades to be replaced by one of an evening view over an ocean. The water is calm and the sky a dozen coloured streaks from orange to purple that fade in brightness towards a dark border.

"Oh," I say, "I've never seen this one. I mean I've heard of it but… This image is priceless."

I turn back to Dodge, confused.

"Who are you?" I ask him. "Why do you live here if you can afford that?"

"I like it here," Dodge says. "All my kilos go on the pictures anyway; doesn't matter where I am."

I look at the picture again. It has a strange effect on me. Perhaps it's the sense of scale; no one sees height and distance like that anymore. Or it could be the sun, lost to us now and out of sight in this image too. When the picture was taken though the sun would have come back again… My breath catches.

"Sorry," I whisper.

I shake my head and turn to see Dodge and Harlan watching me.

"What is it?" I ask.

"I like her," Dodge tells Harlan.

"Er…" I say.

"Dodge has to like you," Harlan says, "for us to…"

He looks at Dodge.

"Hm," Dodge says.

"To what?" I ask.

Dodge points at the table.

"Over there," he says.

We cross to the table. Dodge grows something out of it and picks the object up.

"Payment," Dodge says to Harlan without looking at him.

"Done," Harlan says.

Dodge hesitates, presumably to check his Aerac and then holds out the object from the table. It's a hypo.

"Left or right handed?" he asks.

"Either."

"Choose one."

"Right hand," I say. "What are you injecting me with?"

"This," Harlan says.

He points at one of the empty walls. A red beam of light flickers from his right index fingertip and crackles against the diamond wall. It's the weapon he used on the Blank at Ursula's party.

"And this," Harlan says.

"No!" Dodge shouts, too late.

A white beam from Harlan's right finger disintegrates the wall with a terrific crash that shakes the building and fills the room with smoke.

"You fucker!" Dodge shrieks. "I said to you, I fucking said to you no more fucking obliterate shots in my gaffe Harlan, I said that, did I not fucking say that?"

"You did," Harlan says, "and I ignored you. Now if you please: the young lady."

"I'm getting one of those?" I ask.

Harlan smiles.

"It's a nano-gun or n-gun," Dodge says. "It uses the movement in your body to generate energy. The clever bit is how it amplifies that and fires charged particles down the beam."

He points at the remains of the wall, which begins to grow back as the smoke and debris are absorbed into the floor.

"The obliterate bolt gives a single particle a hint of antimatter at the point of impact."

"A hint?" I say. "That's… not possible."

Dodge looks at me and then at the wall. He shrugs.

"You want it or not?" he says.

There's something wrong with Centria.

"Yes please," I say.

I tug the jumpsuit down to expose the top of my right arm. Dodge presses his hypo against it and I feel the cool jet of smart molecules as they enter.

"It'll take a while to grow," Dodge says.

He drops the hypo onto the table as I do the jumpsuit back up.

"It's a permanent product as well," Dodge continues. "There's no time limit before it's automatically reabsorbed so you never have to buy another one."

"How do I work it?" I say.

Dodge points between my eyes.

"It connects to the seed so you control it with your Aerac," he says. "You've got three levels of power: one is stun and the beam is blue. Two is kill, which has a red beam. Three is obliterate. That's white."

"Okay," I say.

"But be careful," Dodge says. "You need kilos to work the n-gun and too many obliterate shots are expensive."

"Can I still-?"

"Yes you can still pick your nose," Dodge snaps.

I look at Harlan.

"I thought that was quite funny…" I say.

Harlan shakes his head slightly in warning.

"The n-gun won't work on you," Dodge says as if I hadn't spoken. "It's too easy to have an accident. If you want to commit suicide you'll have to find some other way."

"Right."

"Another thing: this beauty won't register on any scanners so use it sparingly. The fewer people know you've got it the more useful it will be."

"But…"

"Get a standard weapon as well and use that as a decoy. Actually, take this one."

Dodge hands me a small, squat fuze.

"It's nearly as powerful," he says. "Another one I designed myself. Thought I'd throw it in."

"Oh, thank you," I say.

I slip the gun into a pocket. Harlan rolls his eyes. I look at Dodge again.

"How much was the n-gun?" I ask.

"100,000 kilos," Dodge says.

"How much?"

"I've made you superhuman, nigh on," Dodge says.

"Yes but Harlan-?"

"Don't worry about it," Harlan says.

"That's more money than I've ever had!"

"I think you're worth it," Dodge says.

"I – thank you Dodge – I will pay you back Harlan."

"No," Harlan says.

"How can you charge that amount?" I ask Dodge.

"That's what it costs," he says.

"But you could charge less and sell more."

"She's from Centria," Harlan says.

"Figures," Dodge says. "I'm not like that. I just sell a couple of these a year to people I like."

"Huh," Harlan says.

"To people I like most of the time," Dodge says and glares at Harlan. "Let's see how it's getting on. Stand behind that."

He points at the opaque screen in the corner and I walk behind it. The screen begins to glow.

"Looks like the circuits are growing up your arm nicely- Jesus Christ!" says Dodge.

There is silence from the other side of the screen. I don't move.

"What-?" Harlan says.

His voice is soft, awed, not like I've heard it before.

"Jesus Christ!" Dodge says again. "Who… what the fuck is she Harlan?"

"I don't know," Harlan says.

"I'm right here; I can hear you," I say, trying to mask panic with indignation.

There is silence again.

"Charity, you'd better come round here," Harlan says.

I walk around the edge of the screen and stop when I see how Dodge and Harlan stare at me.

"Do you really not know?" Harlan says.

I can't think what he means so I just shrug.

"Show her," Harlan tells Dodge.

Dodge looks at the screen and a man's silhouette appears on it.

The shadowy figure has wires woven through his flesh, as we all do. There isn't much, just the bright silver point of the seed between his eyes and a loose nest of silver fibres leading back into the brain. A further set of filigree wires lead to the n-gun at the tip of his left index finger.

"That's me," Dodge says.

Another, bigger shadow appears on the screen.

"That's Harlan."

More shadows appear one after the other.

"Other people," Dodge says as he flicks through them.

Everyone has got a different shape but they all have the same silvery wires, until…

"You."

On my shadow the seed and the wires are gold.

My legs lose their strength and I slowly sit on the floor. Dodge and Harlan watch me. My head seems to shake itself.

"I don't understand," I whisper.

"Would your parents know?" Harlan says.

"I don't know who they are," I say. "I mean I've got a mum and dad but I don't know where I came from originally." I nod at the screen. "I certainly don't know what that means."

"You must be a princess," Dodge says as if it's the only logical explanation.

"No, that's my sister," I say.

The automatic response usually gives me a sense of certainty but it doesn't anymore. Instead the feeling of not fitting in, which is as much a part of me as the heat in my blood, intensifies until it's almost painful.

I have always felt like an outsider, even in a city you cannot leave. The irony of that condition used to be grimly amusing but now it just seems cruel. I stare at the golden threads, which imply a value I do not recognise.

"It's okay," Harlan says.

He kneels beside me, runs the palm of his hand across the top of my head and holds my braid tightly as he kisses my hair. Dodge shuffles nearby and then leans over and pats my shoulder. I have only known him a very short while but I sense that such consideration is rare.

"Whoever you are you're still you," he says.

How strange that this peculiar, difficult man should summarise it so perfectly. I've simply learned something that was there all along. There's no reason to be scared of myself is there?

I breathe deeply and feel... all right.

"Yes," I say and find that I'm smiling.

Harlan straightens and lifts me with him. I look up into his face and remember the extraordinary sex that still tingles through me like soft electricity. I made that feeling with this man who can get any woman but who chose me. I realise I've still got the sense of balance I felt earlier. Perhaps it's here to stay.

Suddenly a little crosshair target sight in a circle superimposes itself on my view of the room. I jerk my head back involuntarily.

"Got it?" Dodge says.

"Yes," I say.

Above the target sight are the numbers 1, 2 and 3. I focus on 1. The little sight is in the centre of my vision and settles over whatever I look at. I feel an unfamiliar but very slight tug in my arm and lift my hand.

"The circuit helps you point your hand and your finger in the right direction," Harlan says.

I take a deep breath and shiver as I feel the tug in my arm again. Almost without realising, I fire and the blue beam flickers from the end of my finger to hit the wall. The gun controls lock as I rub the end of my finger and regard it warily. There's no burn mark there and no hole either.

When I point at the wall again the gun controls come back on. I select 2 and fire. The red beam darts out and makes the diamond wall crackle.

"Nice," I say.

11

I hold onto Harlan as we fly towards Centria. My cheek is against his back and I can feel the contours of his body like I did when we first flew to MidZone. Everything is different now; even New Runcton is tinged with magic.

I feel infused with mystery, as if surrounded by so many secrets I have become one myself. The gaudy terror of Diamond City slips past as MidZone gives way to VIA Holdings and finally to Centria, the enclave drawing me in with its usual ruthless gravity.

"Let me off away from the main entrance," I say. "I want to just walk in quietly."

"Whatever you say, beautiful."

I let the compliment soak in. A response begins to form in my mind-

The bike spins. Blinding light. Centria is in the wrong direction. The outer wall races at me. I'm terrified but there's no time to scream.

Shocking pain crunches in my shoulder. More lights.

People shout in my ear.

Harlan?

I'm on the cruelly hard floor. I try to clutch at it but my arms won't work.

"Charity."

A familiar voice. Who-?

"Charity, get up."

"Harlan?" I say.

"He's gone. He got away."

"…Away…?"

"Charity, it's Anton. Come on now."

Anton Jelka looks down at me. He looks oddly ravaged although I'm the one on the ground.

"Got… got away? What do you mean?"

"You need to come with me Charity."

Anton's voice is firm.

"I can't."

"You can. You just moved both of your arms. Nothing's broken."

"What happened?"

"Come with me, please."

I sit up. I'm surrounded by at least thirty Centrian guards who watch me closely.

"Fuze, right pocket," says one.

Anton looks into my eyes.

"May I have that please?" he says.

I pull the stubby fuze out of my pocket and hand it to him.

"I'd like it back," I tell him.

"Charity, you know there are no weapons allowed in Centria other than those operated by Security."

He half turns to the guard who spoke and says, "Anything else? Explosives, monitors?"

"Nothing," the guard says. "She's clean."

I get shakily to my feet.

"Where's Harlan, Anton?" I ask.

"He left you. Now come with me."

Anton walks along the great ring road away from the entrance to Centria. Up ahead, an opaque cylinder grows with a door in its curved surface. Inside I can see a chair with hand-sized globes on the end of each arm.

"In," Anton says.

I walk into the cylinder, able to see out as if it isn't there. Anton follows but the guards stay outside, surrounding the cylinder and facing it impassively. The door closes, silencing all exterior noise. Anton indicates the chair and I sit on it.

"I need to talk to Ursula," I say.

"We're keeping you outside Centria for now," Anton says.

He stands with a slightly distracted look that tells me he's reading something on his eye screens. Scared now, I look through the cylinder. To the right is the great curve of Centria's outer wall with the ring road's ellipse and three of the eight equally spaced link roads. I think of the train terminal on the other side of the outer chamber wall and people going where they want, a freedom I have suddenly been denied.

"Why don't the trains come into Centria?" I ask nervously for something to say.

"Centria's original purpose was as a final refuge," Anton says distractedly. He focuses on me. "Hold the globes please."

The globes don't convey any sensation when I touch them, even when they start to glow.

"We were able to get footage from the club," Anton says, "and of your journey to the hotel."

I will not feel dirty.

I look up at Anton defiantly. He doesn't seem to notice.

"Other than Harlan Akintan, did you meet anyone else at the hotel?"

"No," I say.

Anton's gaze goes in and out of focus. He nods.

"Did Harlan give you any instructions?"

"No."

"Did he ask you to do anything?"

"Like what?"

"Anything pertaining to Centria."

"No," I say.

"Did you at any time do or say anything you felt could compromise Centria?"

"No."

"Why did you meet him?" Anton says.

"He saved my life. And I like him."

"You mentioned when we last spoke that you were following a lead. What was that lead and how did it develop?"

"I thought he could tell me something about the Guidance."

"And could he?"

"He said it was some kind of ruling authority."

"What evidence did he have?"

"None, it was just something he heard."

"He was at two parties you organised. Why did you invite him?"

"I didn't invite him."

"Then why was he there?"

"For the girls."

"He said that?"

"Yes."

"And no other reason."

"No."

"You spoke to him on both occasions."

"Yes."

"But you knew he shouldn't have been there."

"The Blanks shouldn't have been there either Anton but-"

"The Blanks took us by surprise because VIA Holdings have no concept of security," Anton says. "You've got no such excuse; on two occasions an unknown individual was in close and potentially lethal proximity to a key Centrian asset."

I realise he means Ursula.

"At the first party I had no idea Harlan wasn't meant to be there," I say. "At the second he saved my life. I realise it was a mistake not to have told you Anton but if I hadn't made it Balatar Descarreaux would have used me as a human shield and I would be dead."

"Where did you go after the hotel?"

"To meet a friend of Harlan's called Dodge69."

"Why?"

"Harlan wanted to give me... the gun you took just now. It's more powerful than a normal one. He said it was a gift."

Anton looks worried, then turns abruptly and walks out. Unsure what to do I sit there uncomfortably.

The air before me begins to shine and a male figure takes shape. The head is sleek but looks like it could batter down a diamond wall, the hands resemble balls because they are clenched into fists and the grey light becomes a suit so expensive the patent can only be used once. As Gethen Karkarridan's hologram completes its intimidatingly slow materialisation I'm so scared I forget to breathe.

Gethen devised the policy dictating that failure is punishable by expulsion from Centria. Failure is relative of course. Centria doesn't just buy patents; it researches and develops them so there are acceptable tolerances of trial and error. How acceptable depends on what is agreed in advance and how profit is affected in the long and short term. The commercial seethe of Diamond City makes it hard to determine when a business disadvantage can flip to an advantage or vice versa. Gethen's genius at intuiting financial trends makes him final arbiter of who stays and who goes.

Will I be going?

Gethen glares down at me; it's the most emotion I've seen in him. I remember to breathe again and try to think of an appropriate greeting. Nothing comes.

"Did Harlan Akintan mention anyone else when you were with him?" Gethen says.

His voice is quiet. He does not blink.

"Only Dodge, his friend," I say.

Gethen thinks for a moment.

"Not relevant," he says. "Anyone else?"

"No."

"You're sure?"

"Yes," I say.

"What did you find out about Harlan?"

"He's rich. He rides a big flybike-"

Gethen shakes his head angrily and I stop talking.

"Did he say why he picked you?" Gethen says.

"What do you mean, 'picked'-"

"Did… he… say… why… he… picked… *you?*"

"H-he he said I just happened."

"Meaning?"

"I thought he liked me."

Gethen snorts.

"I haven't done anything wrong," I say.

His look makes it clear he disagrees. I swallow with difficulty.

"All I did was go on a date with a man who saved my life," I say, my voice high as I try and stop myself chewing my lip. "What's this about?"

Gethen isn't listening.

"Gethen?"

He notices me again.

"You're lucky," he says. "If it was up to me you'd be out."

Gethen's hologram fades, his cold, unblinking eyes focusing on me until the last moment so I can still feel his gaze when he's gone.

I get up, shaking. The door opens and I walk out as the cylinder is absorbed. Anton waits nearby with his guards.

"This way," he says.

The guards crowd around me until I follow Anton along the ring road and through the great door into Centria. A Security cruiser waits, its spherical bulk obscuring the view. Anton walks onboard and four of the guards escort me after him. I sit next to Anton as the cruiser lifts off.

I expect us to go straight up to Security Control but instead we fly across the enclave. I look past the impassive guards who sit opposite me and through the side of the cruiser. We are past the Comms Tower and now cruise by the five great silver needles of Gethen's Centrian Business Division. I shiver and turn away.

Presently, I see our unexpected destination is the assembly housing Ursula's apartment. The assembly is an airborne tumble of enormous cubes that reveals a different set of stunning symmetries from every angle.

When we dock Anton gets up but stays where he is. I stand as well, feeling uncertain and clumsy. Anton nods to the door and I walk unsteadily off the cruiser.

Ursula waits on the docking platform outside her apartment wearing a black wraparound with too many tassels. Her worried expression reminds me of Anton's.

"What is it?" I ask her.

Anton is in the doorway of the cruiser now. He and Ursula exchange a look and then the cruiser's mirrored door slides shut. For a moment all I can see is my confused face above the unfamiliar jumpsuit and then the cruiser lifts away from the platform to disappear over Centria.

I turn to Ursula.

"Come inside," she says.

She walks away without looking at me again. Nervously I follow her in.

The volume of her dwelling is at least five times that of Mum and Dad's and twenty times the size of mine. She could have a standalone building or a whole assembly if she wanted but unlike me Ursula needs the proximity of other people at all times.

Of the ten rooms she owns she only uses one, which is the huge living space we stand in now. The others are stuffed with goods she thought she wanted and didn't but can't bring herself to deposit and gifts she feels she ought to keep even though she doesn't like them. She enjoys the big living area because it's got a view over the heart of Centria.

The heart of Centria is a strange, empty space. Diamond City is held up by a variety of devices, none of which is a thick pole connecting the top of the great sphere to the bottom. However, if such a structure existed then the heart of Centria would be at the middle, embodying an almost unimaginable concentration of pressure. The space seems aware of this perspective and a perversely relaxing, otherworldly calm emanates from it.

Ursula feels obliged to counteract this existential void with a staggering amount of over-ornate clutter, all of it expensive and none of it tasteful. Pictures of mythical whimsy, some of them featuring her in various unintentionally comic poses (Ursula The Mermaid! Ursula The Cloud!), clash with earnest sculptures like the brick in a sieve that's there because Ursula thinks it ought to be rather than because she understands anything about it. The floor is a patchwork of tile and gem-studded carpet that radiates like an explosion from a ceramic copy of Ursula's eye.

She turns to me.

"Oh baby," she says.

"What is it?"

"Anton thought it would be better if I told you…"

A grunt of impatience escapes my throat.

"Harlan," Ursula says hurriedly.

She states his name like a fact. I stare at her; she gulps and goes on.

"Anton and his nods have been going through the files Mum and Dad produced and found something earlier today, something deeply coded. It seems… I'm sorry Charity but Harlan Akintan is a spy, a spy for the New Form Enterprise."

12

I twist in some kind of low rent immersive. The visual quality is poor and the content meaningless. The sensurround feels wrong; I seem to boil in my own skin. The only aural input is a series of attempted breaths that fail and fail.

I wake up. Ursula watches me, more concerned than I've ever seen her. The horrible memory erupts again and I'm back in the low rent immersive. There is no comforting darkness. Not even sleep can block out what's happened.

* *

Through a haze I see Ursula in a different outfit that doesn't suit her or maybe it does. She leans towards me.

"Just rest Charity. Here."

Ursula takes my hand and pulls me slightly off a bed I don't remember getting into. She presses my palm against the floor and I feel a drug from the Basis tingle through my system.

"This should help you. Get better. Take all the time you need."

Dark.

* *

"Charity?"

Ursula again, but only her voice this time.

"Wake up honey. Charity!"

"For pity's sake."

Another voice: Bal. Why is he here? My eyes are open but I can't see.

"Charity!" Ursula shouts.

I feel fingers on my eyes. Dull light enters and then flickers out.

"Don't just play with her eyelids, hold them open," Bal says.

More pressure on my eyes. Light again; everything is blurred.

"Charity?" Ursula says.

I try to speak but my throat seems filled with foul sticky plastic. I start to worry about Bal seeing me like this and then realise I don't care. The pressure on my eyes is released.

"No good."

"We're running out of time," Bal says. "It's been two days. I can't believe Ellery is letting this happen."

"It's not Ellery."

Their voices fade with the light.

**

I wake up and look around. Ursula isn't here. I'm on a bed, presumably giffed on the spot where I fell. I feel incredibly weak, as if Harlan has taken something essential from me.

I move and immediately regret it. The most vicious simulated battle loss would not make me feel as defeated, sick and physically sore as I do now. My heart seems to have enlarged itself to become an echo chamber for every unhappy thought.

I push myself upright. The ifarm lurks like a headache; the one part of it I can tolerate is the date. Although I've been unconscious for three days I don't feel rested. Memories of Harlan, Dad, Mum in a coma and the Blanks' attack remain terribly clear. They sit inside me, as undeniable as the end of the world.

I call Harlan. I don't expect him to reply but he does instantly and appears on my eye screen. His expression is hard but has a sadness I realise was there all along.

"Harlan," I say, "are you a spy for the New Form Enterprise?"

"Yes."

My body creases to wring the grief out and tears blur everything so he is just a shadow. It's hard to speak but I force out the words.

"Why?" I say. "Why me?"

"Because I am trying to do good." His voice cracks. "Because we came together as if we were meant to-"

CENTRIA SECURITY INTERCEPT: CALL TERMINATED.

A hologram of Anton Jelka appears in front of me.

"Are you mad?" he asks.

"I had to hear him say it."

"The NFE are opposed to everything we stand for Charity. Harlan Akintan will kill you if you get in his way or if he thinks it will advance his cause. Do you understand?"

"Yes. Am I going to be fired Anton?"

"Not this time, but you are running out of chances." He hesitates. "You need to be much more careful Charity, please."

If I didn't know better I'd think that 'please' sounded almost tender. The hologram of Anton fades.

Out of breath and giddy, I stare dully at an empty patch of wall and then get slowly out of bed. I deposit the now-embarrassing red jumpsuit. Naked, I feel shapeless, stale and small, as if I have been used up.

I shuffle through a connecting doorway into Ursula's shower. Its many heads on multiple waving stalks seek out individual target areas and blast me from all sides. As my hair lifts, fans and ripples in the flow I don't know if it's hot water from the shower or tears pouring down my face. The shower ought to feel good but doesn't so I shut it off and step out.

I grow my usual business suit straight onto me. The familiarity is disappointing. I sit at Ursula's table and look out over Centria, which seems reduced somehow. Still shaky, I grow a mug of Soupergaz and gulp it down. It hits my innards like a cramp.

Ursula calls.

"Charity!" she says when she sees me.

I run the back of a trembling hand over my mouth.

"Food…" I mumble.

"You haven't eaten for days. I was going to force-feed you some canapés I got from this filthy party on Wednesday but Bal said that suit you had on would take care of you, so I ate them. Sorry. How are you anyway?"

"Quite... bad."

"Don't move. I'm nearly home."

I watch the empty mug disappear back into the table and check the call to Dad, which is still unanswered, and the system that monitors Mum, which shows no change.

Ursula walks in and rushes over to grab me. I'm pinned against her awkwardly but don't move.

"You poor little thing," she says. "Men! I mean they're fun but honestly..."

"'S all right," I say.

"You look good though," she says. "Thinner. Very poetic. Very you."

I go to tell her about the golden threads but an instinctive sense of danger stops me. Centrian Security will record every word. Who else will they tell?

I prise myself off Ursula, who stares down into my sore eyes. She thinks if she does this long enough it is somehow empowering. It works on some people but not on me.

"Don't do the eye thing," I say.

"I will ease your pain," Ursula booms.

"You really aren't helping."

She humphs and sits on the chair next to mine.

"If only," I say, "he hadn't been so amazing."

"Yeah," she says quietly and then brightens. "Anyway, look on the plus side. You got properly laid finally and..."

"What is this 'finally'?"

"Shush. Plus you've still got your job and my wedding is going to be such a massive success that everyone will forget this bad luck."

"Bad judgement, more like."

"Charity, he was a professional. You didn't stand a chance."

"That doesn't make me feel any better."

"It should." Her eyes go steely. "Next time you'll know."

There's a pause. I realise the subject is closed.

"How is everything?" I ask.

"Disaster!" Ursula says cheerfully. "My wedding is in two weeks and horrid weather is still clobbering profit. Fights between the

Blanks and the Sons of the Crystal Mind hog so much attention in-Aer I wouldn't be surprised if no one notices my gobsmacking nuptials at all."

"You really aren't worried are you?" I say.

"No," says Ursula. "Now tell me you've got some ideas in that funny little head of yours, something exciting from your experience out in the real world."

My head is comfortably empty so I rub my eyes to disguise a quick trawl through the ifarm. One message stands out. It's from Bal.

Dear Charity

I hope you are better. I regret we were not able to discover Mr Akintan's purpose sooner. We must therefore take responsibility for what happened.

I'm still concerned about Centria/VIA being out of touch and know you understand the problem better than most. I therefore have an idea to address the current bad weather.

Get Ursula to go outside Centria and actually meet people, which will reinforce the idea that she is one of them. We can use the meeting to generate interest and take the focus off the Blanks/Sons. Please call me to discuss details, location etc.

Finally and most importantly, I feel very bad about my actions at the party. I hope one day you will forgive me. I know this will take time but the way forward is to work together, if that is acceptable to you.

Yours
Balatar

I feel a strange mix of emotions: relief, gratitude, anger and above all frustration because I didn't think of the meet and greet idea. I look at Ursula, who watches me expectantly.

"We need to get you out there," I say.

"Me? There?"

"A meet and greet. Outside Centria."

Ursula stares, astonished.

"Why not just mock it up here?" she says.

"No, it's got to be authentic, or as close as we can manage," I say and the words begin to tumble out as I think them. "We can have different kinds of people; the whole demographic spectrum, then have them on vix links so everyone will know it's real. This will dominate the weather for weeks afterwards!"

"Will you be inviting the Blanks?" Ursula says.

For a moment I think she is serious.

"Do you mean we need to have very good security-?" I say.

"Yes I mean that!"

"Of course, everyone present will be screened…" I say.

"Screened until they are transparent Charity."

"Right, yes."

"Ellery will support us. Anton won't."

"Bal will take care of it," I say.

I smile for the first time in days.

13

I lie back on the temporary bed in Ursula's apartment with my eyes closed. I need a new social processing patent; my version has expired so the ifarm is full of nonsense and admin. I start to ask Ursula which one she uses and then remember she's gone to record an ad for a year-life garment range.

I return to the ifarm, notice an unfamiliar name and open the message.

My beautiful darling Charity

What?

I thought long and hard about whether to send you this information for fear of endangering you.

The style is familiar; the formal diction, the long sentences.

But it seems you are in danger anyway and given that fact you would do well to have some idea of what you are up against, even though it is presently very hard to define.
They are after me, the very worst of them, and I won't be able to fight them off forever. Sending this information has exposed me, which is why I have been silent until now. Forgive me for that.

Oh…

I have forwarded everything we discovered to you. It is not complete but may be enough to help. I wish I was there to protect you and Ursula and your mother too, but I fear I will do more harm than good. You will have to protect them for me my

special girl.

I have persuaded someone from the Outer Spheres to send you this message so that Centria will not be alerted to my contact with you. The contents are in a newly patented format, which means that all anyone monitoring your ifarm will see is a set of statistics. Centria will not be able to decode these, or not immediately anyway, so work quickly.

There is so much I want to tell you but it's safer for you this way. Please take care. I hope that solving this problem will also bring you the other answers you seek. You must believe me when I tell you that your mother and I have told you all we know.

Love always
Dad

I gasp in shock. Dad's message blurs as hot tears rise and I strain to see through them while they trickle and cool. My heart feels dented; I rub my chest and breathe deeply. After a while it helps.

I open the first file, which consists of a hundred smaller ones. I hadn't expected so many. I try and scan-read the information in the first file to determine a pattern but none of it sinks in. There are text files, formulae, recordings and accounts in a daunting accumulation of detail. I always thought a benefit of being an outsider was the resource to deal with anything on my own but as the great bulk of mysterious information hangs before me I wish there was someone I could talk to.

**

My neck aches as I look at the long list of unread files again and sigh. My regular work has accumulated as I've gone through a quarter of the mission documents in chronological order. Some of the material is standard surveillance on a vix link; Dad will watch an area out in Diamond City, sometimes with no one in sight, for a couple of hours. Being an ex-soldier, he is able to point himself at an object or location and then not move until he or Mum is satisfied there is no further intelligence to be gleaned from it.

As Mum follows Dad, she analyses data. Surprisingly, the data is primarily financial and concerns transactions with a company in MidZone called Fulcrus. There is no explanation for why Fulcrus is of interest; the transactions involved are not large. I imagined the mission files would be a series of astonishing revelations but the only surprise is how ordinary their contents are.

I move my head to ease the discomfort and realise I'm so tense my body is rigid. I am still lying on my back on the bed in Ursula's room and have barely moved since I saw Dad's message. I sit up slowly and put my feet on the floor, which seems a long way away. I stand, sway slightly and stretch.

I know very well why I feel paralysed and what it is I don't want to do.

As I nervously start to pace I finally decide to look at the last entry and see what happened to Mum. My poor heart goes so hard it actually hurts. I take a deep breath and consider having a drink but instead just access the file.

There is extraordinary strength in my arms and legs as I run at unfamiliar high speed down a long, diamond corridor. Aware of every movement around me, I am more scared than I have ever been. I don't know the nature of the threat, only that it's there.

I'm in a recording of a full-on vix link with Dad, dated ten days ago. Some vicarious links are audio-visual only but this one conveys what Dad feels as well. I hear his breath as he hears it, close and heavy, and feel the strain in his chest that warns this speed is not sustainable for long. I feel/hear a woman's voice and it takes me a moment to recognise Mum.

MUM	Down the end and keep going.
DAD	How many?
MUM	Four.
DAD	How did they find out?
MUM	Unknown.

I don't share Dad's thoughts but I sense them through a series of emotional impressions as they affect his body. When Mum speaks for example, some of Dad's visceral fear reduces, while another tension grows as he carries out her instructions. Behind the action is a sort of calm I can't place at first but realise after a moment is trust.

Dad runs to the end of the corridor and across a gangway. I glimpse the dizzying drop either side before we race into a red building formed by five towers that curve up like a clawed hand. We must be somewhere in MidZone and judging by the light it's day. People either side of Dad register as a series of surprised expressions as he pounds through a blue-lit tunnel under the building.

I've had vix links with soldiers before as part of my training but none were as fast and powerful as Dad. Perhaps the potency is down to my closeness to him, or maybe until now I only saw training as a way to impress my seniors. Whatever the reason, as I move with my father every sense is attuned in a way I have never managed before. I feel realignment in myself; a loosening of restrictions, as if Dad is giving me permission to use my own power. I remember the fight with the Blanks at Ursula's party. I will not freeze next time.

Dad pulls out a fuze. It is reassuringly heavy.

MUM   Go through the wall on your left.

Dad's grip on the fuze is firm and controlled as the weapon spits green fire. The wall becomes a cascade of disintegrated diamond lit with flickering emerald flame and we are through before the pieces reach the floor. Ow! The shrapnel burns; one piece actually sizzles. Dad grunts and suppresses the pain with sheer concentration. I'll remember how to do that.

I feel his legs tense as he slows beside a mirrored panel on the wall. As he checks himself over his familiar profile jolts a little cry out of me. He's got intense blue eyes in an otherwise expressionless face, cropped blond hair and a discretely muscular, agile body. His outfit is combat gear disguised as the scruffy clothes a sub would wear. Some of it smoulders so Dad yanks it off to reveal burns over his chest and shoulders. He hurls the clothes away and looks around.

We are in a large triangular chamber with a slightly curved far wall that forms part of the circular base of the red towers. The wall we broke through is between two of the twenty customised immersion booths evenly spaced around the perimeter, while the entire floor is a pulsating advert for the child pornography experience you can apparently only get here. Dad tuts in disgust and begins to run across the chamber.

MUM	Er…
DAD	Julie?
MUM	There's no coverage in here. Stop!

Dad halts and the view swings as he looks around until he sees the chamber entrance in a wall on the far side. The entrance is empty but Dad watches it fixedly. The only sound is his breathing.

A man and a woman sprint into the entrance. They snap rifles to their shoulders and focus the barrels at Dad/me. I forget this is a vix link, shout in panic and wave my arms uselessly. Dad fires his fuze at the man and woman, who duck back through the entrance out of sight. Dad shoots through the wall to get at them-

MUM   Back!

The view jerks as Dad changes direction. Flesh between my shoulders prickles in anticipation of a shot but I can no longer tell if it's me or Dad who feels it. The wall we broke through has begun to regrow itself and the top rises as Dad gets closer. He leaps through the closing gap headfirst and for a moment we fly.

Dad catches a toe on top of the wall and tumbles down the other side. I feel a terrific muscular clench in his stomach as he kicks away to turn himself in midair and land lightly on his feet.

MUM   Grab the dekpak and go over the side.

Dad turns back towards the gangway. Growing out of the floor nearby is a disc about thirty centimetres across attached to a harness. Everyone in the area has wisely kept out of sight except two ragged-looking men who approach the descent pack eagerly.

| DAD | **GET THE FUCK AWAY OR I WILL WASTE YOU!** |

He fires over their heads. One freezes in shock, the other bumps into him and then they flee. Dad snatches up the dekpak and looks back the way he came, where a wall explodes into a glittering scarlet cloud. I gasp in fear but Dad doesn't as the pursuing man and woman run through the dissipating debris.

Dad races for the gangway but two men with rifles run across the other end of it. There is something familiar about them…

Streamlined, fit and fast, they have the dynamic concentration of soldiers. They fire at Dad, who dives to one side. The floor speeds closer, the view twisting suddenly as Dad lands and turns.

Rifle fire zips past, partially demolishing the base of a red tower. Screams echo as parts of the building fragment and crash to the floor, forcing the man and woman to jump back out of the way.

Dad slides across the floor, snatches up the dekpak and shrugs it on. As the harness lashes itself to his chest Dad is up again so fast I barely register the movement of his muscles.

MUM	Circular corridor to your left, around the outer edge of the building.
DAD	Tower's collapsing.
MUM	No it's not.

A thick diamond column grows out of the floor to reach the gaping cavity in the red tower, which stops swaying. Another shot misses Dad but is so close I feel it burn him. He sprints down the circular corridor and snatches a look behind but the curve of the wall masks him from his pursuers.

He turns his entire body around mid-run, slows to a halt and moves closer to the central wall. Holding the fuze out with both hands he keeps his shoulders relaxed and his breathing regular. He is utterly calm.

One of the men from the gangway runs into sight, all determination and lethal energy. Dad blows the man's head off but his body keeps running for a couple of steps and I can still see his face although it's just a memory.

For a second there is no blood and then it begins to pour down the man's chest and shoulders. His legs fold but he doesn't let go of his weapon, which lands with a light tap as if he is still looking after it. The body thumps wetly to the floor and blood spreads with shocking speed. There is no sign of the other man from the gangway as the one on the floor is absorbed into it. For a moment the gleaming red sheet of his blood remains, then it dilutes to transparency and finally nothing.

MUM   Keep going away from the gangway.

The view jolts as Dad runs down the corridor. He stops at a crossroads with an entrance corridor in one direction and a tunnel through the building base in the other. At the end of the tunnel is a five-way intersection, blue lit with a slow-spinning holomap of Diamond City that looks like a giant crystal ball.

MUM   Stay there and let them see you.

Dad stands at the end of the corridor. His heart begins to pound and so does mine. In the curved corridor across from him a diamond wall grows to the ceiling. Another one grows about three metres behind it and the space between them fills with transparent liquid.

The man and woman run around the corner into the five-way intersection.

MUM   Go back six metres.

Dad jogs back to where he was as the sound of running footsteps gets louder. Another clear diamond wall grows directly in front of him. This one appears to be about a metre thick.

DAD	Have you got enough kilos?
MUM	Yes. The last wall will be thinner.

As the man and woman run around the corner their brutal expressions turn to surprise. The wall behind them shatters to release the fluid and they are submerged at once, thrashing as Mum gifs more liquid to fill the space to the top. A red pulse in the depths indicates rifle fire but it's weakened somehow.

The fluid turns dirty pink. I can't make out the man and woman clearly any more and after a few moments they disappear in a swirl of blood and bone to leave a fizzing soup.

DAD	Acid?
MUM	Hmm.
DAD	And the other one?
MUM	Don't worry about him.

The acid subsides into the floor, followed by the walls. There is no trace of the man and woman. Dad runs for the gangway again, sees movement on his left and turns towards it, fuze raised. Halfway down the tunnel a diamond spike slopes up and away. The impaled body of the last pursuer slides down it, colouring the top half an even red. His head hangs down and only the back of it is visible. I'm glad I can't see his face.

I'm short of breath. My lovely Mum and Dad are these incredible, terrifying people. I ought to be shocked but I'm not. My hand grips at a gun that isn't there so I point my n-gun finger instead.

I'm with you Daddy.

Dad peers over the side of the gangway, which crosses an ornamental shaft so deep I can't see the base. I jerk in fear as he vaults over the side to freefall headfirst. I feel air whistle past him and shout in fear at the immense height. However, his heart rate has returned to a slow, steady counterpoint to mine and eventually I start to relax as he falls past platforms and windows to glimpse people working, arguing, embracing…

Dad calmly goes in-Aer to activate his dekpak. He feels movement against his back and glances from side to side as the dekpak opens out into four thinner discs on slender arms. The discs angle themselves so they are parallel with the unseen floor far below and Dad uses controls superimposed over his rushing descent to avoid another gangway that bisects the space beneath him.

Dad falls out of the shaft into a vast MidZone chamber. He drops towards the throbbing stratum of adverts past a massive inverted pyramid. The first advert is a giant green holographic head with hairs like thick cables and when Dad plunges into it he seems weightless in a green void. He pops through the underside of the jaw and passes a group of huge letters although I can't make out what they say. The adverts get smaller the nearer they are to buildings and Dad falls between rather than through them as if past fragments of a dream voided into the air.

The buildings below are either huge and basic or small and complicated, probably needlessly so. There is no order to the layout and the chaos makes it hard to focus on any one area. It's a horrendous clash like a visual equivalent of the advert racket, which we quickly reach the heart of.

This close, music, words and bits of both implode in a weird roar like the voice of some giant alien. One ad is so loud it hurts and Dad's view snaps around to a free-floating speaker. He shoots it into vapour and the pain in our ears diminishes.

Dad drops closer to the top of a monolithic black building and activates the dekpak's descent control. His fall slows and his legs swing down so he glides feet first. As if aware his reduced speed makes him vulnerable, he tightens his grip on the fuze and his heart rate increases. He operates directional controls to push away from the building and soon floats between six octagonal towers that bend hopefully towards each other over a park whose greenery at this height looks like khaki.

MUM	Oh no.
DAD	What is it?

MUM	Don't set down in MidZone.
DAD	I'm already too low.
MUM	Please let me be wrong.
DAD	Julie?
MUM	I'm not…
DAD	Ju-
MUM	VELOSSIN!

I'm back in Ursula's room, on the bed. When I try to stand my legs give way; I slump down until I sit on the floor and then lean to one side and throw up. For a moment the vomit gleams at me before it's absorbed into the floor.

That horrible scream was the last thing Mum uttered before they got her. I go in-Aer to look up this Velossin. There is no match.

The scream is not the worst thing about the recording, however. The worst thing takes the longest to register, perhaps because it defies reason. I've realised what it was about Dad's pursuers that was familiar.

They wore Centrian Security uniforms.

14

"I'm not calling the wedding off," Ursula says.

"Please," I say.

"Are you insane? No."

We are in a restaurant where she has reluctantly waited for me, her face flushed but focussed. The restaurant juts over one of Centria's rare unpopulated areas and the view is of a clean drop into crystalline emptiness. As the day lights fade into evening, Ursula plays with an empty glass while I look at discarded cutlery. I expect Security to turn up any second.

"Everything about this is wrong," I say.

There is a difficult silence.

"I know you're sad after Harlan…" Ursula says.

"It isn't Harlan," I say, my voice uneven. "I just think we should grab Mum and get out of here."

"Where would we go?" she says. "What would we do?"

"I don't know and it doesn't matter."

"It does matter. How are we going to look after Mum?"

"We'll find a way. We'd be alive at least."

"Why would we die if we stayed here?" Ursula asks, hurt and confused.

"You wouldn't," Anton Jelka says, having silently appeared beside us.

I stare up at him, conscious of the fear and rage in my eyes. He looks back at me evenly. The lines in his tight face give nothing away.

"Ursula," Anton says, "I'd like to speak to Charity alone if you don't mind."

Ursula is suddenly uneasy; she's usually the important one. I try to stay calm but grab her hand.

"I think I'll stay," she says.

To avoid trouble I want her to go but I also need to see her, to make sure she's all right. My gun finger twitches.

I force myself to accept that Anton has got access to soldiers just as lethal as my parents and could have seized me at any time. I kiss Ursula's fingers and let go of her hand.

"It's all right," I tell her.

Ursula hesitates, then gets up and backs away with a warning glare at Anton, which he ignores. I wonder if I will ever see my sister again.

Anton sits opposite me. He is able to appear bigger than he really is by dint of restrained aggression that gives him a kind of charisma. The effect is enhanced by his eyes, which are set too deep so he always looks tired and haunted. His mouth turns down but is very full-lipped, its sensuous contours at odds with brutally cropped dark grey stubble on his head and jaw. As I study Anton I notice his rigidity hides a restlessness, which he must keep under ruthless control.

I realise the usual restaurant sounds of cutlery and talk have died away and glance around. The restaurant is deserted; in this stillness and silence we could be the last people alive. I look back at Anton.

"How did you get the mission files?" he asks.

I try to look nonchalant but fear strains my eyes.

"You searched in-Aer for Velossin," Anton says.

"Is that all you've got?"

"It encouraged us to check your ifarm. A file the same size as the mission document was discovered."

"Dad sent it to me."

"But–"

"He got someone else to send it for him so you wouldn't know, given that you tried to kill him."

Anton frowns slightly as he sends and receives information.

"I see," he says distractedly.

"Well?" I say as anger burns away my fear.

He looks at me again and I feel my patience come to a definite end. I jump to my feet and the chair clatters over. My right index finger trembles so hard that my entire hand shakes.

"WELL?!" I shout.

I hurl a chair at a window and it bounces off. I pick up another one and smash it against the table next to us. My face feels weirdly static. I smash the chair against the table again and look at Anton. He looks back at me without changing his expression.

"Charity," he says.

The tension in his face has gone. As I glare at him, lungs pumping oxygen into me at a terrific rate, I realise I'm building up to a fight that will not come, a crisis that is already over.

"Why did you try and kill Dad?" My voice is quieter now.

"I didn't," he says, "I would never-"

"They wore Centrian Security uniforms!"

"I know."

"Someone attacked Mum inside Centria!"

"And where is Julie now?"

I stare at him.

"In her house," I say.

"Protected by?"

I think of the diamond layer Anton grew to keep Mum safe. Despite the evidence from that last mission file, my anger suddenly feels childish.

Anton gets up.

"Come with me please," he says.

I look at the wrecked table.

"Leave that," Anton says. "Frankly it's an improvement."

He walks towards the exit and after a moment I follow him. Instead of leaving through the front door, Anton heads up a spiral staircase. I walk behind him, watching the back of his legs and the soles of his boots until we emerge on the roof where the mirrored ball of a small Security cruiser waits. The door slides open as Anton approaches and he gets on but doesn't sit. I follow and stand next to him. The door closes and the cruiser rises straight up.

We pass assemblies and the tops of buildings and keep going into Centria's filmy, vaporous clouds. Above them the diamond ceiling is divided into quadrants by four great slots that make it look like a giant targeting sight. We ascend into one.

The ceiling is at least ten metres thick and forms ground level for Security Control, which I've never had clearance to visit. The upper edge of the slot is lined with spherical cruisers, battle planes, troop transports and great red warships, all of which can descend to any point in Centria at a second's notice. As our cruiser continues to rise I can see that the other three slots are armed in exactly the same way.

The view is very different to the rest of Centria. Security Control, which includes all of Centria's armed forces, is a huge, shallow dome with a thick pillar linking floor to ceiling in the centre. The pillar has got a luminous band near the top, bright in the darkening air. Our cruiser slows and stops midway between the floor and curved ceiling and halfway between the pillar and the circular perimeter.

Below us army training camps spread over a series of levels, their varied battle terrains a huge set of brightly lit squares in different colours. Flashes of light indicate work in progress, while nearer by hundreds of troops march in formation across a white parade ground. The soldiers are tiny from up here but their precision is unmistakable; they remind me of the microscopic machines in the Basis.

Anton watches me impassively as I survey Centria's awesome military power.

"If I wanted anyone dead they would be," he says finally.

"I understand."

He puts his hands on my shoulders. His grip is very light, very comforting and very confusing.

"I do not know why the people after Connor were Centrian soldiers," he says. "I would never have authorised that."

After a while I nod. He takes his hands away and waits for my next question.

"Why did they wear the uniforms?" I say.

"I think it was deliberate. Knowing their own side was against them would have undermined Connor and Julie, however skilled they were."

"The attackers must have had Operators like Mum. Can't we

ask them?"

"They didn't have Operators," says Anton. "That ambush in MidZone was off the books. An Operator would have revealed it."

"Who authorised the attack?" I ask.

"I don't know."

"But you know everything!"

Anton throws his head back and loud, surprisingly high-pitched laughter pours out of him. I shift uncomfortably and wait for him to finish.

"I don't know everything," he says finally. "No one does, not really. Look, I'll show you."

The cruiser moves up to the pillar's bright band and docks at a gantry. I follow Anton out of the ship, across a walkway above the unfamiliar landscape and into the pillar, where a circular lobby surrounds the central chamber. Anton's ifarm opens a door to it and I walk beside him into Surveillance.

The vast, high-ceilinged room is full of people. Some are in uniform, some not although everyone I can see wears the Surveillance symbol: Centria's logo inside a stylised eye outline. They create quite a din as they talk to each other, stroll or sit and process images fed by the ifarm to their eye screens from all the recs in Centria.

Anton leads me towards a raised office set into a wall, greeting members of his staff from time to time as he passes.

"We accrue information and search for patterns," he says, his voice raised. "I know more than most people Charity but there are forces in Centria that are much greater than me."

We walk up a short flight of steps into Anton's office and the door closes behind us to shut out the noise. The office is modest with a round table and built-in bench. There are pictures on the wall, some medals in a case and a large screen. I peer at one of the pictures, in which a group of twenty uniformed soldiers pose formally in front of a warship.

"Is that Mum?"

"We were in the same battalion," Anton says wistfully.

He gestures to the table; I sit slightly awkwardly and Anton sits nearby with his back straight and palms flat on the surface. Two drinks grow out of the table; Anton picks one up and knocks it back. After a moment I do the same. Two more grow. Anton stares at his and I move mine around like a chess piece.

"What forces are greater than you Anton?"

"Ellery. Gethen. Keris."

"Why would they attack my parents?"

"I don't know. It may not be any of them. There may be others, hidden even to me."

"Isn't telling me that a bit risky?"

"Riskier not to, under the circumstances."

"What do you mean?"

Anton takes a breath and then another one on top of it as if he can't get enough oxygen into his lungs.

"Do you ever wonder why you always get me when you call Security?" he says.

"I thought it was because of my job," I say.

"Ellery Quinn doesn't speak to me as often as you do."

"So why do I get you?" I ask him.

He scratches the back of his head and then very deliberately places his palm back on the table.

"Because I have watched over you for your whole life," he says.

Astonishment buzzes in my head while the silence around us seems to get deeper, almost like something solid.

"Why?" I whisper.

"I was ordered to. Sealed instructions. On *paper*."

"When?"

"The instructions were there the day I got my first job in the department."

"Who sent them?"

"I don't know."

"Have you still got the paper?"

"No."

"Do you know who I am, who I really am?"

"No," he says. "I'm sorry. Your parents don't either."

"What do you know about the Guidance?"

"I know the words are off limits. I react when they're said under certain circumstances."

"Do you think it's the ruling force in Diamond City?"

"I'm surprised you take what Harlan Akintan says seriously."

"I-I don't, it's just…"

My glass scrapes against the table. I hesitate and then drink the contents, which have no effect.

"What gave Harlan away?" I say to change the subject, not very successfully.

"Your father was tracking an operative who led to Akintan, whose goal was to get access to Centria and let the rest of the NFE in."

"Would that have been so bad?" I say.

"Yes," Anton says.

"But I didn't think we knew their intentions."

"We know they want to take over. We don't know why."

"Who's in charge of them?"

Anton smiles strangely to himself.

"Jaeger Darwin," he says.

"Who is he?" I ask.

"He used to be my boss."

"Here? In Centria?"

"Yes."

"Was he thrown out?"

"No. He's an exceptional man, with access to unique insights. He decided that Centria no longer aligned with his worldview and left."

I know how Jaeger Darwin feels but refrain from saying so.

"When?" I ask instead.

"Twenty years ago," Anton says. "One day he was just gone."

"Have you heard from him since?"

"No."

"How do you know he's not dead?"

"He is basically unkillable."

"What was this view he developed?"

"No one knows except the NFE and they don't advertise."

"What's Jaeger Darwin like?"

"The greatest soldier who has ever lived," Anton says, his voice hushed with awe.

"Then why did he lose the Ruby War?" I ask.

Anton shakes himself.

"It can only be because for some reason he wanted to."

I try to understand but there is too much going on in my head. For a while I look out over Surveillance at all the officers busy watching and processing. Outside, the army is training: people doing the same job as my parents, as Anton, as Jaeger Darwin…

"Tell me about Jaeger," I say.

"He is the most dangerous man in Diamond City," Anton says. "For some reason he is opposed to Centria. That is very bad news for us Charity. You've seen how strong Akintan is. Jaeger Darwin is much worse, on every level."

"Is he Velossin then?"

Anton slumps slightly.

"No," he says sadly. "It would be so much better if he was."

My hands begin to shake. I hold the glass tightly but it still rattles. I push it away and fold my hands in my lap.

"I'm sorry Charity. This is the worst thing I've ever had to say to you but in a way I'm glad it's me doing it. Your dad is as good as dead. If anyone stood a chance it would be him. But he doesn't stand a chance."

I am too numb to respond. Anton Jelka drums his fingers on the table and then makes an odd sneezing sound as he grips at his eyes. He is crying. I don't know what to do or say.

Anton eventually leans back to look at the ceiling, his face mottled and his eyes red.

"You're familiar with the Blanks, how they came about," he says.

"Yes."

He looks at me again.

"There were other experiments," he says.

"People were rushed into production, so to speak," I say.

"Yes, but the technology also enabled some manipulation to

take place. One company was able to combine a particular DNA sequence with certain enhancements to create soldiers of exceptional speed."

"How exceptional?"

"They move so fast you can't see them."

I try to imagine what it would feel like to move like that but I can't. All I sense is growing and powerful unease.

"There were problems," Anton says.

"Like what?"

"The soldier has to be physically lighter and his heart needs to be more powerful to get the blood round quicker."

"So?"

"So a graze could cause him to bleed out."

"Well that's a bother of a design flaw."

"Quite," Anton says. "That wasn't the main problem though; the main problem was control."

"You mean they move too fast to be able to control themselves?"

"No, I mean they get more powerful than the people they are there to serve and become… difficult."

"Like Jaeger," I say.

"Yes," Anton says. "I suspect his DNA was used as the original template."

"What happened?"

"Speed on its own wasn't enough. Something else was needed."

"Control," I say.

"Yes: a failsafe way of conditioning."

"Like brainwashing?"

"In a way," Anton says. "Unfortunately, that in itself was no use."

I think for a moment.

"The troops can only carry out a single instruction at a time," I say, "which is not what you want in a battle."

Anton nods and then swallows uncomfortably.

"It was soon realised there were other applications," he says.

"Tell me," I say although I don't want him to.

"You have someone who moves so fast you can't see them. Someone who can be brainwashed into doing exactly what you want, however dreadful…"

"No…"

"An assassin, Charity. A high velocity assassin."

I shake my head at him but it does no good. Anton squints as if in pain and continues hurriedly.

"There is one of them after Connor," he says. "Someone who can't be bought off or reasoned with."

"Bastards."

"I know. But in Diamond City it's the only way to absolutely guarantee that the target is… I'm sorry."

The office seems insubstantial. I look at Anton for some kind of reassurance but he is just as lost and helpless as I am.

"Which company developed these Velossin?" I ask.

"Centria of course, although now Velossin is a standalone firm."

"Where are they?"

"No one knows. Probably MidZone."

"How do people hire them then?"

"Intermediaries."

"I could talk to them…"

"Forget it Charity. Once the deal is made that's it."

For a while I look at him and he looks back at me. Tears trickle down my face, fast and slow and then fast again.

"What do I do?" I whisper eventually.

"Get your sister married to that shithead. Do your job, keep your mouth shut and get more influence. Understand?"

I feel myself nod. My chest hurts.

"At some point you will be able to do something about what happened to Connor and Julie," says Anton.

He puts his hand gently on mine.

"Will you do those things Charity? If not for you or me then for Ursula?"

"Yes," I say.

15

New Runcton looks the same but feels different. I walk around the perimeter with four Centrian guards and pretend their once-comforting uniforms don't make me uneasy. Each guard stops at a preordained point so I'm soon on my own, which is a relief.

New Runcton sits in a cubic chamber. There are two large, arched entrances at ground level, two more halfway up and three at ceiling height far above. One wall supports a layer of pod-dwellings, each of which is a bed in a tube. The hundreds of lit pods dotted among the dark ones turn the wall into a constellation but despite the lit interiors every pod is currently unoccupied.

People from the pods don't usually venture out of them but when they do it is to visit the Dabs, a set of four interlinked, stubby square towers in a building style abandoned by Centria forty years ago. The Dabs are between the pods and New Runcton's neighbouring settlement, which is similar to New Runcton although even less inspired. Beyond New Runcton an open diamond plain extends to the entrance on the chamber's far side.

The outer edge of the settlement hazards some small originality with a crescent of domes around a sunken garden but all the plants in it are holographic. Some are bigger than they were this morning because they conceal cannons, while the four people who relax amid the green light are actually soldiers.

From the garden's edge I can see the sign swing on its own down in the centre of the crossroads. Beyond that, the train tube elevates into the dark vault above. The tube is empty and will remain so because I have bought every ticket for trains coming through here for the next two hours.

I glance up. I don't expect a star to appear and whisk me away; that is absolutely the last thing I want, truly. No, I am checking to ensure that the four cruisers hovering in the darkness above cannot be seen.

They remain hidden in shadow. No stars appear. Good.

The first of the 'public' arrive. They are not the actual occupants of New Runcton, who have been paid to disappear this evening. Instead, they are an idealised version of residents in a place like this; plucky, bold, a bit cheeky. Meanwhile, Centria people emerge from the houses and begin to mingle.

Soon there is a party atmosphere, as if New Runcton is the social hub of Diamond City. I have created an event that everyone should be at, even though they don't know it exists. Fortunately, they can buy vix links from the people who are here and experience the party that way instead. I don't want to feature in any recordings and keep to the edge so nobody notices me amid the growing crowd.

I call Anton.

"All good," I tell him.

His face is its old tense mask.

"No activity in the surrounding areas," he says. "I'll call again in ten minutes with an update."

He ends the call.

Music starts to pulse gently in the air. Deeply buried in its rhythm is the wedding motif that will soon inform every musical patent coming out of Centria. It builds but sounds slightly empty in the half-filled town.

More people cross the plain to New Runcton from the chamber next door. They have been paid a lot to be surgically altered so they look poor and sick but we need to be careful. The poor and the sick are not victims. They are people on their way back up, perhaps all the way to Centria itself with Ursula leading them like a trashy girl messiah.

The poor and sick don't mingle too much with the style sheikhs and party people; that would be unconvincing. However, a few gestures here and a few conversations between unlikely parties there begin to create a sense of something special happening.

Ellery calls.

"Broadcast in one minute," she says.

"I'm ready Ellery," I say.

I'm impressed with how flat and unexcited my voice has

become. Once I am promoted, I will really fit in. Perhaps the Harlan experience will enhance my status in unexpected ways by making me seem interesting and edgy. It will certainly give my life a story for the first time. No one will actually mention it of course so I can safely forget about golden threads and wicked beards, while the offline n-gun is just so much pointless circuitry. Even his name will fade, eventually, I am sure. I think about how amazing the weather is going to be today and feel better, not that I was feeling bad, not at all.

Ursula struts out of the largest building. When she waves to everyone they seem to forget they are actors in a little play and cheer spontaneously. Pride surges through me. Ursula is the soul of this artifice; she makes everything all right.

Milky light swirls in the floor as she walks across it. As well as decoration to mark the steps of the Princess, it's a gentle drug mix that quickly elevates the mood still further. We must give the impression that the party has gone on for days without spending longer than two hours here. Some of the guests have bare feet while others kneel and press their hands against the floor. Everyone is soon much happier and more relaxed although I keep my boots on and so does Ursula.

I check the weather. It's positive and we already have coverage everywhere. Even *The Cron*, that bastion of tedious conservatism, is squeaking about how Ursula might have grown up and become a proper princess after all.

It's a shame so many of the guests decided to wear black. Hold on. *Black?* That's not on brand. I do a quick count. There are twice the people here I expected, which is impossible. None of the broadcasts give our exact location, which will be announced when we've gone.

There's a sudden flash above and something patters down around me. It's quickly absorbed into the floor but not before I see burned cloth and tiny fragments of…

I look up. There's another flash as a second Centrian cruiser explodes, its gleaming sphere expanding outwards in a blinding cloud of gas and debris. As the terrible sound of its destruction rumbles past us the flash illuminates the last two cruisers as they spin in the upper air. Their confused motion suggests they can't determine the source of attack.

A beam of intense red light licks at one of the cruisers, which spins hopelessly to shatter against the far wall. As the parts tumble to the floor the last cruiser starts shooting. In the light of gunfire I make out a cannon emplacement on the distant ceiling of the chamber's upper entrance. The cannon shoots back and hits the cruiser, which spirals over us to crash into the Dabs. Instead of exploding, the cruiser just smashes through the empty towers with an awful shriek.

The crowd doesn't notice. They are crazed, ecstatic. The floor is bright as more of the drug is pumped into them and now the white has streaks of purple in it. Not everyone dances; the people in black stand among revellers like dark rocks in a frothing sea.

I look around for the security detail but wherever I expect to see them there's a clump of black-cloaked figures instead. The figures surge and swell as the surrounded guards fight back.

I wait for the hidden guns in the sunken garden to come into play but the garden too is full of mysterious dark figures. There are so many of them I doubt anyone watching can even see what's happened. When the groups of black-clad figures disperse the guards have gone, their deaths hidden from the recs that broadcast every horrible moment of this debacle. I try to switch the recs off but the control codes have been changed.

I cry in panic and search for Ursula. Instead, I make eye contact with a bald, middle-aged crag of a man on the other side of the road who watches me with an expression of beady-eyed triumph. He's got a powerful-looking body but there is something petulant, even childish about him. Perhaps it's his expression, which makes me feel like everything wrong in the world is my fault.

I scan him. His name is Thom3 Hobb. His name suggests he is not quite rich and not quite poor but some unhappy median between the two.

I call Anton.

"I know," he says. "We've got ships on their way."

"Who are these people?"

"The Sons of the Crystal Mind," Anton says. "Oh hell, there are more of them. The way is blocked; we are engaging... Charity, sorry, stay alive."

Distracted, he cuts the connection.

The party guests throw themselves around. All reason has left their faces and I doubt they will recover.

I spot Ursula. Black-clad men surround her. We didn't want to look too corporate so she wears a one-piece red dress with black leggings and boots. I've got on something similar but in blue. She is a bright spot of undimmed colour and beauty amid their hideous drabness. I want her to beat these idiots into babbling submission but she can't because there are at least two of them restraining each of her limbs. One of the men pulls out a knife.

My outrage turns to fear so pure it's like a high note amid the din. The man slices Ursula's boot off and presses her foot against the floor. Her head lolls back and she sways. The man drops his knife and slips the remains of Ursula's boot back on. I'm knocked forward. Everything smudges out-

I recover in time to feel myself hoisted up and rushed across the glowing floor to Ursula, who smiles at me. She wears a black cloak over her red dress. I look down and see that I wear a black cloak too. I try and move my arms but they are tied behind me under the cloak.

I remember the n-gun and activate it. The little target sight does not appear. I wiggle my finger and realise the n-gun points at my body.

People bang into us and bloody spit flies out of their mouths as they scream. The BAM BAM BAM of Ursula's song is distorted by volume into something bullying and vicious. Ursula herself is lit from below by the hellish drug. She looks demented.

True to their name, the Sons of the Crystal Mind are all male. They remain motionless amid the tumult and any drug-ruined guest who bumps into one of them is punched to the ground where the crazed dance continues in a smear of blood.

The Sons have formed a thick semicircle that reaches back to incorporate most of the town. Tops of buildings and blocks grown from the floor are used as vantage points to create a kind of arena. The focus is a point in the middle of the street, where a set of ten steps grows. Thom3 Hobb strides up them to look over his silent followers and the unfortunates who jerk brightly between them.

I kick Ursula. Someone jabs me in the kidneys and I gasp at the unexpected pain.

"Don't fucking touch her," a male voice hisses, just about audible over the terrible din. "And fucking look happy."

The music cuts out. Its absence is a shock. The only sound comes from the people who writhe and moan on the floor.

As the drug glow fades Hobb lifts his hands from his sides and spreads his fingers.

"We are honoured," he says.

His amplified voice is a powerful baritone. Unexpectedly, it sounds like an anchor of sanity; people watching in-Aer will think Hobb has arrived just in time to save us. Despite everything I want to trust him, for him to let me know the bad things are not my fault after all.

Hobb breathes deeply. He stares at the floor, his expression a peculiar mix of love and rage. His eyes narrow and he cocks his head slightly as if listening. Beneath the shock I get a sudden sense of profound strangeness.

How do I know the Basis is not a god? I don't understand how the technology works. We have let our knowledge of it go along with so much else as we carry on our insane, cramped little dance amid the glittering ruin of our species. The destruction around me is so overwhelming, the inversion of reality so total that it does feel like I am in the presence of some wrathful deity. Perhaps it too fled into Diamond City and festers down here with us, enraged at the colossal vanity that is our last great achievement.

Hobb finishes his mysterious communion and looks from the floor to Ursula and me.

"The lovely daughters of great Centria have joined our cause today," Hobb says. "The People's Princess herself, Ursula Freestone and her fine sister Charity have heard the call and become part of our great mission."

Around us, the Sons begin a deep, humming chant. Hobb closes his eyes and smiles. He's got a surprisingly nice smile, especially with his eyes closed. His teeth are even, if a bit discoloured, but that just makes him seem more genuine and trustworthy.

Looking at his smile I feel that everything might turn out fine after all. The four ships will reassemble themselves, our soldiers will pop out of the floor shaking their heads in befuddlement and the people on the ground will get up and tell everyone who didn't experience it what an utterly splendid high that was. Hobb takes a deep breath and his large chest gets even bigger.

"The Crystal Mind!" he roars.

Hobb's voice blasts away foolish notions of hope and redemption. His gaze is so intense it nearly hurts and rage has distorted his smile into a terrible sneer. He has clearly got himself confused with the god he is meant to serve.

"The Crystal Mind," the Sons boom as one.

I shake in my silly blue dress under a black cloak that smells faintly of sweat.

"O Humble God in the Floor," Hobb says. "You are the source of all light, of all warmth, of all food and all drink. We thank you for your bounty, for the freedom and the life you give us.

"Forgive our waste. Forgive our foolishness. Teach us the way before it is too late, before we squander your gifts as our ancestors squandered the whole world. In you is eternal life for those who reach the true awareness. We know you will guide the ones who are pure.

"There are many whose greed and folly are such that they would abuse you to breed *monsters* whose existence is an affront to you. Their very being contaminates everyone, even us your loyal servants.

"Our dream is to reside in you as a lattice of bright power, but that dream will never be realised while such creatures exist. We your Sons will hunt them down. In their deaths the horror that taints us will fade, Blank by filthy Blank until we have attained purity for all men in Diamond City."

Beside me, Ursula groans as the drug wears off. She shakes her head and widens her eyes as she tries to focus. Her damp face is pale, her eyes slightly bloodshot. She looks around and then at me.

"Who are these pricks?" she says.

"Shut up, bitch," the nearest Son snarls.

He is a small, weedy-looking man. None of the Sons is particularly impressive in himself, but together they generate a field of danger so strong it's like a tingling on the skin. I look away, scared and see a diamond column grow in front of Hobb. Other objects grow at the base but I can't make out what they are.

I'm distracted by a commotion near one of the buildings. The Sons have got hold of someone who screams at them, his voice familiar.

"Get off me you fucking lunatics!"

The Sons drag the man into view. It's 88 Rabian, leader of the Blanks who seized control of Ursula's party.

I look again at the column below Hobb. The objects at the base of it are blocks of wood. I didn't think I could feel any sicker.

The Sons drag 88 Rabian over to the column where diamond bands grow around his limbs to hold him in place.

"Princess Ursula," Hobb says, "we present the leader of the terrorists who attacked you in your home. We must deal with him but await your final approval. Do you approve, Ursula?"

Ursula is still unsteady from the drug but straightens nonetheless and her eyes narrow. She will use her magic, be it flirting, wit or outright aggression to get everyone out of this awful place. I almost smile and then I see the terrible thing.

One of the Sons stands on top of a nearby building, right in our line of sight but out of the area covered by the recs. He points a rifle so large it needs a tripod at my sister. The shot will leave nothing of her, an absence I can barely imagine.

I realise with terrible cold clarity that I cannot let Ursula die.

"Do you approve, Ursula?" Hobb repeats, smiling.

"Say yes," I whisper.

"Yes," she says without thinking.

Hobb's eyes flare in delight. 88 Rabian stares at Ursula, then at me and then at the wood piled around his feet.

"Please," he says, "Ursula, please! I didn't hurt you-!"

Hobb points something at the wood and it begins to smoke, a rare phenomenon in Diamond City. The herbal smell is strange and evocative. Barely comprehensible impressions of the Old World swirl among it; the sensuous freedom, the richness, a vast and terrible destruction...

88 Rabian coughs and then coughs again as the smoke thickens. He tries to turn and look up at Hobb but the restraints prevent him.

"Hobb, this is wrong," 88 Rabian says, "you know this is wrong."

To my surprise, Hobb looks stricken as if wrestling with some frightful decision.

"My friend," he says, "the means of your unfortunate creation are not your fault. But you are an abomination and must be dealt with."

The burning wood begins to snap as a red and yellow glow lights the dark recesses of the pyre.

"I am not an abomination," 88 Rabian says, "I am human, just like you."

"You are not human," Hobb says, "and you are not like me."

Flames writhe up through the wood.

"Where is the humanity in this?" 88 Rabian says, his voice close to cracking as his eyes stream from smoke or terror or both.

"Where indeed?" Hobb says softly. "I am not an evil man. None of us here is. We seek to avoid violence in service to our God. But our plight requires swift and drastic resolution before we are all doomed."

"Doomed to what?" 88 Rabian shouts. "Being different and living together?"

"We seek more than mere existence," Hobb says. "We seek purity and thus sublimation. It is the only bearable destiny in this realm."

The flames creep closer to 88 Rabian.

"No!" he screams. "NO!"

"There are times when to do great good one must do dreadful things," Hobb says. "Then, when the great good is achieved the dreadful things are transformed and made precious. They are revealed as sacrifices. The sacrifices then protect the great good in the same way as these diamond walls protect us."

Fire rushes through the wood and it seems inconceivable that a human being is in close proximity to such a force. 88 Rabian goes to speak again but he is out of time. The flames begin to burn him; he screams and the sound rises with hysteria.

The Son keeps his gun aimed at Ursula as the other Sons begin to chant again. I make myself watch the pyre as punishment. How did any of this happen?

88 Rabian's clothes catch fire and burn off with astonishing speed. His eyes bulge grotesquely and his whole body goes red as it tries in vain to dump the terrible heat. I wish I could somehow suck the agony off him and take it myself but all I can do is hope he dies quickly.

88 Rabian's skin crackles and spits as the flames move up him. His beautiful dark hair becomes a set of weird bright flames, like a moving crown. He thrashes in the restraints, his expression one of such horror it is barely human. Soon it actually isn't human, just a blackened mask whose melted eyes form thick tears that sizzle to nothing.

As he burns the smell reaches me. Fatty and acrid, it disgusts even more for not being that unpleasant. Thankfully, the flames roar up to cover 88 Rabian's final moments in a searing yellow bulb too bright to look at.

The Sons' chant rises with the flames, massive and unrelenting. Behind the roar of the fire the screaming stops and is replaced with a faint liquid pop. Ursula moans beside me. This time no one tells her to shut up.

Around us, the people on the floor shudder in their nightmare. Hobb stands above the pyre with his head bowed and eyes closed, seemingly immune to the rising heat. I can't blink as the flames begin to die and I see there is nothing left of 88 Rabian at all.

16

The Centrian cruiser stinks of burned flesh. Everything does; I don't think I'll ever get rid of the smell. Ursula stares at the empty seat opposite her and retches sporadically but nothing comes up.

I feel doomed and repulsive; I can't bear to think about myself. The two images scorched into me are that poor burning man and the gun, almost an entity in itself, pointed at my sister's head.

I expected our troops to wreak suitable revenge on the Sons but by the time the first Centrian cruiser arrived Hobb and his followers had gone. I can't understand why only six guards and three cruisers came to get us. The other two were medical ships for the original guests, many of whom are now insane.

The same condition cackles at the perimeters of my own mind, like cold fire. Worryingly, there is a strong temptation to cross over and acquiesce in it.

The cruiser drops but touches down gently and I focus on what's outside for the first time in the journey. The cruiser has landed in a large room, roughly pyramidal in shape. There is a circular entrance halfway up one wall through which I vaguely remember us flying.

A blizzard of adverts tells me we're in MidZone although there are no other vehicles or assemblies in sight. A single building nearby is a rectangular break in the otherwise empty floor and despite the ads that flicker around our cruiser the place is deserted.

One of the guards turns to Ursula and me.

"Get out," he says.

"What?" I say. "Why?"

"You are no longer employed by Centria," the guard says. "You are both exes."

The cruiser door opens. Ursula looks at it dully and then looks at me. I don't think she heard.

I go to check my ifarm but it's gone. Instead, I just have a good old standard Accumulated Experience Realm Account the same as everyone else in Diamond City. I remember the mission files and look for them. Like my kilos and personal messages, they have defaulted to my Aerac. Relief is a warm point, quickly extinguished.

"Ursula," I say.

"Now," the guard says.

The other guards look at us. Ursula shakes her head and her expression doesn't change. I reach for my sister but everything seems slow, perhaps to allow time for things to return to normal. Instead three guards grab Ursula and throw her out of the door.

My disbelief is such that she seems to float in the air for a while, as if even gravity is astonished. Ursula lands clumsily and falls over. I jump out after her and the cruiser lifts off away from us. I barely register the movement as I try and haul Ursula to her feet.

Tears drip off her face as she looks at the ads. None of them feature her; even Vingo is now promoted by another girl, whose hair is light brown.

"Oh…" Ursula says.

Her gaze takes in the ugly building nearby and the walls that slope over us.

"No," she says, "no…"

Fortunately, we are still alone as far as I can see although I don't know how long that will last.

"Come on," I say. "Get up."

She gets her legs under herself and pushes but leans on me, which is quite a weight. I don't care. I put my arm around her.

"How much money have you got?" I ask her.

She finally focuses.

"My ifarm is gone," she whispers.

"I know, mine too. Use your Aerac instead. Now how much?"

"Uh… 960,341 kilos," she says.

"That's good, that's a lot."

"It was less, but my room, all my stuff…"

Ursula was more attached to her home than I ever was to mine. Everything in Centria we bought via the ifarm, from our furniture to Ursula's 'art', will have been automatically absorbed and the kilos transferred to our Aeracs. It's as if we were dead, or had never even been there.

"We need to get out of sight before someone sees us," I say.

Ursula shakes herself.

"Where are we?" she asks.

My Aerac tells me we were travelling away from Centria, not towards it. We are now on the border between MidZone and the Outer Spheres, which explains the lack of company. It makes sense; Centria can get us right out of the way before we mess anything else up.

"Nowhere good," I say. "Someone would have seen us land. Let's move."

I pull her arm and she follows me to an exit from the pyramidal chamber. I activate the n-gun and slowly lead Ursula along a corridor. We stop at the end and look out into another large, empty chamber, this one cylindrical.

"Gif us somewhere to get inside, quickly," I say.

Ursula blinks and frowns. After a moment a square diamond building grows next to a wall nearby. The building is unadorned and looks like part of the structure behind it, which should avoid attracting attention.

We walk in and the door grows up behind us. Ursula darkens the walls until the lighting is low and gifs a large bed in the middle of the room. She stumbles over and gets in to lie on her side stiffly, as if she is injured. I stare at her, trying to remember what I'm supposed to do.

I realise there's nothing. My career is over and so is Ursula's. Our family is shattered and our lives tainted with horror, part of which we caused. The pressure of life in Centria has been relieved but I don't feel free. Instead I feel hopeless, an absence that is paradoxically like a huge weight.

All I can do is follow Ursula to the bed and get in beside her. She's got her back to me so I put my arm around her and she holds my hand. We stay like that for a while. Eventually, Ursula lets go and I raise my head to look across her cheek at one closed eye. She has passed out. I hold her tighter, helpless and terrified.

17

MURDERING WHORE
Delete
I'M GOING TO BEAT YOUR-
Delete
GOOD JOB, BLANKS ARE FILTH-

The day we got here I reset my Aerac to deflect calls and messages. From time to time I check to see if things have calmed down. They haven't. More messages trickle in, which look like the same kind of thing.

The unanswered call to Dad is still open and Mum's monitor shows her condition is unchanged. Since there isn't anyone else I want to hear from I delete every message in my Aerac and set it to reject all communication.

I lie back on the bed and stare at the cubic interior of our new home, which would fit into New Runcton with depressing ease. Beside me, Ursula is unconscious with her face towards the wall. The warmth and movement of her sleeping body are the only constants now.

We haven't spoken much in the last three days. One or other of us will wake, press her naked foot to the floor and let the Basis dispense dreamless oblivion. Sleep hasn't made what we saw any more bearable though, or our involvement in it any less revolting.

Dad's files must have something on Hobb for Mum to have warned me about the Sons of the Crystal Mind. I scan the mission files in my Aerac for Hobb's name and discover a document about him by Mum:

RESEARCH NOTE
There is very limited information about Thom3 Hobb in-Aer, probably the result of a full personal info clean. [Note: check for

traces to indicate who is responsible – not Hobb, it is unlikely to have occurred to him].

Information sources that were discovered include: personal and medical files from Communal Health In Limited Dependents (C.H.I.L.D.) formerly $$$labour, formerly The Rascal Club 6, formerly The Rascal Club 5, formerly The Rascal Club 4 (etc.) and related organisations.

EARLY LIFE

Hobb grew up on a kid farm, which is essentially an orphanage/workhouse. Kid farms are always being sold and resold, hence numerous name and organisational changes. Sometimes owners are kind and well meaning, other times not. Children are therefore educated depending on what is in vogue at the time and what the latest owners plan to do with their new workers.

The prevailing culture on a kid farm is one of constant change, bullying and boredom. From accounts by Hobb's kid farm contemporaries, it is clear that the regular regime changes were regarded as both unnecessary and infuriating. This continuous flux could explain Hobb's need for an absolute, uncomplicated belief system.

Hobb's life was difficult but he was never a 'sub'. The impression gained from my research is that he thought he was meant for better things. However, he didn't seem to know what these 'better things' were or how to get them. He appears to have expected it to happen just because he was quite smart, without being exceptional. In his mid-twenties, something happened to change all of that.

PREJUDICE AGAINST BLANKS

The first Blanks were grown in the floor as adults, which was seen as preferable to wasting years growing and educating children. However, the mysteries of human psychology are such that people need to go through childhood before they can become properly functioning adults. They also need the physical experience of growing. Although later generations of Blanks were allowed to develop naturally, the first Blanks were not.

Another misconception was that Blanks could be clones but even the Basis cannot replicate identical human beings. It can simply create an environment for human embryos to grow, do the job of the placenta and ensure the judicious release of nutrients. The first Blanks suffered from part-replacement of this process with the use of stimulants, strength hormones, hypno-learnings etc.

As a result a race of very strong, hyper-educated psychopaths was created. They wreaked havoc across a large section of Diamond City before most were exterminated at the climax of a very expensive war. [Note: some of the original Blanks are still around. Wisely, they keep to themselves now.]

One of the casualties of this conflict was Hobb's kid farm, where Hobb still lived and worked having married one of the other kids as often happens with institutionalised people. He was not particularly happy, but he wasn't poor or desperate either.

His feelings about the Blanks destroying the kid farm and killing his wife are ambiguous. Anecdotal evidence indicates he had fantasised about what he could achieve without her. In a single stroke he not only had that freedom, which inevitably offered fewer opportunities than he expected, but also a cause. Inspired, he sublimated his confusion and guilt about his wife and projected it onto a perfect enemy.

THE SONS OF THE CRYSTAL MIND
The Sons of the Crystal Mind were originally the remnants of

Hobb's kid farm. However, over time the women were subjugated as 'breeders'. The cause of this prejudice is probably Hobb's resentment towards being an orphan, or abandoned. Details of his parents are not known but the fact his movement is called the 'Sons' suggests Hobb is claiming some kind of birth heritage.

Renaming the Basis the 'Crystal Mind' makes it an abstract, unemotional deity that thinks but does not 'do'. This description is in fact the opposite of the Basis, which is a nanotechnological tool linked to a financial communications system. Such distortion implies Hobb sees the Crystal Mind as an idealised parent figure. That his deity is harsh and demands sacrifice to achieve 'purity' is a reflection of Hobb himself.

So Hobb doesn't know who he is. I can relate enough for a plan to assemble itself with little conscious input.

I will spread a rumour in-Aer that Hobb himself is really a Blank, the worst of the original psychopaths. The notion is so outrageous it's actually likely. I will also suggest that the Sons of the Crystal Mind are not a cult at all but dedicated instead to extortion.

I start to put the story together and then hesitate. Ursula and I have served our purpose to the Sons of the Crystal Mind; they will leave us alone now. If Hobb finds out it's me behind a lie about him…

I remember the extraordinary vix link with Dad on his last mission. I remember too how Mum dealt with the attackers: with a diamond spike, with acid. Filled with dark inspiration I set to work on Thom3 Hobb.

The Aerac is much less cluttered than the ifarm and I realise the latter's complexity was another distraction, a means to keep Centria occupied. I sense Ellery's influence behind it and use my experience of working with her as I plant key concepts of the Hobb rumour in-Aer. There are plenty of opportunities; the Sons are a source of near universal revulsion and people quickly pick up on the story.

Mum's document is still open and there is a final paragraph:

It is not certain whether the Sons of the Crystal Mind would continue to exist without Hobb. However, the Sons have an income far in excess of the usual contributions from supporters, which suggests well-hidden links to big companies. There may be connections with Centria and definitely with VIA Holdings. Evidence indicates the latter may even use the Sons of the Crystal Mind as a proxy army to enable the spread of commercial influence.

I sit up at that last sentence. The meet and greet was Balatar Descarreaux's idea. What if the Sons' attack was too?

"Ursula," I say. "Wake up."

Ursula opens her eyes and looks at me. The grief in her face magnifies my despair.

"Do you dream?" she says, her voice hoarse with disuse.

"Yes," I say. "It's all horrible. Did Bal-?"

"I dream we fought them," Ursula says.

Her sleepy voice has an edge. I wonder if she actually dreams that or if she just wants to.

"We tried," I say.

"I dream we saved him."

"We couldn't."

"They weren't really going to shoot me were they?"

"I think they would have shot you and burned him anyway."

"Are you sure?"

"No Ursula I'm not sure; I'll never be sure and neither will you. I'm sorry."

"I don't like being awake," she says.

"You can't sleep forever."

She doesn't look convinced.

"I made you say it," I say.

"No baby," she says, "you didn't. I wish I could think as fast as you."

She sits up and holds me tightly.

"Did Bal what?" she asks.

It seems less urgent now, in Ursula's arms. I can smell the natural oils in her hair and the warm aroma of her body. For a moment I don't move.

I remember Ursula is not a princess like she deserves to be anymore. Someone took that from her. Someone put Mum in a coma, sent an assassin after Dad and arranged for 88 Rabian to burn alive in front of us. Rage stabs through me like ice. I pull away from Ursula.

"I think Bal set us up," I say.

"Bal? Why?"

"The meet and greet was his idea."

"So?"

"VIA Holdings bankroll the Sons of the Crystal Mind and use them as a kind of army. Hobb does what Loren and Bal want."

"How do you know?"

"Dad sent me the mission files; it's in there. Also, very few people knew we were at New Runcton and Bal was one of them. Did he ever mention the Sons?"

"No."

"Suppose Bal is behind it, for whatever reason. Did anything about him seem strange?"

"No," Ursula says. "It was all about the merger. He was... very professional. I don't know why he would sabotage me like this."

"I think Mum and Dad found something out while they were monitoring the New Form Enterprise," I say.

"What have the NFE got to do with the Sons?" Ursula says.

"Nothing," I say, my ideas becoming words as I think them. "It all comes back to Centria, something being wrong with Centria. The NFE, the Sons, they're just symptoms of something else, something bigger."

"Why go through all that shit in New Runcton?"

"Mum and Dad were attacked because of what they discovered," I say. "You and I were about to become a lot more powerful; whoever is behind this couldn't allow that. You were too public to kill so you had to be destroyed some other way. Disgrace in

Diamond City is just as devastating."

It's very odd not to be part of the wedding anymore. However, the ease with which Centria simply replaced us depresses me less than I expected.

"Ursula, I've got some... other news."

She looks up. I don't want to do this.

"There's an assassin after Dad," I say.

"Dad will fuck him up," Ursula says.

"Not this time," I say. "The assassin is brainwashed into doing it and can move faster than you can see."

She looks at me with such disbelieving anguish it causes me physical pain, like a cramp in my heart. I think she is about to cry but instead she gets up.

"So," she says, "what are we going to do about it?"

I let my mind drift over the mission file contents.

"Mum was obsessed with a company in MidZone called Fulcrus," I say. "I think we start there."

18

Fulcrus is a hundred floors up in a broad, cylindrical building that connects the floor and ceiling of a wide, circular chamber. Four large evenly spaced openings reveal neighbouring chambers, the nearest darker than this one and full of moving assemblies shaped like planets. Well-populated and expensive, the Fulcrus chamber is clear of adverts and illuminated by the glow of two round-sectioned circular assemblies. They ring the tower and move slowly up and down it, away from each other towards the floor and ceiling and then ascending/descending to meet at the centre.

Fulcrus has no Aer presence and doesn't advertise its location; I had to get the coordinates from Dad's mission file. As we walk into the elevator I glance nervously up at Ursula.

In a headscarf and large dark glasses she looks like someone doing a bad impression of her but anything more permanent would be a waste of kilos. She can change her face but not her Aerac so anyone who scans her will know who she is, while her ID will show on every transaction. It is only a matter of time before someone challenges us over 88 Rabian's death.

I tap my leg with the n-gun as the elevator fires us up one hundred floors.

The elevator slows, stops and its doors open. Fulcrus extends to the building's transparent circular periphery. Opaque, brightly coloured geometric shapes fill the huge open area, their tops just shy of the ceiling. Red cubes, green pyramids, blue cylinders, orange cones, purple rhomboids and yellow spheres are spread in no discernible pattern from one side of the great room to the other. They look like toys, except any child who played with them would have to be twenty metres tall.

Ursula and I walk out of the elevator and stand self-consciously. There are hundreds of people working in here. Few employees make eye contact with each other and none look at us; many just recline in tense positions to work with rapid eye movement behind closed lids. The sibilant rustle of many whispering voices gives the bright room a strange, haunted feel.

I start to regret coming. Ursula grunts like Dad does and walks toward the centre of the room, her usual confident strut only slightly diminished. I follow her.

A stocky, ferocious woman whose red hair is the only soft thing about her strides out from behind a green cube towards us. She holds one of her eyes slightly more closed than the other and the muscles in her jaw are visible. Grotesquely, her mouth is an exact cosmetic copy of Keris's.

As we focus on the tall woman, seven large guards in old-fashioned blue business suits surround us. Undaunted, Ursula keeps going as if she can break through. I grab her arm. She spins round, sees it's me and stops, confused she hasn't got her way. I scan the red-haired woman, whose name is Lin Lin Lin.

"Well look who the fuck it is!" Lin Lin Lin says. "Hey, you'll have heard this one. Why does Ursula Freestone never get pregnant? Eh? No? All right: her boyfriends all fire Blanks!"

No one laughs. I feel Ursula tense and tighten my grip on her.

"That's genius that is," Lin Lin Lin says, her mismatched mouth twitching.

"Funny," says one of the guards, female I think.

"My girlfriend's a Blank," a male guard says, glaring at us rather than at Lin Lin Lin.

"Look," I say, "we didn't want that poor man to get killed. The Sons of the Crystal Mind are insane - one of them had a gun pointed at Ursula…"

Ursula snatches off her scarf and glasses.

"We don't have to justify anything to you lumpy dickheads," she snarls.

Seven fuzes aim at us. They will shred me and Ursula before anyone in a blue business suit is even grazed. I try to put the insult to Ursula out of my mind and imagine what Dad would do. My gun finger wants to twitch against my leg. I don't let it.

"We'd like to hire you," I say, finally.

Lin Lin Lin is not impressed. I thought everyone in Diamond City was for sale.

"Oh?" she says. "To do what?"

"To do... financial... services," I say.

Ursula slowly turns to look at me without expression. I ignore her. Lin Lin Lin relaxes her tense eye as she gets a message from someone we can't see.

"How did you find out about us?" she asks.

"I had sufficient clearance for..."

"Don't lie to me."

I chew my lower lip and swallow. Lin Lin Lin's eye narrows again; she looks like she wants to rip my head off. I sense the others get closer.

"I worked with Balatar Descarreaux," I say. "He mentioned you."

"That's not it either," Lin Lin Lin says. "Tell me how you know."

"Or what?" Ursula says.

"Or I will make you tell me," Lin Lin Lin says.

Ursula doesn't look scared, just annoyed at the presumption of these people. She has forgotten she's not a princess anymore.

"We'll just go," I say.

"You just won't," Lin Lin Lin says.

I try and force myself to relax. It's impossible; I am helpless, helpless...

"Well?" she says.

I think of Dad in the vix link, the feel of his simple practicality. He assessed each occurring moment without panic or distraction no matter how terrifying. His conscious decision to remain calm enabled him to spot opportunity in chaos.

I take a deep breath. I take another.

I realise I am punishing myself for some reason. Perhaps it is for being in a place where I am not welcome. Perhaps it is for simply being. I decide to stop that, now and for good.

At once I remember the mission files. I get one up about Fulcrus and send it to Lin Lin Lin with a message:

I WILL SEND THIS TO EVERYONE BEFORE YOU CAN KILL ME

Lin Lin Lin's expression does not change. The guard with the Blank girlfriend growls softly. I activate the n-gun and set it to level 3 as the target sight settles on Lin Lin Lin.

"Well?" I say.

"Come with me," Lin Lin Lin says.

Some of the guards move off although unfortunately not the one with the Blank girlfriend. Randomly, I wonder what sex with a Blank is like. The same as with anyone else I imagine. The whole belly button thing sounds a bit of a distraction. You probably get used to it.

Lin Lin Lin leads us into Fulcrus. The floor and ceiling throughout are white and the space is evenly illuminated. The only features are the large coloured shapes and the furniture that supports people as they work. The whispered conversations get louder but I can't make out individual words. The voices are angry and cold.

I glimpse a man sitting on the floor. He sobs and shakes his head as blue-suited guards surround and dwarf him. We are past the scene before I can make sense of it and I know better than to ask.

After a while the floor begins to move us and we speed past the brightly coloured geometric shapes. Close up I see shadows inside each one and immediately wish I hadn't.

The coloured shapes contain people. They are motionless and suspended in a variety of positions: upside down, at angles, supine as if floating. The geometric shapes are solid structures, as if they have formed like crystals around the people at their hearts. The people don't look conscious, thankfully.

We arrive at the centre of Fulcrus, where geometric shapes create a discrete barrier so there is no view of the windows. In front of a large yellow cone that contains the small figure of a child a man stands and watches us arrive. As the floor eases to a stop a few metres away from him, Lin Lin Lin and her remaining entourage move silently out of sight although I sense they're not far. The man waits a long enough to make me uneasy and then comes forward, solemnly extending his hand.

I scan him. His name is Steeber Loke.

Steeber is of indeterminate racial heritage with a bulky, powerful body that moves with deceptive grace and utter control. His hair looks attended to in a last-minute sort of way and his skin is oily with scars across his forehead and cheeks.

I shake his hand. His palms are dry and unusually coarse.

"Sorry about the ceremony on the way in," he says.

His quiet voice is scrupulously polite and every word seems measured.

"So I should fucking think," Ursula says.

"My sister is… ah, still troubled by recent events," I say.

Steeber nods understandingly.

"Horrible," he says, "just horrible. Please, sit."

A ring of three chairs grows out of the floor, one red, one yellow and one blue. Steeber sits and slowly crosses his legs. A large glass blooms from the arm of each chair and fills with a matching liquid. Steeber picks up his drink and sips with a strange, absent-minded expression as if the taste doesn't quite register.

I lower myself into the chair opposite and tuck my legs to the side. Ursula glares at Steeber and then sits as well, her legs spread like an invitation, a challenge. She snatches her glass and gulps the contents. I sigh inwardly and hope it wasn't drugged.

"Was that nice then?" I ask her.

"It was all right, yeah," she says.

I ignore my drink. Steeber puts his down, meshes his fingers contemplatively and regards the small circle of empty floor between us.

"Lin Lin Lin sent me your document," he says. "What concerns me is that it was created in utmost secrecy. I am aware of your new circumstances; if you let me know how you came by the document I could be of help to you."

"Help how?" Ursula says.

"We have many opportunities in Fulcrus," Steeber says.

"You're offering me a job?" I say.

"Yes," Steeber says. "You should take it; I know what happens to exes from Centria. It's very different out here in the rest of Diamond City."

"What is it you do?" Ursula says.

Steeber looks at her finally.

"We assist," he says.

"I don't understand," Ursula says.

"The nano-finance system in Diamond City is so simple and so fair that it's almost impossible to make decent money out of it," Steeber says.

"Hm," I say.

Ursula looks at me, then at Steeber and nods slowly. She's got no idea what we are talking about.

"Alternative revenues must therefore be found," Steeber continues.

I glance at the encased human figure behind him.

"You have like for like kilo exchanges," he says, "a kilo of plastic for a kilo of metal for example. Then you have relative values, which are where the profit is."

"Are you brokers of some kind?" I say.

"Not quite. Brokerage is all very well but I find that the market determines most product values."

"People won't pay over the odds for something whose worth they already know," I say.

"Exactly," Steeber says. "So companies create products whose wealth is hard to quantify. We assist them in these ventures financially."

"How?" I ask.

"We buy the product from them for an agreed price, usually a very high one. That purchase sets a precedent that enables them to sell for more."

"What if it doesn't sell?" I ask.

Steeber waves at the shapes around him.

"That is where they come in," he says.

"Hostages?" Ursula says.

"Securities," Steeber says. "Everyone has somebody they

value."

He smiles at Ursula and something cold clutches at my heart.

"Do people actually agree to this?" I ask.

"Sometimes they do," Steeber says, "sometimes not."

"So you kidnap their families?" Ursula says.

"Not whole families, we haven't got the space. But someone important, yes."

"Do they always pay?" I ask.

"One way or another."

"I'd be tempted to blow you into the Outer Spheres," Ursula says.

"As would I," Steeber says. "Hence our secrecy, although people who need us still seem able to get in touch. That's why we keep the securities here."

"As human shields," I say.

"Exactly," Steeber says. "The containers let you see that there is someone inside but not who it is. You would never find your loved one in time and launching an all-out attack would be even riskier. We always get our kilos back, plus substantial interest. Charity, you look confused."

"It seems so much trouble," I say. "Why not just exchange terms?"

"Terms?" Ursula says.

"You can grow most things out of the floor but not all," Steeber tells her patiently. "Services, for example, fall into a category that is hard to quantify. How do you avoid getting ripped off? Trust is a very rare commodity in Diamond City."

"Right," Ursula says uncertainly.

"Exchanging terms is like buying trust," Steeber says. "Suppose I've got something that can't be grown by the Basis, like an Old World item. I need to get it to another location but can't go myself because, say, the journey is too dangerous. I need a courier to take it. What's to stop the courier from stealing the item and selling it?"

"Nothing," Ursula says.

"Diamond City abhors a commercial vacuum so a solution has been found," Steeber continues. "Terms are patents in which you write the details of your agreement. Once the courier and I buy the completed patent, he commits to delivery and I commit to pay him.

"The terms contain instructions to the Basis. If the courier does not deliver the item to the agreed location at the agreed time then something bad happens."

"How bad?" Ursula says.

"The bad thing could be as simple as transferring every kilo in the courier's Aerac to mine. Or the terms could instruct the Basis to grow a cannon next to the courier and blow his head off.

"In common with most of Diamond City, we don't like terms. Both parties have to agree to them and once agreed, the terms can't be changed or cancelled. Then there are in-Aer records, that sort of thing. Our solution is more open-ended."

"Do you ever give the people back?" I say.

"Yes. There are many different ways to make money out of people Charity. Coming from Centria, you should know."

"Centria is different," I say, not quite convinced.

"Centria likes publicity," Steeber says. "That's the only difference I can see."

I feel more alienated from this man than I ever did in Centria.

"I don't think we can work for you Steeber," I say.

"Pity," Steeber says, "especially now you know so much about us."

"We won't say anything," I say.

He looks at Ursula again and then smiles at me. I want to run but instead I grip the chair so my hands won't shake because whatever is wrong with Centria somehow involves Steeber Loke.

"Tell me how you got that document," he says.

His face holds no expression, the state in which I think Steeber is most comfortable.

"My dad is a Centrian spy and he sent it to me," I say.

Ursula looks at me. I hear her swallow.

"Who was he spying on?" Steeber says.

"The New Form Enterprise," I say.

Steeber looks surprised.

"Were there other files?" he asks.

"Some more like the one I sent you," I say.

"Has anyone else got this information?" Steeber says.

"Dad and one other."

"Who?"

"Someone in Centria."

Lin Lin Lin and the guards surround us.

"Who?" Steeber says again with that polite, otherworldly calm.

For the first time Ursula looks scared.

"Our mother. She's Dad's Operator. They're soldiers. If you kill us they will-"

"Yes, yes," Steeber says. "Where is your father?"

"I don't know."

I feel a gun against the back of my head as two guards seize Ursula's arms. She kicks her long legs ineffectually. Lin Lin Lin punches both of Ursula's thighs in terrifying quick succession. Ursula's feet thud to the floor as the feeling leaves them. Lin Lin Lin jumps onto Ursula's lap, pinning her to the chair.

"Hmm, hmmm, mmm," Lin Lin Lin says with dead-eyed intensity.

She grabs Ursula's throat as a small knife with a serrated edge grows out of the floor. The guard with the Blank girlfriend picks up the knife and hands it to Lin Lin Lin.

"Ah," Lin Lin Lin says, "Budget Stabmaster 5000. Lovely."

"Wait!" I say.

The gun barrel traces a scratchy little circle in my hair. Lin Lin Lin taps the knife against her chin thoughtfully as she examines every contour of my sister's face. Eventually, Lin Lin Lin nods to herself and holds the point of the knife against Ursula's left eye.

"Dad's hiding!" I shout.

Lin Lin Lin grunts and seems to restrain herself reluctantly.

"Why?" Steeber says.

"There's a Velossin after him," I say.

Steeber's gaze doesn't waver but something changes in the tense atmosphere, as if he has come to a decision. Lin Lin Lin slowly moves the knife away from Ursula's eye and turns to me.

"We can find you," Lin Lin Lin says.

"Understood," I say.

Lin Lin Lin takes her time getting off Ursula and steps back. Shakily, I get up and so does Ursula. Steeber remains seated.

"Your father must be quite a problem for someone," Steeber says.

"How so?" I say.

"Velossin are incredibly expensive," Steeber says. "Part of the deal is that if you do manage to kill the one after you – and you won't by the way – another is despatched in his place."

I try not to stumble as I grab Ursula's arm. The floor whisks us back to the elevator in a traumatic blur.

19

Our vehicle is a graceful silver lozenge, six metres long by three across although the interior is smaller to hide the Basis interaction pads. The hull can be one or two-way-transparent and is currently set to reveal a strip of MidZone view around the sides with another across the ceiling and floor. Operated in-Aer with a set of backup controls at the front of the cabin, the ship will get us out of trouble fast although the patent commission was a ruinous 15%.

In the three hours since Fulcrus we have tried to get over our experience there with limited success. Ursula slumps on the long seat opposite mine, her expression glazed. At least she has stopped shaking.

I feel less shocked than depressingly resigned. Everyone outside Centria seems so much more cunning and worldly than I am. How are we going to last long enough to learn basic survival?

I look down through the window. We are on an unplotted, unpredictable course and fly equidistantly between the ceiling and the floor. This part of MidZone is called Gereleye. Diamond roads, mezzanines and graceful buildings curve gently away. With its subtle, almost muted colours, Gereleye lacks Centria's dizzying glamour or the dark pulse of other MidZone districts but is more calming for it. Daylight is standard throughout and adverts appear to be planned so they don't deteriorate into a storm of blinding noise. The even spread of landscape has a pleasant effect and I actually start to relax.

Suddenly I get a strange feeling. Ursula hasn't moved; the ship's interior is unchanged so I look outside. A few other vehicles are on courses similar to ours but none are close. In the distance a dark green warship drifts behind a set of assemblies that descend from the ceiling like giant frozen waterfalls. I turn to study the area behind us. There's nothing there, which surprises me because I now recognise the sense of being followed.

"What a dick," Ursula says.

Her voice is a welcome interruption to my unease.

"Who?" I say.

"Loke. Why would Centria do business with someone like him?"

"I don't understand that either," I say. "The answer is in the mission files."

I get them up and go through anything to do with Fulcrus, which is easier now I know their business model. The accounts detail payments from Centria to Fulcrus for a product called 'Zero'.

"Did you ever hear about anything or anyone called 'Zero'?" I ask Ursula.

"No."

I sink back into the data.

There's no pattern to the payments from Centria; even the timings are off. Remembering what Steeber said about interest payments I factor those in but the information still doesn't make sense. Increasingly frustrated, I buy an advanced accounting program and feed it the numbers. They tell me Centria's payments to Fulcrus total nearly a million kilos.

I find a new focus, partly from fear and partly from Ursula. I look over at her. Scruffy and scared she is no less wonderful and here with me alone, just how I always wanted her. She sees me looking and bugs her eyes. I smile. Everything seems easier.

I start again. With effort, I don't project any expectation onto the figures and try instead to understand what is actually there. Soon I settle into a rhythm. Comfortable on the seat, I concentrate all my energy on analysis and fly over the data like the ship over MidZone.

* *

My head hurts despite fatigue adjustments made by the eye screens. In-Aer coordinates show the ship is still in Gereleye, where we have flown in a long loop for the past hour.

I open my eyes to look past the data at Ursula. She lies on her front looking sadly down at the seat. I want to put my comforting arms around those familiar shapely shoulders and stroke that shiny dark hair, which is kinked on one side now that Ursula has abandoned her rigorous beauty regime.

I will give the data ten more minutes, after which we can land and get a drink. I close my eyes and start to work again. Distracted by the prospect of relaxing with Ursula I skip over a familiar name and read on.

The name tugs at me. I go back to it and gasp as my eyes fly open.

"What is it?" Ursula says.

"Fulcrus is owned by VIA Holdings."

Ursula jolts towards me as the facts jostle in my mind.

"Bal suggested the meet and greet," I say. "The Sons of the Crystal Mind sabotaged it. Bal's company, VIA Holdings, secretly backs the Sons. VIA Holdings also owns Fulcrus, a company that seems able to hold Centria to ransom."

"What has Fulcrus got on Centria?"

"Whatever is wrong with it I suppose."

"And Mum and Dad's mission uncovered VIA Holdings using Fulcrus to blackmail Centria…"

"Just as VIA Holdings and Centria were about to merge," I say.

We stare at each other.

"The merger will benefit VIA Holdings enormously," Ursula says.

"Yes…"

"It will go from a crappy tenth-rate outfit to the most powerful company in Diamond City."

I watch Ursula put it together.

"Mum and Dad's discovery could properly screw that merger up," she says.

"So Bal and Loren had a strong motive to attack Mum and Dad and discredit us," I say.

After the icy calm of analysis, rage lights up inside me. I shout and thump the ship's wall. The impact on the light craft satisfies.

"Let's go and fucking beat it out of them," Ursula says.

As the ship changes course and accelerates I picture 88 Rabian's burning face. Balatar Descarreaux was the architect of that atrocity and the cause of everything that has happened since. Loren is as guilty but inspires less hatred; unlike her, Bal has never bothered to hide his contempt. He considers me a minor being he can take his frustrations out on. Something about his disdain chimes unpleasantly with my ignorance about myself, confusion Bal obviously regards as weakness.

Ursula doesn't feel this despair; she just wants to destroy them. Her aggression is a tangible force, simple and beguiling. It gives me clarity. I let my rage build.

Ursula climbs onto the front seat while I slip in beside her. She engages the ship's controls and opens the front view until the great curves of Gereleye spread before us. They begin to streak past as Ursula increases our speed, her expression fixed and ferocious.

We finally leave Gereleye and swoop through a glowing cavern hung with slender white spires that taper down, their pointed tips suspended just above the surface of a motionless black lake. The ship yaws automatically to avoid the spires or I'm sure Ursula would just smash her way through.

I grip my seat as we pitch forward and then bank right through an arch into a more familiar MidZone chamber: big, noisy and full of clashing adverts. Speed breaks them into bright fragments and my restraint vanishes in a blinding kaleidoscopic rush.

I've got the n-gun up and its target sight jumps around my vision. I swat at it. I could kill anyone. For the hell of it I go to fire-

I stop. Slowly, I force myself to relax. I have to protect Ursula and stop her doing something mad that will get us both killed. How many more chances are we going to get? This is Diamond City, where luck is as rare as trust.

Also, Mum said there was something wrong with Centria. VIA Holdings is outside Centria, so whatever Bal and Loren are up to relates to the wrongness but is not the main problem. I've got more work to do on those files and less on obliterating Bal, which is a pity.

"Ursula," I say.

She doesn't hear.

"Ursula," I say again. "They'll cut us to pieces."

She looks at me. Our brief exhilarating link is broken.

"An excuse to get rid of us permanently might even be what they want," I say gently.

The ship slows down.

"I've got a plan," I say.

"Go on."

"We buy part of a building… in VIA Holdings."

The ship speeds up again.

"Ursula!"

"Seriously Charity? Buy a building? That's your plan?"

"We need to outsmart them!"

"By giving them business? Fuck no!"

"We can spy on them from there! They both move freely around the complexes. We get closer to the centre, room by room so we're there at the right time and-"

"We waste them," Ursula says.

"We question them! Don't you want to know what's really going on?"

"That could take years!"

"We're hardly busy!"

Ursula's mouth is tight and her breathing heavy with anger. She blinks a few times and calms down slightly.

"They won't sell to you or to me," she says eventually.

"We can set up a trading identity so someone else can buy the building for us…"

"There isn't time Charity. How long are they going to keep Mum hooked up in Centria? And Dad…"

"You need to help me Ursula," I say quietly.

She huffs and stares out of the window. Suddenly, she looks at me.

"I know who will buy the building," she says.

"Who?"

"Ruben Toro."

"Really?"

"Oh yes," Ursula says. "He genuinely loves me, not like those other phoneys."

"The ifarm will alert Security if you call him."

"I'll ask him to meet us near Centria. He can lose them long enough for us to let him know what we want."

"Will he really risk becoming an ex?"

"Never underestimate obsessive love Charity."

Why do I think of Harlan? He's not obsessed with me and I'm not obsessed with him.

Ursula's eyes go out of focus for a moment as she sends Ruben the message. I think she grasps the uncomfortable truth that this plan is all we've got. The alternative is an entropic spiral to the Outer Spheres, looking behind us all the way.

"Ruben says he's coming," Ursula says. "We're on."

The ship changes direction. I shift on the seat uneasily, conscious that even if we do find out what's wrong with Centria we will never be able to go back there.

20

I look out of the ship's window as we touch down at the edge of a square bordered by three giant buildings on the inner curve of MidZone. One building is a tower of green tile facing another whose featureless white facade is partially obscured by a sheet of milky liquid. The liquid pours unendingly from the ceiling four hundred metres above us to hit the floor nearby with an uncanny lack of spray. The third building is a sensuous cylinder that rises to a blunt point. Every imaginable colour pulses in it and there are no dark areas; the colours bloom alongside each other in a slow riot of gorgeous light.

The cul-de-sac opens onto the rest of the chamber, which is filled by a wooded park. Light blue trees are sculpted into loose knots above dark blue grass. A pink lake glows softly in the centre.

We sit and watch the colours change in the cylinder as the white liquid falls in silent majesty. People cross the square from one of the three buildings to another and at one point a man with a dekpak lands, which gives me a little start of sadness.

"There," Ursula says.

Ruben Toro walks into the square from between the green tiled building and the coloured cylinder. Although Ruben wears chunky dark clothes that obviously contain armour he still manages to look scared and needy, while his surgically rendered Ursula-beauty makes me even more uncomfortable here than it did in Centria.

"We should take him up in the ship," I say.

"I can't see Security yet."

"Stick your head out for a second then."

Ursula opens the ship's hatch and stands there.

"Come on," I hear her mutter.

"What?"

"I don't know. He's stopped."

"Has he seen you?"

"Yes!"

A strange pulsing, metallic hum has grown subtly in volume. Ruben starts to back away, staring in fear at something above us. I look up and see the dark green warship I glimpsed in Gereleye. This close I can see how huge the craft is, much bigger than the ones Keris had in Centria. Its name, visible on the lower hull, is Wrath Umbilica.

It must have been waiting for us to land.

A flash jerks our ship from under me. For a moment there is silence and a peculiar sense of suspension as if time has become physically tangible. The ship's inner wall recedes with alarming, inexorable speed until my back hits Ursula's seat and the air is thumped out of my lungs.

The base of our ship is now its side and through the window strip I see Ursula scramble to her feet. Ruben stands as if frozen and then begins to run towards Ursula. The silent white fluid drops obliviously behind them both.

The view changes again and I feel a sickness in my ears. The brief screech of another shot cuts through it, then I'm in freefall before slamming down. All air leaves my body again as the ship scrapes across the square and judders to a halt. I feel heat close in and turn to see a wall of energy buzz towards me as our attackers burn the ship millimetre by millimetre.

Suddenly it melts as Ursula deposits the remains to prevent our precious kilos from evaporating and I fall beside the last fragments as they're absorbed into the floor. The awful buzzing heat disappears; I roll over to see Wrath Umbilica hanging above us and glimpse Ursula run toward me. I want to tell her to get away but haven't got enough breath to speak or move.

Ruben backs off and then stops. Something grows out of the floor in front of him. From this angle and distance it's hard to make out but when Ruben grabs the handle and swings the thing around I see it's a cannon, so large that the barrel rests on a stand embedded in the floor. At any other time the weapon might look impressive but not against that warship.

I mentally urge Ruben to run but instead he fires a volley of shots over our heads. A blinding white flare from Wrath Umbilica removes Ruben's arm and blood sprays over a luminous yellow pulse in the cylindrical building. Ruben spins and falls to his knees, sagging towards the floor until he puts out his remaining arm to stop himself. He looks at Ursula and then uses the cannon controls to pull his bleeding body up. He actually gets a shot off before another blast from the green warship vaporises him and the cannon completely.

The seconds are long and packed with incident. It seems to take an age to register grief for Ruben, whose love for my sister drove him to try and help her even with his arm shot away. It takes even longer for Ursula to complete her facial expression: rage I think and also terror.

The local security systems finally open fire on the warship, which shoots back. Gunfire is a grid of crackling energy as diamond shards drop slowly towards us.

I reach for Ursula, remember the n-gun and select level 3. There is a flash and Ursula falls in front of me. Something hits-

21

I feel my eyelids move as they open and close but I can't see. Everything is white. A slap to the side of my head shocks a hoarse, pathetic shriek out of me. I try to move my arms and legs but can't.

"Wake up."

It's a woman's voice close by, charged with the kind of rage that smoothes out all inflection.

"Who are you?" I say, shaky with fear.

"Scan me why don't you, you stuck up little bitch?"

"I can't," I say, "I can't see."

There's a charged pause as blindness enhances my other senses, especially touch. I feel the woman nearby, coiled and ready. When the second blow thuds into the other side of my head it should be a relief but she knows how to hit. Echoes of it lock my trembling neck as I cry out and stinging tears crawl down my face.

"Stop it, stop, please."

I try and shift my whole body to get out of the way of more attacks but I can only move each limb slightly. The back of my head bumps against a hard surface, while aches in my knees and bottom let me know I'm held on a seat. I screw my eyes shut and then open them. After I do this a few times I can make out indistinct shapes.

"Charity!" Ursula's voice sounds slightly further away than the woman's.

The shapes resolve into people, standing still. Some look at me and some at Ursula, who sits facing me about three metres away secured to an upright pole. There is a red hand mark on her wide-eyed face but I can't see any other injuries. Thick diamond bands restrain her arms, legs and neck.

I'm held in the same way. My bare feet are pressed against the floor of a featureless diamond box about ten metres square. People line the walls four deep, watching us silently and without expression.

The woman stands looking at Ursula with her back to me. She

has Ursula's height and the physique I would possess if I spent six hours a day working out instead of two. Thick, almost black hair tumbles down her back and whips out as she turns to glare at me.

Her face is heavy-featured and almost brutally sensuous. The delicate tone of her very pale skin is offset by a sense that she doesn't bruise easily, while the furious, unblinking stare of her dark eyes seems to reach the back of my head. She uses her whole body in her movements as if she is powered by so much fierce energy she has to constantly try and use it up but never can. She grips a fuze with sufficient force to make the whiteness of her knuckles visible from here.

Her name is Ashel 5.

My gaze moves from the fuze to the ridged musculature of the Ashel 5's exposed midriff. She hasn't got a navel. I look at the heavily armed crowd that surrounds us. Not one of their proudly exposed bellies is marked by a navel either.

Ashel 5 sees the realisation in my face and a small contemptuous smile flickers across her full mouth.

"Get it now do you?" Ashel 5 says.

"Yes," I say, hearing the resignation in my voice.

"88 Rabian was a beautiful man," Ashel 5 says.

"I'm sorry," I say. "Please understand…"

"He was my husband."

Shame presses down so hard I'm actually glad the restraints are there to support me. I can't look at Ashel 5 but feel her rage like radiation. It echoes my own anger at the Sons of the Crystal Mind although that's a weaker force, like the rifle fire of Dad's MidZone attackers as they dissolved in acid; a hopeless gesture, not even impressive.

"You must know we didn't kill him," I say. "We never wanted that."

"Really?" Ashel 5 says.

I make myself look up at her and see despair in the contempt. Did I want her husband dead? I try to focus on what was behind that decision in New Runcton. Bizarrely, Ashel 5's merciless presence helps; she will sense if I'm not honest.

"I don't know," I say finally. "You're the first Blanks I've ever met. You've always just been there in the background."

"We're hardly a mystery Charity. I think if the Sons of the Crystal Mind hadn't forced your prejudice out someone else would have."

"I didn't want to hurt anyone," I say. "I never have."

Unexpectedly I relax. I'm telling the truth.

"I don't believe you," Ashel 5 says. "To me it looked like you wanted to teach us a lesson for spoiling your sister's party."

"No," I say. "Never."

"I don't care about the stupid party either," Ursula says.

I can tell from Ashel 5's expression she has stopped listening.

"My husband was a peaceful man," she says and her voice wavers with grief. "He didn't want bloodshed. Despite everything that happened in his life he was determined no one should die on our account; that we should be a source of hope, not loathing."

She looks down thoughtfully and I feel a flicker of hope.

"I am not my husband," Ashel 5 says.

The venom rises in her voice as she looks up again and her eyes brim with hate. I go in-Aer to buy shielding for me and Ursula but it doesn't work. Ashel 5 owns this building on closed protocol so I can't gif anything out of it.

The n-gun is still set to level 3. I point my gun finger at the armrest but can't get the angle right; if I fire there's a good chance I'll blow my own legs off. Level 2 will kill one Blank but what about the other hundred? And do I really want to do these people any more harm?

"We will deal with the Sons of the Crystal Mind," Ashel 5 says. "But first we need to give a small demonstration of our seriousness."

"It was my fault," I shout, "I told Ursula to say it…"

"But Ursula didn't have to say it, did she?" Ashel 5 says.

"She did Ashel."

"Ashel 5."

"I'm sorry, Ashel 5. One of them was pointing a gun at my sister. They would have killed us too."

"I think there is something you could have done," Ashel 5 says.

"What could we have done?" I shout.

"You could have said no and taken a chance that with most of Diamond City watching, the Sons of the Crystal Mind would not have been stupid enough to publicly execute the People's Princess."

I look at Ursula, who sobs quietly.

"You love your sister don't you Charity?" Ashel 5 says, her voice quiet now.

"Yes," I say.

"If you'd been alone in front of the Sons you would have taken that chance wouldn't you?"

"Yes."

"I believe you. Steeber Loke thought the same."

"How do you know Steeber?"

"He offered us your whereabouts for a rather large sum," Ashel 5 says, "which we need to replace."

"We can help you with that," I say. "Take all of it."

I access my Aerac, transfer every kilo I've got to Ashel 5 and look over at Ursula. She nods as much as the restraints will let her.

"Have you got it?" I ask Ashel 5.

"Yes," she says, "from both of you. Thanks."

I strain expectantly against the structure holding me. It stays in place. Ashel 5 contemplates the ceiling and the other Blanks watch Ashel 5.

"What are you doing?" I ask her.

"It's not enough," she says, almost with regret. "I thought leaving you without kilos would be sufficient but… it isn't."

Fear seeps through me like weight in my blood. Ashel 5 turns to Ursula.

"I have sent you a file Ursula," she says. "I want you to open it."

"What-what is it?" Ursula says.

"It's a recording of the full-on vix link made by my husband as the Sons of the Crystal Mind burned him to death. You will experience that Ursula."

"No!" I cry. "You'll kill her!"

"Maybe not," Ashel 5 says. "Some of the intensity has been

reduced by elongating the file. It's locked though, so once you're in you stay until the end."

"Send it to me!" I shout.

"No Charity," Ashel 5 says, "because that is what you want. Open it Ursula."

Ursula's whole body shakes. Tears make shiny zigzags down her cheeks and her upper lip is wet where her nose has run.

"Open it," Ashel 5 says. "Open it and know what my husband knew."

"Please," Ursula says.

"Come on Ursula," Ashel 5 says. "We're recording this for everyone to see later. I thought you'd like that."

"I don't," Ursula says. She sounds like a little girl.

I send a message to Harlan with our coordinates:

THE BLANKS HAVE US. PLEASE HELP AND I WILL GIVE YOU EVERYTHING CENTRIA KNOWS ABOUT THE NFE.

"Ashel 5, listen, please," I say.

"Open the file Ursula," Ashel 5 says.

"Don't," I say.

"OPEN THE FILE URSULA!"

Ursula sobs and shakes her head. Ashel 5 raises her fuze and shoots me through the right elbow-

Pain like the worst thing ever known condenses to a point.

A trillion of those points appear calmly and quietly in my body.

A nova of agony blasts everything, everything-

AAAAAAAAAAAAAAAAAAAAGGGGGHHHH!

Stop stop stop stop stop stop stop stop!

PLLLEEEAAASE-!

Aftershocks excruciate as the pain overwhelms me. I will do anything to blot it out, distract it or beat it down. I want to punish myself for feeling it but rage is like a blow to an open wound. I try and smash the back of my head against the diamond pole but can't move enough to do it. I scream myself silent but rawness in my throat fades against the torment blazing in my elbow. I try to resist it, manage it and even make friends with it but it comes back at me again and again.

Ursula cries something that sounds like my name. Ashel 5 speaks too although I can't understand what she says. She closes in and smashes the grip of her gun into my right cheekbone, the blow ricocheting across the bridge of my nose. I try to scream again and choke on rushing blood. I manage to spit it out and some hits Ashel 5. Her expression twists into a snarl; if the pain had a face, it would be hers. She jams the barrel of her fuze into the crook of my left elbow and turns to stare at Ursula. Ursula's eyes widen and she jerks slightly as she accesses the file.

Sweet relief eases up from my bare feet and soon I no longer feel my shattered elbow or cracked face. Ursula doesn't move; she stares in my direction but I know she doesn't see me. Instead she sees what 88 Rabian saw when he was tied to that post in New Runcton.

Ursula flinches; this must be the moment when Thom3 Hobb shot the ignition into the pyre. Ursula tries to shy away from it but the restraints hold her. She whimpers.

"Ashel 5," I say. My voice is thick and barely works through the painkiller rising from the Basis. "Please stop. I will do anything."

"You're doing what I want you to do," Ashel 5 says.

"This won't achieve-"

Ashel 5 shoves the barrel of her fuze into my mouth.

"Shh," she says.

Ursula screams; a short piercing sound like an alarm. I imagine her/88 Rabian's point of view: the terrible crowd, the rant from Thom3 Hobb and worst of all the heat, a terrible thoughtless energy that gets closer by the second and by the millimetre. Tears blur my vision into abstract shapes. Ursula is a streak of light in front of me, Ashel 5 a large dark block to the left and around us the Blanks are a silent grey border.

Ursula screams again, for longer this time. Sweat runs and drips as her body tries in vain to cool itself down. She wants to thrash from side-to-side but all she can do is tremble furiously. Her eyes are wide with horror and her flesh reddens. She coughs furiously, thinking her lungs are full of smoke. Will her body believe she has burned to death and therefore die? Like the flames, it is the unknowing agent of a universe hidden far above us that knows no love, only physics.

My eyes come back into focus and I become conscious of the hard plastic texture of the weapon resting on my lower teeth. Ashel 5 watches Ursula with a slight frown and presently pulls the fuze barrel out of my mouth. I try and call to Ursula but can't; the pain-killing drug has anaesthetised me completely.

I send her a message:

STAY IN REALITY

It doesn't work; she can't see anything except the flames. Suddenly she presses her throat against the restraint. She is going to choke herself. Clever girl. It will be a victory of sorts.

The structure holding Ursula dissolves. She falls onto her back and writhes blindly, flipping over as if the floor is red-hot. The movement is ferocious, desperate; Ursula looks like she is trying to jerk out the agony in glistening droplets of sweat.

She stops writhing; her hands hook and tighten into claws as her legs draw up. For a while she stays in that clenched position, her inhuman gulping much worse than the screams. Every muscle in her body twitches visibly as if her trapped flesh is trying to flee. Slowly, the expression goes out of her face. She seems to become a simpler organism, one consisting entirely of tormented sense.

The burning goes on and on, longer it seems than at New Runcton. I wonder how close Ursula is to the moment of 88 Rabian's death. How will she deal with infinity, my happy lovely sister? I picture the sunny avenues of her character darkening in the face of it, the shadow spreading through her.

Finally Ursula goes limp. After that awful tension it looks like she's melting. Her long legs spread out and her arms slide off her chest. Her eyes are dead.

Ashel 5 grabs the front of Ursula's jacket and pulls her up to stare into her face. I try and intuit what our captor will do but her rigid pose gives nothing away. She seems no less crazed; torturing us does not look like it has eased her grief or her rage.

Ashel 5 lets go and Ursula's head thunks against the floor. Transparent slime oozes off her; I can smell its sour, rancid odour from here. My sister is in an unknowable place and I don't know how I will get her back.

The structure that holds me is absorbed and I slump into a position where I can no longer see Ursula. Instead, the ceiling opens and the walls lower as the Basis takes them apart. The Blanks disperse without a word but Ashel 5 remains.

As she stares down at me I don't feel anything except terrible regret. My mouth works but no sound emerges. I wish she would come closer. I use the last of my strength.

"Forgive me," I say.

"No," she says and walks away.

22

The painkiller still works but I don't know how long it will last. I move my head, which rolls to the right like a huge weight barely within my control. I look down the side of my body. Shards of bone poke revoltingly from a burnt-edged hole in the jumpsuit's right elbow, wet with seeping blood. Hot, sour fluid bubbles in my throat. My eyes flutter.

Time skews slightly...

I look up between two plain square buildings at a great dark vault lit by the glowing vertical line of a train tube. Beyond my splayed feet a sign swings in the middle of a crossroads. Further away a diamond plain extends to an unremarkable entrance through a wall whose height is in shadow.

We are in New Runcton. How very fitting. This is my third visit here and each one has been a disaster. I will *never* come back, providing I live.

Ursula lies motionless nearby, her face turned away. I can't move my shattered arm and for some reason the other one doesn't work either. My legs are more responsive so I press my feet against the floor and push myself across it.

"Ursula," I whisper. "Baby?"

Ursula's body is a range of soft curves. I manage to get my head onto her shoulder and damp heat rises against my cheek. Her shallow breaths gently lift me up and down as I hear the ooze drip thickly off her, its heartbreakingly strong burnt smell hinting at new and unwelcome otherness.

"Oi oi!"

It's a male voice, to our left. Footsteps approach: more than two people and less than ten. Perhaps they will help.

"What the *fuck* is this?"

Or perhaps not.

I should be frightened but I haven't got the strength. Even if I was able-bodied there would be little I could do; with no kilos I can't fire the n-gun let alone gif a shelter. Ursula is a silent, immovable weight beneath me as the footsteps halt beside us.

"Fresh gash? On a Wednesday? Is this a fucking trap or what?" says a third male voice.

"The little one's got a fucked up arm."

"She won't need her arms," says a fourth man whose calm voice is nonetheless full of hate.

"Shit! Ain't that Ursula Freestone?"

"Fuck me it is!"

"She fucking stinks."

"I got something to wash her with."

A few barks of insincere laughter peter into silence and then I feel the atmosphere charge with decision. A booted foot shoves me off Ursula. My shoulder cracks against the floor and I hear myself groan. The men around us stare down.

There are five, none of them older than me. They are too well-fed to be subs and their bland faces are vicious with bored resentment. One of them grabs Ursula's front so her head hangs back, exposing her neck. The man grunts, his eyes cold as he looks up at the others.

"Can we ransom them?"

"Got chucked out didn't they? No one gives a fuck now."

"Let's do this."

"Here?"

"No, get 'em inside. We don't want any interruptions."

Ursula is dragged away and I hear the juddering squeak of her boots get fainter with distance. A hand grips my ankle with grimly indifferent strength as I'm swung around and pulled across the floor.

My precious sister and I are mere objects now; all we have ever achieved a minor enhancement to the cruel pleasure of strangers. The great space above New Runcton seems to move with me, a mocking reminder of my first time here when I was taken into the air to be loved, or so I thought.

My right arm tingles menacingly each time it bangs against the floor. The resulting bloody spatters make prickles of nausea drop through my gut. Soon the tingling becomes unbearable-

I convulse to a fanfare of agony that explodes out of my elbow as Ashel 5's painkillers finally wear off. The pain is so excruciating it chokes my scream and the light around me seems to become blindingly intense.

"Don't worry Charity," the man says as he drags me, "I'll give you something to take your mind off it."

I try to stay silent but instead of willpower there's just dreadful numb hysteria and I moan through clamped lips. Bitter, useless tears are acid in my broken cheek.

I'm hauled inside a building, glimpsing plastic table legs and a stained cardboard chair on its side. Both pieces of furniture are kicked away to clatter out of sight against the walls. I want the pain from being dragged to end but I'm terrified of what will happen when they get me where they want me.

We reach the wall furthest from the door. The man swivels me around again so my head faces the wall and lets go of my foot. I try and stop it hitting the floor but strain causes more agony in my elbow. Clamping my teeth together I manage to slowly turn my head.

Ursula lies on the floor to my left but I hardly recognise her. She has always been so funny, so alive but now her face is rigid with shock. Her skin shines as her poor confused body tries to cool a heat that was never there. Her eyes do not register me.

A door grows to seal us in with the five men. They hesitate for a moment as if unsure how to proceed and then one leans down to pull at Ursula's top. Another joins in; the top is ripped off and hurled away. The men crouch beside Ursula and fondle her breasts. One man grips Ursula's hair and licks her face. Two others pull Ursula's trousers down, which snag on her boots. The men punch Ursula's legs furiously in frustration as if it is Ursula's fault. Afterwards they yank the boots and trousers off together.

One man is left out. He's not the smallest but he seems to lack even more than the others. His face twists in frustration as he looks down at Ursula. Then he looks over at me.

The other four walk out of their clothes, which remain standing as if worn by invisible men and make the room seem even more crowded. Two of the men are already erect. One gets on his knees and shoves Ursula's legs apart; another crouches by her head.

The man looking at me walks over. He kneels down and tears at my jumpsuit.

"Fuck," he spits.

The man between Ursula's legs hesitates, his cock poised.

"For shit's sake, what is it?"

"This slag has got armour on."

"Just wait can't you?"

"No!"

"I swear I'm going to... Rompy! Don't you get in her mouth before I've... Honestly, I fucking..."

His words break into grunts of rage. He gets up, snatches a small cylindrical device from the pocket of his clothes and throws it at the man beside me. It bounces off his chest onto the floor; he scrabbles the device up and jabs it into my shoulder. There's a snap and my jumpsuit becomes much lighter.

"Killed it," he says happily, as if this is the one success he's managed all day.

I kick at him; he punches me in the mouth and my lip suddenly expands. It's nothing beside the almost deafening torment in my elbow, which is so powerful that every few seconds it blinds me although sadly not for long.

He grabs the front of my jumpsuit and tears it open. My shoulders hit the floor one after the other as I'm jerked from side to side. I scream as the impact jolts my elbow; he ignores me and doesn't even pause. I try to pee so he won't want me but I can't. My legs twitch in panic; I want to throw up but nothing comes. He knows I can't move so he takes his time.

My mind tries to outrun the horror but every loathsome detail is too clear. There is a rash on his neck and his breath smells rotten. In the background I hear the others breathe too, some louder, some faster. One man inhales through his nose with a faint rattle of dry snot; another clears his throat and then does it again. Someone's knee clicks.

They shift around and close in on Ursula. There is a vile

efficiency to the dreadful unthinking movement, which is accompanied by wet sounds and grunting. All I can see of my sister now is her left arm, which jerks back and forth, the hand flopping. Please let her stay unconscious, please…

Their lust is contemptibly small and ordinary for something so destructive. They don't appreciate the value of the person they are violating; someone who loves Ursula should be holding her, touching her. The unfairness and waste are unbearable, the damage hideous. It's nearly impossible to feel any emotion; just deep, silent rage like the beginning of a devastating illness.

The one on me is not in yet; he seems to like the delay as if feeding off the trauma of it. He stares into my eyes, his expression almost as dead as Ursula's but energised by awful determination.

Suddenly his gaze darts to the right. All movement stops and the room falls silent.

"What was that?" one of the men who squats over Ursula says.

An explosion outside shakes the building. The man on me grabs my throat as if to hold me in place.

"Fuck or fight?" he snarls at the others.

"Fuck," comes the reply.

He smiles down at me and tries to shove it in. I jerk my hips and he misses. He tries again.

"Don't you struggle," he says, more excited than angry.

There's another explosion, this one nearer. From the other side of the room the sounds of friction and mean enjoyment intensify. I suspect the men want to finish before they are interrupted.

A third explosion sounds like it's demolished the building next door.

"I'm suiting up," one of the men raping Ursula says.

There is a general murmur of assent. The man on me watches them and his lip curls into a sneer.

"Pricks," he says.

He thrusts at me again. From somewhere I find incredible strength and kick him so hard in the balls his breath stops. I nearly pass out with the effort; his groan is a faraway sound and I barely notice him slump against me. For a moment I feel like I'm drowning in air.

We recover at the same time with the unwanted synchronicity between victim and perpetrator and he looks up, his entire body puce with rage. He grips my right elbow and squeezes. A huge scream rips out of me and I throw my head back so hard I hit the back of it against the floor. He laughs. I slump back with nothing left except grief…

The wall with the door bursts inwards. The man rolls off me and jumps up. A tall figure in the smoke emits a red beam from one hand that knocks my attacker off his feet. He hits the floor to my left with a slap of flesh and clunk of skull. The remaining four men rush at the intruder but a white flash reduces them to red vapour and flying body parts that crash into the furniture.

The open eyes of the man beside me stare back into mine. I hold his dead gaze. Soon he sinks into the floor and I continue to watch his eyes even though they stare blankly at a point underneath me.

His skin dulls and shifts as the Basis gets to work. Its tiny machines travel into the body from all sides, shunting molecules, spreading them, making the lump of matter light enough to move. There is no gore and no brutality; the man simply expands until he is transparent and then becomes nothing. I wonder who he left his kilos to; if they will care he is gone.

The figure in the smoke resolves into Harlan. He walks over, kneels and gathers me gently.

"My beautiful," he says.

The darkness of his face engulfs my vision until all I see is him and then nothing.

23

I wake up slowly, wary of that pause where the previous day is forgotten and everything seems all right. Soon the painkillers will wear off and the agony will commence. Soon the sickening assault will begin again. Soon I will start to scream.

I wait. Nothing happens. I let my mind focus along with my eyes. I'm under a soft sheet in a single bed. The room is dimly lit. I move gingerly but there is no warning pain.

I realise I am deliberately breathing shallowly. I inhale; in… in… all the way. I wait again. I breathe out. My memory twitches with snapshots of horror.

Foul breath, dead weight, crashing furniture, crashing limbs… And worst of all Ursula's hand, jerking helplessly nearby with me unable to save her. I reassure myself that our attackers are all dead but the knowledge doesn't make me happy so much as sick. I squeeze my eyes shut. Now Ursula writhes on the floor as the Blanks look on and the world ends in my elbow…

I shake my head and check the Aer. For a moment nothing I read makes any sense. I persevere with the familiar ritual and after a while my mind steadies.

I have been unconscious for five days.

I grit my teeth as I stretch my right arm but even in the low light I can see my elbow is healed. No scars, not even a mark show where Ashel 5 shot me. I touch my cheek and that feels fine as well. The swelling, the blood, the acid sting of my tears are all gone.

I hear slow breathing nearby and turn towards a second bed next to mine. I can just make out Ursula lying on her back under another sheet with tubes going into her arms.

Wary of enfeebled limbs I carefully climb out of bed and am surprised to find I stand without trouble. My hair tumbles into my face and I push it away. I expect a lank curtain but it's glossy and smells sweet. Someone has looked after me.

I lean over Ursula. She is clearly not right. Although the awful frozen expression has gone there is a shocking vacancy to her as if she's there but not there. The disquiet in me coalesces into a sense of loss so strong I gasp. I don't know how Ursula will deal with this. I suppose that means I don't know how I will deal with it either.

I want to get drunk and take drugs and pull men with her. Why did I never do any of those things? Maybe it was because of my precious career, my thwarted journey to perfection. I suspect that's an excuse however. I think I feared if I misbehaved like Ursula then Mum and Dad wouldn't want me anymore.

I put my hands to my face and sob, the tears jerking out of me. Soon I have to crouch by Ursula's bed, rocking on my bare feet until my legs cramp. The tears flow on and on. It helps to lose myself in them, as if I am an Old World engine pumping hot salty water from a dark and terrible well.

Eventually, I just run out of energy. Exhausted, I slowly stand, rubbing my wet face on the sleeve of the gown. I climb into Ursula's bed and the warm air under the cover is rich with her old familiar smell. I lie pressed against her; I want to hold her but she's heavy and I'm wary of pulling the tubes out of her arm. Instead I stroke her warm cheek.

"Ursula," I whisper, "Ursula…"

A door opens and I look across Ursula to see Harlan. He waits in the doorway for a while. I'm not sure what to say. His presence eases me but with it come confusion, questions and remembered fury at the betrayal that seems a long time ago…

"May I come in?" he says.

"Oh. Yes."

Harlan walks towards me. I realise I'm so pleased to see him I want to smile but all I do is stare. Honestly, a *spy?* For the New Form Enterprise?

He stops by the side of the bed.

"Thank you for saving us-" I begin.

Harlan shakes his head almost angrily. He looks down at Ursula.

"We don't know why she's still in a coma," he says.

"The Blanks made her access a full-on vix link of one of them getting burned alive."

He looks genuinely shocked, but then he's very convincing. I sigh.

"Where am I?" I ask.

"With the New Form Enterprise."

"As a prisoner?"

"No," he says. "You can leave any time."

"I suppose you want Centria's files on the NFE," I say.

"You don't have to give me the files if you don't want to," he says.

"Come off it Harlan. You didn't save us just because you like me."

Our eyes lock. My face feels tight.

"What do you think is happening?" he says finally.

"I think what you did to me was not much better than what those bastards in New Runcton were going to do."

"You're alive aren't you?"

"Only because you want something."

"You mentioned information about the NFE. You didn't say what it was. Believe me, that's not the reason I saved you."

"You spied on me! You were using me!"

"True," he says.

"If I'd brought you into Centria would you have killed me?"

"Like I killed you in New Runcton? As I recall I saved you and your sister, who has no value to me or the NFE."

"I don't understand."

"All right," he says, "I did want you so I could get into Centria and I would have let the rest of the NFE in. But we aren't killers."

"What was the Ruby War then?"

"A mistake."

"I'll say – you lost!"

"Hmm," he says, contemplative rather than angry.

The slant of his eyes is perfect, their lashes long…

"Stop looking at me," I say.

"I like looking at you."

"Too bad."

"You've got the best hair in Diamond City."

Oh, that was low; right below the belt, right… *there*….

"I mean it," I say, slightly out of breath.

"Why?" he asks.

"Because you're the enemy."

"How am I the enemy?"

"Because-because I'm from Centria and you're in the New Form Enterprise."

"You're not from Centria," he says, "not anymore."

I go to speak and realise there's nothing to say. I rest my face on Ursula's chest and hold her tight. It should wake her but she doesn't move.

Harlan stretches out on my bed. I try and pretend he isn't there so I can get my thoughts organised.

I realise with sudden clarity that my thoughts are as organised as they're ever likely to be. I'm recovering from something. I'm in trouble that remains stubbornly undefined. I love Ursula. I want Harlan. Things will probably always be like this.

I let go of Ursula and climb out of her bed, then walk over to Harlan and kneel on the floor beside him.

"Whenever I'm with you I just want to be stupid," I say.

"Good," he says. "You could do with more stupid in your life."

I get up the mission files, take a breath and then send them to him.

"Thank you," he says.

He rolls over onto his elbow and looks into my eyes.

"Check your Aerac," he says.

My Aerac still reads 0. Harlan's name appears in the sender field and my account level increases to 50,000 kilos.

"How rich are you?" I say.

"Very."

"Thank you," I say, hesitant.

He laughs.

"Stop thinking!" he says.

"I can't help it," I say.

I transfer half the kilos to Ursula for when she wakes up.

"It's fine," Harlan says, "but you think about things that don't need to be thought about."

I go to disagree but can't because his lips are on mine. Unexpectedly, every sense floods to my mouth. The smooth floor under my knees, the gown's rustle against my skin and even the weight of my hair become delightful, overwhelming.

I feel desperately triumphant. My just-liberated sexuality has not been destroyed. If that is intact perhaps everything else is too. I let the sensations rise and envelop me, a delirium sweetened by recollected trauma as if in reaction against it…

Harlan pulls away. He swings his legs off the bed and puts his hand on my shoulder.

"Jaeger wants to see you," he says.

24

I walk beside Harlan along a white corridor with a large oval window and pause to look out. A broad surface curves down away from me, moving past diamond walls so high I can't see their tops.

So the New Form Enterprise base is a mobile assembly. No wonder Centria couldn't find it.

We pass enormous mezzanines jutting like shelves over an empty plain. The expanse down there is broken by a few massive but forlorn blocks, which perhaps indicate where something should have been grown but now never will be. There are no buildings or people visible, just unfinished architecture and eerie blue light. The view has a haunted quality born of emptiness and unseen horror.

We are in the Outer Spheres.

I wear my red and yellow jumpsuit again, giffed anew with armour intact. More comfortable and secure than anything I've ever worn it seems especially charged next to Harlan, who must recognise the outfit from when we visited Dodge69. Harlan has the same clothes on too. Perhaps he's trying to tell me something.

Four men and two women all wearing orange jumpsuits jog out of a side corridor. I stop with a gasp. I have been trained to fear and attack anyone in that uniform but I'm too confused to move. The six people disappear down a corridor. I stare after them.

Harlan puts his arm around my shoulders and guides me into an elevator. As the doors close he takes his arm away and my shoulders tingle where he touched them. Faint pressure through my boots tells me we are going up. I look at Harlan, who is uncharacteristically quiet. For the first time since we met I sense tension in him, as if he is apprehensive.

"What does Jaeger want from me?" I ask.

"He'll tell you. Just be honest. He'll know otherwise."

"Anything else?"

Harlan hesitates.

"Best you find out for yourself," he says. "It's easier that way."

The elevator doors open and Jaeger Darwin is right there.

He wears an orange NFE jumpsuit with no insignia to differentiate him from his troops. A big man although not as big as Harlan, Jaeger nonetheless seems incredibly compact. It's as if his musculature has been built and compressed, then built and compressed again, over and over until he hums with daunting strength. Only Keris has a similar effect but with her it is abstract, almost spiritual. Jaeger looks like a weapon. His intelligence glares from the coldest, hardest eyes I have ever seen.

He is still. He could be a statue but for those grey eyes that seem to take in every detail of me. I sense him work out my depths, like light in a shadowy chasm. It feels revelatory, even soothing, as if Jaeger knows more about me from one glance than I've learned in twenty-three years.

I imagine his voice, ruthless and frighteningly reasonable as he evaluates how long I can fight for, my optimum position in an engagement, ideal weaponry for a female my size, whether I would ever give up and if so when… His aura of absolutism, of finality, terrifies me but I already want to follow him.

"Charity," he says.

Jaeger's actual voice is quiet and cultured but not that different from how I imagined. It brims with violence. He extends a hand. Inspired rather than cowed I take it, relieved my palms are dry. Jaeger's hand closes gently around mine with the quiet but awesome strength of the walls holding up Diamond City.

"Jaeger," I say and smile. "I've heard… so very little about you."

He smiles back. His teeth are even and efficient-looking although his thick chestnut hair seems slightly long for a soldier.

"Please come in," he says.

I step into a large multi-levelled room full of Old World artefacts.

"Thank you Harlan," Jaeger says.

The elevator doors close, leaving me alone with the leader of the New Form Enterprise. I resist the urge to look back. Jaeger gestures at a pair of wooden chairs by a floor-to-ceiling window onto the Outer Spheres. I cross the room and sit on the chair to the right. Jaeger arranges himself into a seated position opposite me. His movements are like choreography.

The chairs are slightly uncomfortable. They are Old World so won't respond to the sitter's physiology. I think Jaeger has got them because he doesn't like to be too relaxed. The ornate, beautifully carved wood has a peculiar shiny surface that seems deep, as if I'm staring into the past. I look up. Jaeger's intense gaze hasn't left me.

"These chairs are lovely," I say.

"Thank you," he says. "May I offer you anything?"

"No, thanks, I'm fine."

We look at each other for a moment.

"This must seem very strange," he says.

"Yes. I've fought so many simulations against, well, you."

"Are we what you expected?"

"I didn't know what to expect."

"We were just the enemy," he says with a hint of humour.

"When you say it like that it seems silly."

"We fought a war against Centria don't forget."

"Why?" I ask him.

"To get inside."

"But you were inside weren't you? Before? When you were their general?"

He looks out of the window.

"Do you know what a soldier is Charity?"

"A warrior," I say.

"Partly. A soldier is an extension of another's will: an amplification of their power. A soldier can't really question that will, or he ceases to be a soldier. And yet I did question it. Am I therefore still a soldier?"

"No."

Jaeger looks at me again. Despite his obvious power he is not intimidating.

"Correct. And that was intolerable Charity."

"I know exactly what you mean."

I watch a subtle play of strange emotion flicker across his lean face.

"Yes," he says, "you do don't you?"

"What can I do for you Jaeger?"

"Talk to me," he says. "Tell me about Centria."

"I haven't got any information about Security…"

"I know about Security. Tell me anything else, however random. How is it there? How does it *feel?*"

I pause, conflicted.

"You're struggling," Jaeger says, not unkindly. "I understand. I have found that you never really leave Centria, even when Centria leaves you."

"My parents would have died for Centria," I say, not so much evading the point as trying to work out what it is.

"Indeed," Jaeger says.

"You know my parents?" I say.

"Both good soldiers. You're very different from them."

"They… Well they are my parents," I say with the familiar sense of odd disloyalty. "I mean they brought me up. I don't know who I am really though."

"A changeling princess," Jaeger says.

I flush. His interest emboldens me to ask the fundamental question.

"Jaeger… What is the Guidance?"

Crack!

For a second I think I've been shot with one of those old guns we train with in Centria and then I notice blood run down Jaeger's arm. He has snapped the armrest off his chair; the broken strut has dug into his hand. He breathes heavily as if my words have winded him. His eyes are fearsome now and I gulp in fear; it's like sitting opposite an exploding bomb. I should get away but I can't move.

Jaeger looks down at the broken chair as if it's a friend he has lost. He tries in vain to put the arm back.

"Can't the Basis help?" I say nervously.

"No. This chair is Old World. The Basis can only manipulate objects it has created. Each molecule of everything it grows is marked with the Aerac ID of the person who giffed it. My chair, like any Old World object, has no such imprint. Without the Basis no one knows how to fix anything. We are helpless."

He gets up, puts the chair arm down and grips his open wound. I wait for him to push his hand into the floor so the Basis can heal it. Instead he stares out of the window at the Outer Spheres, whose vacant crystalline structures are a moving pattern of bleak geometry far below.

"The Guidance," he says almost to himself. "I haven't heard that for a while. Who told you about it?"

"Ellery."

Jaeger grunts. He notices blood drip through his fingers and puts the wounded side of his hand in his mouth. I've never seen anyone do that before and lean forward, fascinated. He notices and locks eyes with me. I hold his gaze.

"You should get that healed properly," I say.

He doesn't move. Presently, he takes his hand from his lips and I see the bleeding has stopped.

"Often," he says, "I have to quickly decide whether to trust a person. Other lives depend on those decisions. I have always been good at it and over the years become much better. I want to trust you. Is that wise would you say?"

"Yes."

"You seem important somehow, as if we've met before."

"I would have remembered," I say.

"What is it about you? Like you're part of something…"

He shakes his head and for a moment seems undecided.

"The Guidance is me," he says finally.

I am numb and astonished at the same time. A weird metallic taste creeps up my throat.

"You?" I whisper.

"Well, I'm part of it," Jaeger says. "One of twelve people bred to be the absolute best at a specific job. Together we were meant to form the supreme government although that's rather a quaint idea now.

"Each of us has a different ability. Together we possess all the skills needed to run anything, hence 'the Guidance'. Obviously I'm the ultimate soldier. Ellery Quinn is the ultimate communicator, Gethen Karkarridan…"

Jaeger pauses as if unsure how to describe Gethen.

"Well, you've got to make money haven't you?" he continues. "Gethen could sell us diamond if he wanted. And then of course you have the leader."

"Keris."

"Yes. I can command troops but Keris can lead everyone."

Something in his voice…

"You and Keris?"

"I've loved her for over a hundred and seventy years," Jaeger says.

It takes me a while to absorb his words.

"How old are you all?" I say.

"More than two centuries."

"Do you use longevity patents?"

"Even we would struggle to afford those over that length of time. No, with us it's natural. We were created before Diamond City was built to save a world that no longer exists. So instead we came down here and made the best of it."

The incredible facts move in my mind like elemental forces. Jaeger watches, allowing me to take it in. I don't feel obliged to comment or even react and something of this ease reminds me of how well I get on with Keris. As the second vital question forms I notice Jaeger looking expectant and almost guilty.

"Jaeger, are you and Keris my parents?"

His face trembles for the tiniest instant and is then still. He doesn't speak; I suspect he is not able to. This moment is the longest of my life.

"No," he says finally. "It's not possible."

"Why?"

"Our… creator decided it wouldn't be ethical to allow the super race to breed and so ensured we can't."

There is a very long silence.

"I'm sorry," I say.

"No. I am. That I can't tell you what you want to know."

I relax back into disappointment.

"It's okay," I say although we both know it isn't. "Is that why the Ruby War ended the way it did?"

"I didn't think Keris herself would come at us. That was out of character. She knew I could never harm her."

"Why did she do it?" I ask.

"Because there is something in Centria she cannot let me have."

"What?"

"An unlimited supply of kilos."

The structure of Diamond City is substantial enough to accommodate its own weight, the Basis and all the kilos but... unlimited?

"I don't know how that would work," I say.

"All you need to understand is that Centria controls far more than it should, which must change. If that supply is lost then eventually we will starve down here."

We sit for a while as I consider.

"So the Guidance is you, Gethen, Ellery, Keris... Who are the other eight?" I say.

Jaeger looks troubled.

"In Centria?" he says. "The scientist, Sol Bassa."

I know the name but I've never met him. Jaeger's eyes narrow.

"What about outside Centria?" I ask.

I keep my voice bright and naïve but I doubt that will fool Jaeger.

"Louis Ruckingham, the artist. The others..."

He frowns again. There is a long pause. I take a deep breath.

"Mum said there was something wrong with Centria," I say.

Jaeger leans forward.

"Wrong?" he says. "Wrong how?"

"She didn't have time to say."

"Have you found anything else out?"

"Not yet. I'm still going through Dad's mission files."

"Can you make sense of them?"

"No."

"Nor I. Will you tell me if you do?"

I hesitate.

"Just think about it," he says.

"All right," I say. "But what is the New Form Enterprise? New Form of what?"

"Humanity."

"I don't follow."

"Will you join us?" he says.

"I'm not sure."

"Then that is all I can tell you."

I nod. Jaeger watches me.

"You can trust me not to say anything about… anything," I add.

"Not even to Harlan."

"Agreed."

Jaeger Darwin stands and so do I.

"Thank you," I say.

"Think about joining us," he says. "You would be extraordinary."

I feel my face get hot and look away.

"Goodbye," I say.

I hurry out and don't look back.

25

Harlan gets up from an incongruous purple armchair as I walk out of the elevator. He smiles at me understandingly.

"All right?" he says as the Basis dissembles his chair.

"I-I suppose so, yes."

"Meeting Jaeger for the first time is always intense."

Harlan sounds fond of Jaeger although he is clearly scared of him.

"I'm reeling inside…" I say.

"He can do that," Harlan says.

"I've got to see Ursula."

"She's still asleep. I checked."

I shake my head and then shake it again.

"I want to go home," I say.

"I know."

I go to speak but losses and revelations crowd in and I can't…

"I understand how you feel," says Harlan. "I'm an ex as well."

There is a long pause. He reaches over and gently closes my mouth with his forefinger. My teeth click together.

"Drink?" he says.

"Are there any bars in the Outer Spheres?"

"Not exactly."

Harlan takes my hand and leads me along the corridor past groups of NFE operatives until we reach a ramp. Harlan doesn't slow as he strides up and I match his speed despite our difference in height. We emerge inside a transparent dome on top of the NFE assembly, where a generously upholstered sofa grows out of the floor. I sink gratefully into it.

Outside, the terrible silent beauty of the Outer Spheres invites me to fill its emptiness with dreams but only nightmares come: people frozen in giant coloured shapes, people in the floor just before they're taken apart, people in flames… I close my eyes to block it out.

When I open them I've slept for two hours.

"Better?" Harlan says beside me.

"I am," I say. "I don't know why, but somehow... yes. Better."

I get up and stretch. Harlan watches, which I like a lot. As I wander round the dome Harlan takes off his jacket to reveal a blue t-shirt that's actually faded. A few necklaces of gold, rope and bits of runic bone encircle his corded neck. His clothing and adornments seem earned, as if lesser objects have been swept away by ceaseless violence and adventure. I sense his being here is a pause in some greater journey that will soon resume.

We have left the huge walls behind to drift through a long empty corridor. Its ceiling is a mere five metres above the top of the dome, which seems inadequate protection against such vast and terrifying stillness.

"You're spending a lot of time with me," I say. "Haven't you got missions to go on?"

"My lady before my cause."

"I'm not your lady."

"Ah. Well, you do love someone else."

I stare down at him.

"Who?" I say.

"Ursula."

"Of course I love her, she's my sister!"

"Not your biological sister."

"That doesn't matter!"

"I think it does."

I struggle to understand for a moment and then the implication hits me.

"That's an awful thing to say Harlan," I say, hot-faced and upset.

"Your life is absorbed by hers. You obsess over her."

"That's my job," I say. "Was. Was my job."

"I've seen the way you look at Ursula," Harlan says. "I wish you looked at me like that."

"Then you shouldn't have betrayed me."

"I didn't betray you."

"You... Well. You sort of did."

He leans back, slips his hands behind his head and watches the gloomy ceiling glide past.

"Have you ever found another woman attractive?" he says.

I try and remember; anything to get him off the subject.

"When I was younger I was, you know, curious and... nothing happened you understand..."

"Perish the thought," Harlan says. "What did she look like?"

"Tall, pretty."

"Dark-haired?"

"Yes," I say.

"Long, straight dark hair?"

"Yes," I say again, surprised.

He watches me.

"Oh, I see..." I say.

The dome seems to shift. Swaying, I reach for the edge of the sofa and lower myself onto the edge of it. I think back a few hours to when I held Ursula in bed. A dark part of me rejoices that she needs me, that she is mine alone. I feel sick with guilt.

"It's all right," Harlan says and I love him a bit more for not judging me. "Your sister is beautiful and charismatic. I can understand why you love her the way you do."

"I thought I had it worked out."

Harlan laughs.

"People thought they had it worked out with the Blanks. Look what happened there!"

Despite myself I laugh with him and he puts his arm around my shoulder. I want him to hold me tighter but instead he sits by my side like a friend and presently gifs us both a drink. I sip and feel slightly better. Harlan watches, amused.

"Only in Centria do people still booze," he says. "You people and your traditions."

"You can't say 'you people'. You're an ex yourself."

"My parents were really," he says. "I was too young to remember."

"They threw a little boy out?"

"They'll throw anyone out. You don't get to rule Diamond City by being nice," Harlan says, a trace of anger in his rich voice.

As he lets go of me and leans back I remember Jaeger's description of the Guidance. They don't sound quite human. I finally sense the contempt forcing that churn of people out of Centria's front door and the paranoia behind the recs everywhere. For all his troubling ambiguity the man beside me feels closer and more familiar.

"Who are you Harlan?" I say.

Harlan gazes into his glass.

"My parents were brokers," he says. "Pop was ambitious but not good with people, which meant that although he was great at what he did he never really got anywhere. Ma was the other way around so they complemented each other.

"Pop was an idealist. He believed that Centria should be more of a force for good than it was. Unfortunately, he wasn't important enough for anyone to care. So he decided to make them listen.

"He overvalued a patent, to change your tongue shape of all things. He created a network of people to buy into it, traded related products against each other and made a fortune, which he proceeded to give away to some kid farm in MidZone.

"Then Pop told Gethen Karkarridan about it, like he was going to teach that fucker anything about dodgy finance. I think they marched Pop out before he had time to tell Ma. My earliest memory is my parents shouting at each other outside some big round building, which must have been Centria.

"Pop quickly found out that doing good for Diamond City is a lot easier when you're safe inside an enclave. He had some kind of breakdown. All I remember of him after that is this ragged loon following me and Ma around. Then he just disappeared. I know he's dead because Ma got his kilos but we didn't see it happen.

"She had to use Pop's kilos to trade with but being a broker is much harder without Centria behind you. Ma had to work all the time just to keep us fed and when she wasn't working she drank."

He puts the glass down and glares at it as it's absorbed.

"We lived with different men, all of them idiots and some viciously so. It was as if she was punishing herself for still being alive when Pop had gone. I think the only reason she bothered was because of me.

"One of these... men went too far with her and-and then I got Pop's kilos and hers as well. I was seven. I never found the bastard who did it. Any time I need to kill anyone I pretend it's him."

"Any time?"

"If you grow up in the Outer Spheres you kill a lot very early on Charity. I was a sub-human, as the richer citizens of Diamond City like to call us."

He smiles at me. I feel my face redden.

"I had a feral childhood," he says, "mainly alone and moving fast. I spent enough time in kid farms to pick up the basics but always ran away, usually when the place changed hands.

"One day I had a few people with me. I don't know where they came from, why they wanted me to lead them or where they thought we would go. I suppose Ma's looks helped, along with Pop's ridiculous idealism.

"And... I accepted who I was. Many subs don't; they think their lives are a mistake but I felt my identity was valuable even though most people considered it worthless. Does that make sense?"

"Yes," I say.

"It's easier to make money when people follow you, so I made money. Then I made more. I finally realised why Pop failed: he thought the rules meant something. And, Charity, they don't. This whole place is proof of that. I don't mean you can just ignore the rules but you don't have to be trapped by them either. You need wit, determination and you need to know what you're good at, because everyone has at least one gift. Mine is-"

"Seduction."

"Yes."

"What's mine?" I say.

"I don't know. I think it's probably to do with resourcefulness but... It may also be that your complexity is the truest reflection of our world in anyone I've ever met."

"I think you're trying to seduce me."

"I'm not," Harlan says.

"Not what? Trying or seducing?"

"Do you want to hear my story?"

"Go on then."

Harlan shifts as if making himself comfortable and then he shifts again.

"Eventually I got rich," he says. "I moved into MidZone but there was no let-up in the constant fear and tension. I could never stay in one place for long because by then I had a lot of enemies."

"What was it like?"

"It was like being alive and dead at the same time."

"That sounds awful," I say.

"In a way. But it was also incredible. If you know the second you're living through might be your last you become so aware it's almost supernatural."

"What happened to your enemies?"

"They-they're all gone."

He hesitates.

"I beat them because of everything I knew, everything I understood about Diamond City. It took time, money. Friends."

His energy, usually so inspiring, seems a bleak thing now as if he has led me somewhere dreadful.

"I remember when that part of my life ended," he says. "I stood in a street between two MidZone sectors, where it was noisy and mad. The last man who wanted me dead had just gone into the floor and I had a hole in my leg that should have stopped me standing but didn't.

"Then, thanks to some oddly appropriate timing, everything around me went quiet. I stood in the silence and knew that was it: I had survived. In the same instant I also realised to do so I had committed terrible… I'd…"

Harlan hesitates and swallows, his eyes haunted. I take his hand and he grips it.

"Although I walked away from that spot I've never walked away from that moment," he continues. "It created change in me. Instead of just surviving I wanted to do good. Unfortunately I didn't know what it meant.

"I did what I could for people, especially the ones who came with me from the Outer Spheres. I also sought learning, culture, refinement; everything I thought Centria would have given me. This went on for years; it was like an evolution. One day I simply came to the end of it, like I'd reached a plateau. What was I meant to do now?

"And then Jaeger found me. It was in some MidZone penthouse full of vacuous beautiful people, feeling worse than I did in the Outer Spheres where at least my life had purpose. The room was packed but Jaeger had a big space around him. And his eyes! It's like he was more than human…

"He sizes up your soul and I wanted my soul sized up because I wasn't even sure I had one. We talked and he asked me to join the New Form Enterprise as an agent."

We sit quietly for a while.

"What is the New Form Enterprise?" I say.

Harlan rubs his cheek thoughtfully.

"It isn't a cult or even an army," he says.

"Really?"

"It's got elements of both," he says. "But in fact the NFE is an idea, a means to enable the last people alive to deal with our circumstances."

"Sounds a bit vague to be honest."

"Everyone is in stasis down here Charity. It can't last. We will simply die out if we don't establish a sustainable way to thrive."

"How does Jaeger want to do that?" I say.

"Only he knows."

"That's trusting."

"There's an element of faith."

"Well, yes Harlan, and for all we know the Basis really is a god called the Crystal Mind."

"I don't mean faith in that way. The NFE is an evolving philosophy, something I'm part of and am helping to form."

"Jaeger is generous like that then is he?"

"I've seen Jaeger do incredible things," says Harlan, "and with him I've found such truth."

"But you lost the Ruby War."

"There was never meant to be a war," says Harlan. "We would have just taken what we wanted and gone."

"The kilo source."

"Or its location. I don't think it's in Centria."

"Are the NFE just thieves then?"

"Diamond City doesn't have to be the way it is Charity."

"You sound like your dad."

Harlan laughs.

"You're shaped before you've got any choice in the matter," he says.

"How were you going to get access to Centria?" I ask.

Harlan smiles bitterly.

"Someone already inside was going to let us in," he says.

26

I wake up with my cheek pressed against the soft, ridged cushion of the sofa. A faint play of warm air across my shoulders reminds me I'm naked. Through the dome I see a static view of distant curving walls, which border an empty plain beneath a huge concave ceiling. The Aer tells me I have slept for ten hours.

I stretch to ring out the last sleep and enjoy the slow spreading aches. With them come wonderful recent memories. Conscious of what happened at New Runcton, Harlan spent a long time gently kissing me better. I had expected to shut down; that trauma would have done for my explosive desire. However, the kissing went on, as did the stroking and the holding. Eventually, I was able to let go and blossomed again in his arms. I found I had more capacity than I thought and rewarded Harlan in every way I could think of. Afterwards he introduced me to more ways, then more again.

Dressed, he watches from a chair nearby. I stand and smile as if responding to him automatically. A cylinder grows around me and fills with hot soapy water. It goes to work like a million tiny hands that massage away the nice pain and the sweat. I duck under and enjoy the same feeling on my face and scalp. I surface and hang there in the lovely warmth, studiously ignoring Harlan as he watches me.

"So," I say, "I was meant to be your next way in to Centria."

"Yup," he says happily.

I swish my hair in the water.

"Why me?" I say.

"Jaeger favoured Ursula actually."

"Typical!"

"He thought she was less ambiguous. Jaeger doesn't like ambiguity."

"So I'm ambiguous?"

"Even you don't know who you are!"

I look at him finally.

"Did you research me?" I ask.

"Yes."

"How?"

"Your decisions made a readable pattern in-Aer."

He points at the cylinder.

"Are you done in that?" he says.

"Yes."

The water drains straight into the floor and the cylinder follows. My jumpsuit walks onto me. I pull my hair dry and push my face into the crook of my elbow to emerge fully made up. I favour a heavy layer today.

"Mmmmm…" Harlan says.

He gifs a chair beside him. I sit and he hands me a mug of Soupergaz. I start to sip but it's like I haven't eaten in weeks. I take bigger mouthfuls and feel the gratifying spread of nutrition from my centre out.

"So what did you 'read' about me?" I say as I put the empty mug down.

"You don't make any sense."

"I could have told you that!"

"I mean," Harlan says, "that it was like a lot of different people making decisions rather than just one, which made you unpredictable."

"Didn't that make your job harder?"

"Not if your loyalties were less secure than you thought."

"Why aren't I angry about all this?"

"Think back eleven hours."

I do, to when his thumbs stroked the front of my hips and his long fingers were splayed over my cheeks, holding me in place as I shook and howled while his tongue made soft electrical bolts between my legs that crackled to the tips of my fingers and toes and nipples and every hair on my head…

He clicks his fingers a few times and I'm reluctantly back in the present.

"Right," I say. "So what did you think when you met me?"

"You were the right one."

"To be a traitor?"

"No. You would never have found out."

"Would you have stayed with me afterwards?"

"Does it honestly matter now?"

He takes my hands and looks into my eyes.

"What happened to you and Ursula was horrible but at least you called me. Know this, Charity Freestone: there is no way I will leave you, unless you want me to. Do you want me to leave you?"

"No," I say.

He looks relieved.

"I'll probably never really trust you though," I say.

"I will do everything I can to earn your trust," he says.

His eyes are so sad, so full of terrible experience, regret and longing it's hard to meet his gaze. I look down. His hands tighten on mine as if he's trying to get me to look at him again but I can't. I smile nervously.

"I wonder how Ursula is," I say.

I feel him stiffen.

"Ah," he says, "my rival."

I laugh, but it's a bit forced.

"Come on then," he says.

We get up. He keeps hold of my hand as we walk down the ramp. His grip comforts as we walk through the assembly, two lovers in their own clothes amid a clan of orange-clad warriors.

I'm jumpy with eagerness as we reach Ursula's room. I remember then how I set my Aerac to reject all communication. What if she tried to call me? Well, she can talk to me now if she's awake. The door rises, I rush in but Ursula… Ursula is gone.

I make a weird sound that's half grunt, half shriek and slump against Harlan. He puts his arm around my waist, which keeps me upright. I set my Aerac to accept messages, see one from Ursula and open it. The message says:

Baby, I am so sorry. I let them shoot you before I did anything. It is my fault. You are better off without me. You always were. Forgive me. I love you but do not try and follow

me. I will be all right.

Ursula xx

No! I try and call her. She doesn't reply. I picture my sister as she stumbles into a gang of hungry subs…

I'm out of the room so fast I have to duck under the door. The corridors of the NFE assembly are a jolting blur as I run through them. Soon I pound down a ramp onto the diamond plain. I speed up, barely aware of the impact of my feet on the hard floor.

The plain is bigger than it looks and I don't seem to get anywhere. The only point of reference is the long diamond tube of the NFE assembly, which is now half a kilometre behind me and hard to see in the strange blue light. Distant walls form a yawning oval and the dizzying concavity far above swallows all sound. Overwhelmed by scale and exhaustion I slow to a halt, panting.

"Ursula!" I shout, my tiny voice futile. "URSULAAAA!"

Squatting on the ground I pull at my hair and groan like I'm injured but feel nothing, nothing… The sound is close in the space between my head and the floor.

Running footsteps close in. I jump up and point the n-gun but the runner is Harlan, who stops as I let my arm fall. My eyes ache; I realise they are stretched wide. Harlan spreads his hands in a calming gesture but Ursula's absence is like a physical pain and my breath comes in jerks.

"She's gone Harlan," I say finally. "She said I was better off without her. I'm not though. I don't want her to go."

"I know," he says.

"She's lost," I say.

"She isn't."

"What do you mean?"

Harlan looks around the empty plain uneasily.

"You won't find her like this. Come back inside. It's not safe out here."

"Harlan…"

"She giffed a flybike and headed for MidZone. I don't think

she's even in the Outer Spheres. She's got friends Charity. Let her go."

"You saw her?"

"Our security recorded it. Look."

He sends me a file. I access it, shut my eyes and see Ursula in a dark outfit walk through the NFE assembly. She looks gaunt and ill, with shiny skin and limp hair. Her movements are slow but controlled, as if they take an effort to coordinate. A flybike grows out of the floor; Ursula gets on stiffly, starts the flybike and cruises down the corridor. A door opens at the end and the view changes to one from outside the assembly. Ursula passes overhead and recedes into the distance. I stand with my eyes closed and look at the recording of the empty plain. After a moment I watch the whole thing again.

"Charity," I hear Harlan say.

I shake my head. Again, Ursula flies into the distance. Again I watch the empty plain. I feel weak suddenly.

"Come inside," Harlan says.

I open my eyes. The view is the same as the one at the end of the recording. I try to call Ursula once more but there is still no reply. I let Harlan lead me back to the ramp and into the assembly again. The door closes behind us like a diamond knife that cuts me off from my sister.

We make our way down a level to an area set off from the rest of the assembly. A door opens into a room that can only be Harlan's. The décor is dark with more than a touch of chaos but it's tasteful and relaxing. There is a very thick pile carpet in alternating rich orange and brown stripes, through which a series of rough bronze poles emerge to support a low-slung seating system. The ceiling is black with spots of amber luminescence that keep the darkness gentle at the edges of the room. Through a door to the right I glimpse the side of a large wooden four-poster bed and wonder abstractly how many other girls he has brought here. He sees me look.

"None," he says.

I nod, only half-hearing. He leads me to a large chair. I sink into it and stare at nothing. I don't know how long I sit for. Harlan is a quiet presence nearby.

"Charity," Harlan says eventually.

I focus as if seeing him for the first time.

"Do you want to know how I dealt with it, when I was in your position?"

"Yes."

"It's in you," he says. "You think you're lost. You think you don't know what you're doing."

"That's right."

"But you do know what you're doing Charity."

"There's just… nothingness in my head."

"No," Harlan says. "The answer is there. Don't go trying to solve it all at once. Just think about what you need to do next."

An answer comes but it seems too trivial.

"Well?" Harlan says.

I feel silly and self-conscious, which seems extraordinary given the way we make love so…

"I could look at some messages," I say.

"There you go."

I access my Aerac. Although it's only accepted messages for a short time I've already got hundreds. I filter out those from people I don't know and look through the remaining twenty. One is from Keris Veitch.

"What-?" I hear myself say.

I open the message. It says:

Charity, there has been a terrible mistake.
Come back to Centria now.
I will tell you everything.

27

The flybike is a faster one than usual. It handles well so I fly hard and nobody gets in my way. I bank right and soar over the broad, light MidZone chamber. Its building layout is pleasingly complex. Angular blocks form whorls and lines to link circles, a pattern that is simultaneously mathematical and mystical.

The landscape starts to change. One company has taken over another and is altering the environment accordingly. A delta of people floods out at ground level as a building that stretches along the wall to my left calmly sinks out of existence. Meanwhile, the complex pattern of blocks descends into the floor. The movement is not uniform; blocks disappear at different times as their kilos flow to new owners.

The buildings disgorge more people who run panicked into the changing streets. They flee on foot or in fast-giffed roadsters, which speed away to bump over panels that were roofs a moment ago. From up here the rush of humanity on the ground looks almost orderly until gunfire lights the shifting walls. To my left an explosion shocks and blooms amid the graceful orchestration of moving structures. I pull the flybike higher and speed out of range.

A circular tower grows ahead, sides adorned with rich gothic patterns. As it reaches the ceiling it spreads a vein-like ornamental network that flows and darkens in all directions. The last of the blocks disappears and simple yellow buildings form to radiate across the floor from the tower like petals. The movement of people below becomes less frantic as weapon fire dies away. There is a sense of calm or perhaps resignation.

Anton Jelka calls. I smile when I see his name and slow down, hovering beside the chamber's triangular exit to take the call. I know immediately that something is wrong. He looks terrified.

"Charity, please," he says, "I'm sorry I couldn't find you, I've been looking for you for weeks, I- oh no…"

"What is it?"

"The Sons of the Crystal Mind. They've got me like they got you... Look, if you can do something I'm at these coordinates. It's not a trap, they won't expect you, just-"

The call is cut off.

For a second I sit there, stunned and then I send Anton's coordinates to the flybike. It tells me that at maximum speed I will reach Anton in fifteen minutes. I put in a direct route, cross-reference it with occupied buildings in MidZone and set a course to avoid them. The new route will take me seven minutes. I set the n-gun to level 3 and fly through the exit.

A large grey building spans the next chamber. I grip the joystick with my left hand and point the n-gun. I open fire from ten metres away and the structure's outer wall shatters inwards. The debris seems to hang there.

I realise I'm too close and duck. Particles sting my head and hot fluid trickles down my scalp. I race through a long vacant room as blood drips off my brow towards my eyes. I shake my head, scattering red drops. As I approach the next boundary wall I shoot earlier so it's completely destroyed by the time I reach it.

I fly through the gap and over an open space. Unexpectedly, it contains a circus. I glimpse bright lights, costumes, people in flight... After the circus I soar over a range of low-lying green buildings under a high crystal roof. With no obstacles I can put the flybike on autopilot and go in-Aer.

Predictably, the Sons of the Crystal Mind are broadcasting their latest atrocity. Again, people writhe on a glowing floor amidst black-clad figures, while Hobb repeats the same nonsense. I spot Anton. He stands near a pyre surrounded by Sons. Tied to the pyre is a little girl.

I'm six minutes away and the flybike won't go any faster. Ahead is a large, free-floating dome assembly whose surface is a flowing pattern of orange and blue. As I approach it moves aside. Suddenly, there's a flash-

I yank the joystick hard left as a thick energy beam grinds off one of the flybike's runners. People on the assembly think I'm attacking them! I swerve right. Another beam hits a white conical building in front of me and shears through a quarter of it. I dive to avoid the assembly but the angle is too steep. I brace myself and haul back the joystick.

It's not enough. A terrible screech tears at my ears and hundreds of burning points hit my left leg as the flybike's other runner tears a plume of sparks off the diamond floor. Another energy beam blasts through the ground in front of me; I can't get the flybike up in time and fall into the red-edged, dripping hole.

I do a slow somersault in the weird, hissing well. It glows with damage and starts to close in as it repairs itself. I shudder as the scorching cylindrical surface approaches but drop without contact into the chamber below.

As I corkscrew towards a park with a lake in the centre I gently shake the joystick between thumb and forefinger against the direction of the turn. The spinning whips up a blinding nausea and I hear myself groan. After more coaxing I stop the corkscrew but can't change direction. Hobb drones over the Aer as I race towards the chamber floor.

The engine stutters. Both of its back-up systems are damaged. I scan the ground to see if I can gif some sort of cushion but someone else owns the park. All I can do is head for that lake and hope for the best.

The bike hits the surface and flips over. Blinding water smacks into my face, forcing its way down my throat. The flybike's in-Aer controls flicker then vanish. Nothing works and the almost invisible restraints that secured me in flight now drag me down.

The flybike bumps against the bottom of the lake. I hang there, too stunned to move. My throat burns and my lungs feel heavy. I feel my mouth open; the water tastes flat and metallic. Hobb's voice in my ears is strangely unaffected.

"Perfection will make us worthy," he says.

I try to deposit the flybike. However, the lake floor is on closed protocol ownership so the dead vehicle stays obstinately put. I struggle weakly against my restraints and the flybike rocks against the bottom of the lake, then settles again. Darkness creeps in from the edge of my blurred vision.

In my last moment of calm I remember the n-gun. I point at the restraints but there seem to be too many. Meanwhile, my sense of direction is coming apart. I begin to forget what I'm doing and realise I'm out of oxygen, out of time…

I select level 3. I've got no idea what a hint of antimatter will do to my surroundings but can't think what else to do; even the panic is weak now. Clear in the knowledge that if I don't disintegrate I will drown I jam my finger against the flybike and fire.

Instantly there's a terrific roiling and I'm heaved up amid enormous pressure that stabs my ears. Water spurts from my throat and nose as I glimpse a weird silent perspective. Bright globules stretch and shatter; buildings hang upside down; a gleaming yellow banner swings…

I'm in the air, bent over. The banner is my wet hair; the globules are the lake. I reach a height that has no context and turn almost lazily. I take half a breath and wonder how much water remains-

I slap into the lake again, the impact jarring my back. I go rigid to slow my descent but still hit the bottom hard enough to bounce off. I float briefly, too dazed from another battering to notice the pain. Soon however my lungs become insistent and I make myself flail against the water until I burst through the surface.

I'm not far from shore and the lake only comes up to my waist now. Gasping, I fight through the shallows to stumble onto dry land. Water vents from the jumpsuit and I spit bloody hair. As my feet steady I begin to run towards clear floor a hundred metres away.

The flybike is just metallic vapour; I won't get those kilos back. Nonetheless, I gif a top range flybike that costs nearly all I've got. As it grows I pump more energy into my straining legs and sprint.

The flybike settles just as I leap onto it from behind. I send it Anton's coordinates and the Aer tells me I'm four minutes away. I lift off, still spraying water.

Hobb reaches his crescendo but this time it ends differently.

"We know our cause is just because we have such support from Centria," says Hobb. "The People's Princess lent us her favour and as a result the Blanks tortured her into insanity. Rightly disgusted by this barbarism, the legendary Head of Centrian Security is with us today to bless our latest triumph."

I glimpse Anton's stricken face on the Aer feed. I have to concentrate on flying because there's another building ahead. This one is occupied but I'm going through it anyway.

I call Anton.

"Nearly there," I say. "Stall them."

I switch to audio as the structure looms like a great diamond cliff. When I fire level 2 n-gun bolts at it I'm relieved to see people run out of the way. Moments later I spray the wall in with level 3 and duck under the jagged edges. Sound closes in as I speed through the building. Calm but almost dizzyingly focussed, I glimpse workspaces, discarded food and other fragments of people's lives with perfect clarity.

"Anton Jelka," Hobb says, his voice euphoric, "you guard the very heart of our society against evil and misrule. Like us, you must make difficult decisions in the name of the greater good. Do you agree that the creature before you should be burned before it can reach maturity and spread its vile influence throughout our realm?"

I hear Anton clear his throat.

"Well," he says, "that is a great responsibility and I'm, er, honoured that you should consider me worthy of…"

"Yes or no, Anton Jelka," Hobb drones over the booming chant of his followers.

One minute away. I jerk forward in the flybike seat in a vain attempt to make it go faster.

"In my capacity as Head of Security I often have to weigh up…"

"YES OR NO?" Hobb screams.

I will not get there in time. I call Anton.

"Anton?" I say.

The room is a blur. Ninety seconds.

"I love you Charity," Anton says and cuts the call.

I still hear him over the Aer broadcast.

"NO!" he roars and my heart burns with pride. "Never! I will never agree to anything you say! Your religion is a joke and you are a fool! There is no Crystal Mind…"

I hear the shot as I blast through the final wall.

28

A cloud of shattered diamond falls past me to the floor below. Anton flies back and I catch his eye. Is he smiling? Hobb aims his device at the pyre. The little girl screams. The Sons look up at the debris tumbling towards them as the pyre smokes and then catches fire.

I see the Son who shot Anton, rifle still aimed in Anton's direction. I fire level 3 and the man disappears in a bright flash. The instant I fly past is long enough to reflect that I've killed someone. It feels terribly strange. I've never killed anybody before and neither have I wanted to. I'm not happy about it but I'm not exactly sad either. Weird power blazes through me.

I fire at Hobb but miss and destroy his steps. He stumbles, trying to bat away lacerating diamond fragments. Some just miss the girl on the pyre so I switch to level 2. I aim at Hobb's midriff. Hobb jumps aside; I keep firing until two closely spaced shots take his right arm off. He topples from the column, lands badly and rolls on the floor screaming.

I fly over the little girl, register her coordinates and turn back for another go at Hobb. He looks astonished as he realises who I am. I take aim but the flybike jolts as the Sons of the Crystal Mind fire at me. How dare they! I speed up and ease the flybike around in a wide arc.

Even from here I can smell burning and the pyre is a horrible brightness to my right. I scan the floor; it's not owned by anyone so I use the girl's coordinates to gif a large bathing cylinder. The diamond tube glints with reflected gunfire as it slides up around her and for a moment she is obscured by thick white smoke. I try not to think how she feels as the container fills with water. By the time it stops the girl is completely submerged and bits of blackened wood float on the surface.

A few shots glance off the cylinder so I leave it where it is and bring the flybike around behind the Sons. Level 2 bolts kill three and they fall past the people writhing on the bright floor. I close in on Hobb again, who stops roaring obscenities and crawls into a small plane. I reset the n-gun to level 3 and blast the plane in half. Hobb falls out again, screaming and on fire.

The Sons rush at me. I bring the flybike down until it's a metre off the floor and let them come. Soon they have left the drugged people and the little girl behind and I open fire with level 3. As white n-gun bolts cut through my pursuers I deposit the cylinder and the water. The glow in the floor disappears along with the post holding the Blank girl; Hobb must need his kilos for medical treatment now he's only got one arm and half a face.

The girl jumps free and runs. She is hampered by a limp and the flapping wet remains of her burned pink dress. Ugly red-black gashes mark her skinny legs and the right side of her long dark hair is crisped away. She stumbles to a halt, coughs and rubs her eyes. When she runs again it is with almost hysterical abandon.

The Sons get too near so I haul the flybike out of range. Undeterred, they run after me, shooting. Hobb has managed to put out the fire and waves his followers in the direction of the little girl but they don't notice. The girl runs towards a rec. She's about seven and her face is crumpled with sobs. Behind her, more Sons close in.

The Aer feed shows a red figure soar above black-clad rabble who shoot uselessly up at it. The rider fires dazzling beams that almost flare out the recs. The rabble scatters and explodes amid gouts of broken diamond.

I get a weird sense of dislocation as I realise the scarlet rider is me. My face and hair are soaked with blood and my movements are methodically lethal. I hesitate self-consciously for a moment and the Sons below start to regroup. The feed shuts off.

I pull the joystick back to loop up and over so the floor looks like it's above. The impression is of chaos attached to a dull blue ceiling. Hobb leaves a broad trail of blood; people run from buildings to pull their helpless colleagues inside to safety; Sons grow bikes and take off in pursuit.

I swoop down to skim half a metre above the floor. My bike is faster than any of the Sons' but as I approach the girl I have to slow down. A bolt hits my right hip and the flybike spins. I hear a terrible crackle and feel electrical heat so intense it seems icy cold. I wrench the flybike straight and pump my right leg in panic. Despite the agony it still works thanks to the jumpsuit armour and my distance from the shooter. I gasp and press on.

Finally I reach the girl and lean over to slip my left arm around her waist. She struggles and her face locks with terror; I have to use both arms to hold her and let go of the joystick. The flybike begins to drift.

"It's all right," I say, "I'll save you."

We are heading for a wall at high speed. I use all my strength to lift the girl in front of me, grip her with my right arm and grab the joystick again with my left. The girl wriggles around, scans me and goes still.

"Your name's Charity," she says.

"Yes."

"You shot the wankers."

"I did," I say. "Hold tight."

The flybike wraps restraints around her and we start to climb. Another hit spins us again. The backup system kicks in and we stabilise but now face our attackers. They race closer at frightening speed so I bank right and show them the flybike's underside, which acts as a shield for the next volley. The flybike shudders at the impact and I notice we are down to our last backup.

I want to land but the Sons are beneath us. Instead, I pull up until we are too high to make anything out on the floor. The airborne Sons come at us again and I let fly with a burst of obliterate shots. Two Sons explode but there are still a dozen left. Desperate now, I keep on firing and another Son goes down. Twenty more rise towards us.

We are close to the perimeter of the open area, bounded by buildings that reach to the ceiling. Out of space, I swing around to aim at the nearest Son as he closes in, his face bright with hatred. I fire the n-gun. It doesn't work.

I check my Aerac. The kilo account is at 0. The previous

flybike, this more expensive model plus all those pricey level 3 bolts have left me with nothing.

I drop us out of range and fly down at a steep angle, heading for the buildings so we can escape into one of them. However, when we get closer I see they are now shielded and inaccessible so I turn towards the portal that leads to the next chamber just as three enormous cannons grow from the floor in front of it.

I jerk the flybike left but cannon fire is a blinding corridor. I try and shield the girl with my body but now there is gunfire in both directions. A shot hits my back and breath leaves me with a hoarse animal screech. Again I'm preserved by distance and armour but it's still like being punched by a man twenty times the size of Harlan.

I can only go up and climb at a daunting angle. My chest aches while trickling blood scalds my injured back. The flybike jolts with another hit and then it cuts out.

For a terrible instant we hang there, as if we can stay airborne if we figure out how in time. Worse, the flybike still has power but not enough to keep us up. Gravity clutches horribly at my sex as we begin the sedate drop. The girl starts to scream.

Suddenly, I have kilos, 91,284 of them. The name of the depositor appears: Anton Jelka. He has left me the kilo value of his body and that of everything he owns. Rage, love and hope inspire me.

I gif a large crash pad directly below us and watch the circular shadow get bigger as we plummet towards it. I grab the girl, release the restraints and vaporise the flybike so it doesn't land on us. Soon we are only a few metres away from the ground, the familiar perspective made dreadful by velocity.

We hit the pad and the girl's weight knocks the wind out of me but I still hold her tight as we crash through layers of material to shed the energy of our fall. A momentary pressure from below tells me the pad is still growing and then my entire body crunches to the floor-

It takes a while for the impact to register. Stunned and gasping, I lie with the girl on top of me. My head has walloped the floor with a ghastly high-pitched thump. Flashes of light, more abstract than gunfire, rip across my vision. My brain feels like it wants to vomit and is sickeningly angry that it can't. Instead, more pain charges through me. My ribs feel crushed and my scorched back broken.

Gunfire shreds the edge of the pad so I deposit it. I gif a thick, high diamond ring around us and a thin layer over the circle of floor inside. It's closed protocol; only I can gif anything in here. The girl rolls off me. Ignoring the pain, I struggle to my feet and pull her up. The fort keeps Hobb's cannon fire off but gives no protection from the airborne Sons. They swoop, fire and another hit punches my left shoulder numb. I feel the hot spray of blood against my cheek.

I push the girl behind me and use short, controlled bursts to pick off Sons with level 3. Their gunfire explodes around us as Hobb's cannons pound the fort. Nearby, another group of Sons takes to the air. The hundreds on the floor start to climb on top of each other to get over the fort wall. One of them lobs a grenade and I shoot it.

That grenade… I try to focus on an idea as I aim and shoot, aim and shoot. As I do I realise how to get out of this nightmare. I just need to fight with one part of my mind and go in-Aer with another. I select a bomb, a medium-yield explosive I once used in a simulation, remember the coordinates of the entrance portal, click, buy…

The n-gun tugs my arm to assist the aim as years of simulations pay off. Somehow I'm able to balance these forms of violence; one immediate and the other strategic. I don't have space for nerves but I am very aware of time running out. Soon one of those shots will hit me in the heart or the head. Even if that doesn't take me then exhaustion and blood loss will.

The Basis completes the bomb. Between shots I detonate it via the Aer. There's a dull crump. Hobb's cannon fire stops and hard debris clatters to the floor in the distance. Immediately I realise my mistake as the Sons on the ground encircle us completely. They gif steps against the fort wall and run up them as their airborne brethren close in.

"Charity?" says the girl.

"It's all right," I say. "Kneel down."

She kneels. I pull her close and grow a dome around us. Its two quarter spheres rise as the airborne Sons open fire and the first of the men on the ground jumps down inside the fort. I shoot through the closing gap and shove the girl against the concavity opposite. The dome begins to close over us as a second grenade is thrown. I shoot this one as well-

"Charity!" screams the girl.

I look up to see a third grenade caught between the closing sections and close my eyes. I hear a brief crunch as the growing walls crush the bomb and then silence from outside.

The space beneath the dome is tiny because the wall is so thick and our frightened breath sounds very loud. The dome pulses with blinding light as the Sons around us open fire.

I go in-Aer and find a missile whose complexity means it will take longer than usual to assemble. It costs 54,796 kilos. I definitely won't get those back. The little girl whimpers. I gif a thick, dark viscous fluid that quickly rises in the small space.

"Hold your breath honey," I say.

The fluid tickles over us until we are submerged and we float just off the floor. Gunfire pounds distantly. I go in-Aer again to find the missile nearly ready. I try to stay calm in the glutinous murk but tension saps my oxygen as impacts from outside increase in number and intensity.

Finally the Basis completes the missile. I enter coordinates, fire and detonate it at once. Even submerged in darkness the nuclear flash reaches our eyes. The girl panics and wriggles but I hold her tight. Heat, shockwaves and deafening sound are safely absorbed by the fluid. Soon the noise and light fade but I do not move.

My heart begins to thunder and my lungs ache. When it becomes unbearable I deposit the fluid and feel it slide down over me. My damaged jumpsuit struggles to get rid of the residue and the girl isn't wearing smart-clothes so we lie panting and sticky in the semi-spherical space.

I gif a rec just outside the dome. The rec melts. I wait a few minutes and try again. The next rec lasts and through drifts of thick grey smoke I see the surrounding buildings cracked and streaked with sooty residue. Weird light flashes and pulses in the ground as the Basis tackles the radiation. There is no trace of the Sons of the Crystal Mind.

Presently, the smoke is sucked into the floor while around the periphery buildings begin to repair themselves. The rec lets me know there is no more radiation outside so I deposit it along with the dome and we lie there in the open. I smell something strange: part explosive, part scorched metal, part burned meat. Then it's gone.

I read the auto-message from the Basis that appeared with Anton's kilo notification:

ANTON JELKA CAUSE OF DEATH:
GUNSHOT TO CHEST
T-42 TASLA PULSE RIFLE
12 METRE DISTANCE

The Basis took Anton apart molecule by molecule so is best placed to establish how he died. At least the Sons of the Crystal Mind didn't burn him.

"Thank you Anton," I whisper.

I roll onto my knees, climb painfully to my feet and put out my hand. The girl takes it and pulls herself up. Smeared and shiny we limp towards the exit.

I get a message from Hobb:

WE WILL MAKE YOU SUFFER CHARITY FREESTONE.

I look around but there's no sign of him.

Suddenly, the fearsome bulk of Wrath Umbilica eases into the huge room. I leave the n-gun at level 3 and keep walking. The girl laughs and waves at the warship. I look down at her.

"What's your name?" I say.

"Ashel 6," she says.

A hologram of Ashel 5 appears in front of us.

"Very slack," I tell her.

29

I rise from the Basis to lie naked in a small chamber on Wrath Umbilica. Since the battle, three days have passed in a series of half-registered fragments. When I woke up in the floor on the first day I thought about Anton. His death is another layer of grief, another unresolved mystery. What did he mean when he said he loved me? Wasn't there anyone else he could leave his kilos to? I will never know him properly now. I always fail to seize the moment, wrapped up in concerns that turn out to be pointless or trivial.

As I healed I spent the next forty-eight hours drifting in and out of consciousness. When awake I lay in the floor unwilling to move, my mind agreeably sluggish. I accessed one of Wrath Umbilica's viewports and saw that we drifted peacefully through an unremarkable sector of MidZone. Community with the warship felt uncomfortably apt given the number of people I killed. I tried to think what advice Anton would give, or Mum, or Dad. No imagined words of reassurance came. Instead, I found myself thinking of Jaeger for some reason.

Ashel 6 called a few times and I told her I would see her soon. I sent Harlan a message to let him know I was all right and another to Keris telling her I was on my way. As the Basis did its work I began to fade thankfully out of consciousness again. This was going to be the last time I would sleep before Keris's information changed everything...

I stand slowly and feel the ship's gentle hum through the floor. The chamber is about three metres square by two high with a milky glow in the walls. The one on my left slopes to the floor, suggesting I'm near the hull. Another is inlaid with an equilateral triangle that points down. At first I thought it meant the warship but now realise the symbol represents a human torso unmarked by a navel. Wrath Umbilica indeed.

I grow a new red and yellow jumpsuit and relax into its now

familiar shape. The viewport interface shows the side of a wide rectangular shaft as the ship rises up it, rotating slowly. I disengage from the viewport and step to the door, which opens into a short corridor.

Ashel 6 jumps up and wraps her arms around my waist. I take her little face in my hands and we rub noses like Mum and I used to. It feels good to have someone to care about again, however briefly.

She pulls away and looks at me. She's in pink leggings and a t-shirt with a flower on it. Her dark hair is cropped to match the burned area so her elfin ears stick out, while residual marks on her arms show where the flames reached her. My confused guilt about the battle with the Sons of the Crystal Mind is overwhelmed by a surge of fury.

Ashel 6 sees it in my eyes and draws back slightly. I take her shoulders and kiss both her cheeks repeatedly until she giggles. Naturally pale despite the vitamin D beamed into her by the Basis, she appears to be constructed primarily of knees. Her wiry frame is the result of constant, bouncy energy, which delights but also makes me feel a bit old.

Ashel 5 enters and stops when she sees me. We have not spoken for the duration of the trip although we made uncomfortable eye contact when I first came on board.

"We're at the train station near Centria," she says.

"All right," I say. "Good."

Ashel 5 holds out her hand and Ashel 6 takes it. I follow them onto an observation deck at the front of the warship. Ten people sit or stand in the circular space. Four have their eyes closed as they guide the ship and the rest stare at me. I recognise a couple from New Runcton and meet their gaze. Some look down, a few don't. It's awkward.

The train terminal's huge sphere reaches into blue distance beneath its curved ceiling. Train tubes spine out of the terminal at regular intervals with boarding platforms like shelves beside them. Huge walls hold the great edifice in place and tubes pass through them like bright veins. Wrath Umbilica weaves gracefully between the structures as carriages fire through them almost too quick to see.

Finally, the warship descends and Ashel 5 turns to me. She exudes a strange nervousness at odds with the vengeful rage that possessed her in New Runcton. She tightens her grip on Ashel 6's hand and clumsily indicates the door to an elevator. We enter and the elevator takes us down to a port, which opens straight onto the road. I can see Centria through an archway in the terminal.

Ashel 6 gazes up at me solemnly. I give her a little wave. She gives me a little wave back. I turn to go.

"Charity," Ashel 5 says.

I look back over my shoulder.

"Forgive me," she says.

"Yes," I say.

I walk out of the ship. There are no crowds to push through because everyone at the busy train station avoids Wrath Umbilica. I hear the warship lift off behind me and keep going until I leave the station behind.

I head along the road to Centria and stop in front of the familiar sphere, bisected by its wide road. The place seems less like home now.

It suddenly looks like giant closed eye. I imagine the great lid slowly opening and the bright inhuman pupil turning to focus on me, malevolent and vast.

30

The door to Centria slides up and I walk in, every sense alert. I expect Bal or some other obvious enemy but there isn't even a security guard. The door closes behind me.

Ahead is the beautiful Centrian vista, which today favours slim graceful buildings that angle off the spherical outer wall and point at the middle. The centrepiece is a huge assembly formed by three hoops that slowly rotate through each other. They surround the void at Centria's heart, where a luminous cloud emits dazzling coloured light.

I expected to find the view a relief after the crowded lunacy of MidZone and the haunted vaults of the Outer Spheres. Instead, Centria seems smaller than I remember. The glamorous architecture seems a touch overdone and those sleek buildings glitter like knives in the fake daylight.

A small ship lands beside me. It's a slender dart with a transparent front, curved delta wings and a tail that rises to a point. The hatch opens. I step inside and sit on the plush seat, which moulds to the contours of my body. As the ship rises towards the middle of Centria I set the n-gun to level 3.

Presently I see my destination is a great pink disc, glowing softly as it drifts above a park. A port opens and the ship enters to settle without a bump. I breathe deeply a few times and then climb out. As I step down, the floor begins to move.

It carries me through the assembly amid soft shapes that pulse and bloom in violet. I quickly reach the centre, which is a huge chamber like the heart of some great organism. Keris waits there, her beauty perfectly lit.

The floor takes me to her and stops. Keris has her hair down; like mine it is unadorned. She wears a simple white dress that leaves her arms and legs bare. White should wash out her colouring but the pink light prevents it. Instead, she looks wholesome, delicious even.

Slowly, Keris extends her hands which are warm and slightly damp when I take them. She pulls me close and I feel her unnatural strength as she puts her arms around me. We fit together very well and I inhale her natural scent, which is sweet like biscuits. Wait…

She pulls away and looks at me.

"I'm sorry about what happened," she says.

"Which part?" I say.

"You're angry."

"Yes!"

"You were never meant to be an ex Charity. That was a mistake."

"A mistake? In this place?"

"Anton went to find you…"

"Anton is dead. The only reason I'm alive is because of him. Now tell me what's going on."

"I don't know."

"How can you not know? You're in charge!"

"I'm not in charge Charity," Keris says. "I'm just a very good politician."

"What does that mean?"

"It means…"

Her face registers a strange kind of grief. Unexpectedly, I feel terrific sadness for the Guidance; stunted individuals whose incredible gifts are not quite enough. I relax my unblinking stare and look down.

Keris takes a deep breath.

"It means I'm like a filter through which everything flows," she says. "From time to time I decide what is filtered out and what isn't. If I make enough right choices then I get to carry on.

"But most of the time I don't instigate anything. I need others for that and I am only as good and as powerful as those others. If they have an agenda of their own there actually isn't much I can do about it."

"Really," I say, unconvinced.

"Power is like learning Charity. The more you get the more you realise how little you have."

"Is that what all this is about?" I ask her. "More power?"

"Not for me," Keris says.

The pink glow changes intensity as it reacts to our emotions. Keris's eyes are huge and mournful. I could let my mind drown in that gaze of hers.

"Are Security listening?" I say.

"No," Keris says.

"What do you want Keris?"

"To tell you about the Guidance."

"I know about the Guidance."

"How?"

"Jaeger told me."

Her eyes widen.

"Hah!" she says and then regains her composure. "You met him. How is he?"

"Fine, as far as I can tell. He told me that you and he… er… were lovers."

"Oh he did did he?" she laughs.

I watch her, slightly unnerved.

"Jaeger is strange," I say, "like you."

She laughs again.

"We are strange," she says. "You haven't even met all of us yet. Do you want me to tell you about them?"

"No."

"I think you do."

"Why?"

"Because you're changing. You're no longer just Charity Freestone are you?"

"I… don't know. Who am I?"

"You're mine."

"No! I'm not. Jaeger told me the Guidance are sterile."

Keris blinks.

"Yes," she says softly, "and all the surgery in Diamond City can't change that. But there are other ways."

"What do you mean?"

"Our time must come to an end Charity. We have been alive for so long and we were meant for a different world to this one. We don't understand Diamond City. We do our best but it always slips away from us… and now we have slipped away from each other."

She sighs and gazes above my head.

"What did Jaeger tell you about the Ruby War?" she says.

"That he stopped it because he saw you on the battlefield," I say.

"He probably thinks that's true but it isn't really. He lost the Ruby War because he just ran out of ideas."

"I can't believe that," I say.

"We're old Charity. Two hundred and thirty years. We need someone to take over, someone who is the best of us. A different paradigm."

She's looking at me again. I feel very strange, as if I know what she is going to say.

"Keris?"

"It's you Charity."

I try and process that absurd statement. How can it be me? I'm nobody. I shake my head.

"Yes Charity," Keris says. "Sol Bassa, the scientist, used elements of all twelve of the Guidance to create a new person, a new kind of person, formed in a matrix that would give her all our advantages in one."

"But how? Is Mum my … er… my birth mum?"

"Not birth," Keris says.

Her whole being seems very still, as if she is the silent centre of the universe.

"We couldn't have a surrogate for someone as complex as you," she says. "The only, ah… facility that could handle it was the Basis."

"No…"

"Yes."

The world spins around me. Its burned and empty corpse is a shell around Diamond City and Diamond City is a shell around me, suffocating…

"You're a Blank, Charity," Keris says.

All I can do is open the jumpsuit, grab Keris's hand and press it against my belly button. She smiles sadly and shakes her head.

"Cosmetic," she says. "The Sons of the Crystal Mind haven't always owned the patents for false navel surgery."

The great chamber sways and I have to kneel on the floor. I touch my face, chest and legs to prove I'm real but my hands shake so much I can't feel anything. Keris kneels beside me.

"Don't be afraid," she says. "You are beautiful. You are a wonder."

She strokes my hair and runs her hands over my body. It feels strange to be touched by her, but also right.

"Only Sol, Ellery and I know," she says. "Anyone else might see you as leverage or a threat. I couldn't risk it.

"Besides, I wanted you to have a normal family life. I wanted you to be able to understand people's hopes and fears; appreciate things in their lives that are ordinary and sweet. I never really knew any of that and... It's a void in me Charity, a void in the Guidance. We were an emergency measure that lasted too long."

As I sit frozen before Keris I become aware of a transit at my very core. The movement is like madness, a storm of fragmented impressions; it feels like a conjunction of past, present, future and dream. Voices and sensations I once imagined would take place exist now beside me, as if experienced by someone else. Physical stimuli have no reference and I don't know whether to come or throw up.

Everything multiplies, like mirrors reflecting each other only instead of images I sense dimensions unknown yet familiar. Infinity zooms in both directions at once, down to the atomic essence and out to the distant reaches of space.

Scale and comprehension give way.

    My fragile mind stretches

                          stretches...

31

"Come back Charity…"

Keris's voice is a fixed point in the chaos.

"Come back my lovely one, my treasure…"

The intolerable rotation of galaxy and nucleus resolves into her face. We lie on a long chair that supports me in her arms. She looks kind but lost and her gaze triggers something-

It's as if a giant, invisible hand begins to shake me. I sob into Keris's chest and she holds me to her. The terrific shaking continues, massive and exhausting. I feel like a conduit for some elemental power I can barely accommodate and Keris strains to keep me in place.

If she lets go I will fly off through the side of the assembly, through Centria and the walls of the city. I will fly through the outermost sphere to brute rock. I will fly through the dead Earth's crust and up through the stumps of ruin. I will fly into the venomous sky, the agony of space and the terrifying emptiness beyond.

The darkness of that lost sky is a new gravity. It pulls at my clattering heart and swirls the wanton riot of my hysterical mind.

The great hand that shakes me does not let up.

88 Rabian burns.
I let him die.
He was one of my own.
Instead of his face that burns it's mine.
My eyes melt but I still see-

       I can't take any more…

I look up at a swirl of galaxies. Time has passed without me noticing. Keris's hand is in mine as I lie under a blanket, silvery with reflected starlight. Most feeling has been shaken out of me. The only thing left, barely perceived, is relief.

So now I know.

I sense Keris in me. I sense Jaeger and Ellery and Gethen. I sense others, undefined because although I want to know them I am at my limit for now. Still, the names tantalise: *Sol Bassa, Louis Ruckingham...*

"You talked about stars," Keris says.

Her profile is a lovely shadow against the backdrop of ancient light. I don't know if it's my state of mind that gives me vertigo or that incalculable distance. I turn on my side to face Keris, her head ringed with the soft gold of forgotten suns.

"I remember stars," she says. "You could just stand there at night and see them. Imagine!"

She strokes my face. A crystal glade grows around us and the huge space becomes intimate and mysterious. Faint coloured lights run through the sensuous curved structures in rivulets of purple, violet and blue, their radiance warming the ruthless beauty of the stars.

I sleep. Wake. Sleep again.

When I wake up fully once more Keris's fingers touch my dry lips. She murmurs, concerned and holds a glass to my mouth. The water is amazing in its simplicity. I drink it all and Keris refills the glass. There's an odd moment when she clearly doesn't know whether to hold the glass for me or hand it over. We giggle nervously. I reach for the glass and finish its contents. The blanket slips off but I don't mind.

"How are you?" she asks.

"I don't know," I say.

My voice is hoarse and unfamiliar. I have survived again, or have I? I feel so utterly different. Is the old Charity dead?

"You didn't kill 88 Rabian," Keris says. "There's nothing you could have done for him. Can you begin to accept that?"

I nod, wary of easy resolutions.

"Ask me what you like," Keris says.

"Am I sterile too?" I ask.

"No," Keris says. Her expression is enigmatic as she puts her hand between my legs to cup my sex protectively. "You can have babies. You can do anything."

She leans back. Her eyes narrow slightly.

"What?" I say.

"You're wondering if I decided your parents were in the way and 'removed' them so I could have you for myself."

"Well…" I say.

"I didn't hurt them. How could I when they had done such a good job?"

I nod, breathe. She watches me.

"Jaeger thinks you've got an unlimited supply of kilos," I say.

"I know. He's wrong."

"Why does he think it?"

"He needs a reason for what he does. Other than that I don't know."

There's a pause.

"Keris, Mum said there's something wrong with Centria."

"There is something wrong with it Charity."

"What? What's wrong?"

"That, my Golden Princess, is what I want you to find out."

"Princess?"

"Yes," Keris says. "We ensured Ursula had the career she did so you could see what it was like. Of course, Ursula has her own way of doing things…"

"So," I say, "I'm some sort of… er…"

"Saviour," Keris says.

"Right," I say. "Well. I'd like a pay rise then please."

"Of course. How much?"

"50,000 a month?" I say.

Keris laughs. I try to keep a straight face.

"You can have 20,000 kilos a month with an advance now for operating expenses," Keris says.

"Okay," I say. "I don't want an ifarm though. I need to be able to move around Centria without one."

"Agreed," Keris says.

"Thank you."

"I would keep this to yourself for now," Keris says. She goes to speak again, hesitates and then says, "Be subtle."

I nod solemnly. We both get up. I stand for a moment with the most beautiful, powerful woman in the world. My sort-of-mother. My twelfth of a bio-parent. Hn.

I step back and do up the jumpsuit. Keris and I regard each other for a while. Finally, I give her a little smile and turn to go.

"Charity," Keris says.

I look at her.

"I love you," she says.

32

A doorway in the crystal shroud protecting Mum and Dad's house opens and I walk inside. Repelled by the silent glistening contours I hurry upstairs to where Mum lies in bed, unchanged as the structure around her.

"Wake up Mum," I whisper, "I've got so much to tell you."

Mum's chest rises and falls. Her eyes stay closed. I climb onto the bed but can't relax without Ursula so I call her. She isn't taking calls or even messages. Thwarted, I cuddle Mum with such love its warmth should wake her. When it doesn't I'm gripped again by the now familiar anger.

I remember who and what I am. The knowledge is a brightness in me; a small but astonishing tension. I hold it in my mind and look at it in different ways, as if it is a precious object. Excitement is balanced by dread though. What will I say to people?

It's funny how life just goes on despite revelations like this. I continue to breathe, my hair grows a tiny bit, I digest the food I ate… whenever it was I last ate. I gif a plate of Centrian Old World-style Plugger and eat the six warm yellow and green strips slowly. The familiar rich savoury melt has a loamy texture and sharp tang that helps me to focus.

I know the following: Fulcrus deals in money lending and hostages. VIA Holdings owns Fulcrus. Centria is paying Fulcrus but Fulcrus hasn't got a Centrian hostage as far as I can tell. The only name in the files is 'Zero'. Who or what is Zero?

VIA Holdings and Centria are to merge although have not yet done so. The delay is due to bad weather about 88 Rabian's death, which was orchestrated by VIA Holdings or at least by Balatar Descarreaux.

However, not only do the payments to Fulcrus by Centria predate Bal's appointment as Director of Security, they total a higher value than anything he could authorise. Who does have authority?

Gethen? Gethen's job is to make money; it's what he was created for. Why, then, would he be pouring money out of Centria?

How is the New Form Enterprise involved? Mum and Dad were attacked because they were spying on the NFE, but the NFE has no involvement with Fulcrus or VIA Holdings and nothing to do with the Sons of the Crystal Mind either.

I now know that Jaeger and Keris are linked. They were lovers and Jaeger was Centria's military chief before he left to found the NFE. Why did he do that? Surely it would have been better to carry out research here in Centria, with all its resources.

Jaeger said he was looking for a new form of humanity, whatever that means. However, he was bred to be a soldier. Why does this change in role worry me?

His last fight was the Ruby War, the war that was never meant to happen. Someone in Centria was supposed to let the NFE in. Who? And Jaeger lost! It can't just be because he loves Keris or he would never have left Centria. I don't accept he simply ran out of ideas either. There's another reason but what is it?

Jaeger believes the story about the unlimited kilos. Keris says he's wrong. She's got no reason to lie to me. Who is right?

I think about Keris's description of the Guidance as old and not in control. They are in charge though, as much as anyone in Diamond City can be. In charge but not in control.

In charge. Not in control…

Zero…

I wake up snuggled against Mum. It is dark out and I see I have slept for twelve hours. That isn't surprising; it's been quite a week.

Mum and Dad's room is a series of round-edged shadows lit by occasional washes of red and blue from assembly lights over Centria. I look around. That lump over there is a diamond-shrouded cupboard full of things made by Ursula and me when we were children. In the cabinet by the bed are Dad's medals and Mum's two Old World Harvest Day stars. The big block next to the door is a wardrobe although there will only be a few items of clothing in it.

Lying in the familiar but strange place I go in-Aer for signs of Ursula but there's nothing recent. Instead I see footage of my fight with the Sons of the Crystal Mind, most of which shows an airborne red blur lashing stupid little black-clad figures with a net of white fire.

"Mystery saviour," the feed says.

There's that word again: saviour. Keris said to be subtle so perhaps this saviour should remain a mystery for now.

Feed from Hobb at a rally shows him recovered from his injuries although he's left his face scarred for effect. I'm astonished at the number of Sons present; the Aer says three thousand.

I am part of a group despised and misunderstood by the general population. They won't let ignorance of who I really am get in the way of forming idiotic, vicious opinions. I could do without the bother but at least only I know for now.

I cut Hobb off as he shouts the word 'abomination'.

I will give him abomination.

33

Ellery and I stand opposite each other in her vast office at the top of the Comms Tower, which rises from the centre of the enclave's curved base. The tower is directly beneath the rotating assembly and is so tall I fancy I hear those enormous rings whoosh by above. Centria gleams through a great cylindrical window around us and the vista is such that no other ornamentation is necessary. I used to be impressed by the scale and the view but now it just reminds me of Fulcrus.

"Hn," Ellery says. "All right?"

I go to say yes with automatic politeness but the word comes apart in my mouth. When I slept again at Mum and Dad's I had nightmares about my fight with the Sons of the Crystal Mind. There was a horrible sense of falling, worse than when the flybike cut out. It was like that unknowing, panicked lurch I sometimes get on the point of sleep but this time it went on and on.

Through a disorientating sheen of terror I saw the men I killed but the memory had varying degrees of detail. The men I remembered looked at me with weirdly accusing indifference and I made up faces for the others, who looked at me in the same way.

"I know about the Guidance," I say to Ellery.

"Figures."

"I met Jaeger."

"Hn."

"Why don't you like him?"

Ellery's eyes move as she searches the room for something to focus on.

"Gethen," she says finally.

"Why?"

Ellery looks out of the window and then back at me. She is restless and her expression worried.

"Guards," she says. "Soon."

"Tell me," I say.

"Gethen thinks Jaeger is the only predator greater than he is. Jaeger knows but doesn't care. I love Gethen but-but he isn't constant. Jaeger is just another, another... one."

There is movement in the distance, coming this way. Ellery gives an odd, strangled cry and runs forward. I step back, confused as she throws her arms around me. Her body shakes; she's crying but even her sobs are silent.

"Sorry," she mutters, "I'm so sorry."

"Why?" I say into her crazy red hair.

She pushes me away but grips my arms. Through the window I see three spherical Security cruisers approach.

"No time," she says. "Can't begin to-"

"Ellery, tell me about Fulcrus."

"Lot of work to hide Fulcrus," she says. "Takes as much to keep someone out of the Aer as make them the focus of it."

"Centria is funnelling thousands of kilos to them because of someone called Zero. Why are we doing that?"

"Fulcrus don't just take human hostages, they take information hostages as well," Ellery says.

"Blackmail?"

Ellery looks frightened. The cruisers surround the tower and disappear from view as they land on the roof. There are voices outside.

"Yes. We pay them not to broadcast something and help keep them hidden."

"What do we pay them not to broadcast?"

She hesitates. The guards are here for me, not her. Why is she so scared?

"Who is Zero?" I shout.

"Not who," she says.

I hear the boots of the guards behind me, turn and bring up the n-gun.

Be subtle.

I let my hand fall. The guards surround me.

"Are you all right Ms Quinn?" the squad leader says.

"Hn."

"We need Miss Freestone. It's urgent."

"Fuck off," Ellery says.

"Orders from the Director of Security Ms Quinn." The squad leader's voice fails to hide a sneer of menace.

The change in Ellery is sudden and astonishing. Her green eyes blaze, her shoulders go back and her chin comes up. She doesn't look like a madwoman now; she looks like an empress.

"Your uniform is a disguise that doesn't work," she says.

Her voice is a thrilling whisper. It's the only sound in the room as the guards unconsciously stop every movement to listen.

"You thought it would cover your small mind the way the Basis has given you muscles to cover your small body," Ellery continues. "You didn't earn it. You didn't earn anything. You are the man who will do what others find repulsive because that is the only way anyone will ever notice you."

Ellery's words are like blows and the squad leader groans. He shakes his head, his arrogance battered away as the other guards watch confused.

"Get out," Ellery says.

The squad leader looks like he's about to cry. His gaze darts around the room and suddenly stops. He's on a live vix link; someone is listening in and giving instructions. It can only be Bal. The squad leader's mouth twists and then he points his fuze at Ellery.

Ellery ignores the fuze and her nostrils flare with contempt. She doesn't think anything will happen to her because she has never been in a situation like this before. She goes to speak again just as the squad leader shoots her.

I scream as if the bolt lances into me. Ellery is thrown back but scarily her eyes don't leave the squad leader. Ellery's expression barely changes, even when she thuds against the window. The squad leader tenses to shoot her again.

"I'll come," I say.

The squad leader breathes heavily with excitement as we walk to the elevator. Its doors open and we enter the large white circular car. The guards in front glare down and I feel the hostility of those behind like an almost painful pressure. I stare ahead and don't meet their eyes.

After a thankfully short journey the doors open onto the tower roof, surrounded by the tops of buildings grown from Centria's spherical inner surface. They reflect the coloured illumination of the glowing cloud, which is snipped and recast by the rotating assembly. Beyond the cruisers an ornate railing outlines the roof perimeter and glints in the moving light.

The guards back onto the roof and I follow them. The mirrored surfaces of the three cruisers reflect triple versions of the scene, my jumpsuit a slash of red amid the dark blue Centrian uniforms. Two of the guards take my arms.

"There's no need for that," I say, "I'm not going to cause any trouble."

One of them laughs; three more grab me and push me towards the railings. I struggle and kick, but there are too many of them.

"You're going to commit suicide," the squad leader says, "over your poor mum and dad."

My n-gun flickers blue on level 1 and the guard on my left falls, stunned. An instant later so does the one to my right.

"Get the fuck up!" the squad leader screams at his two unconscious men.

I use level 1 to stun him and get two more guards before the last three even raise their guns. When they finally do I dive to the floor and wriggle beneath the squad leader.

One of the guards shoots straight through him and I get a nasty jolt as the jumpsuit absorbs the charge. I shoot the guard; the other two pull the dead squad leader off me and he sinks into the floor. One of the guards stamps on my right wrist and keeps his boot there.

"Shit," he says and points his gun at me.

"The Basis will record my cause of death," I say and he hesitates. "If you shoot me it won't look like suicide."

The other guard kicks me in the head with a dull thud. Stunned, I feel them haul me up and grip my gun arm. Before they can twist it

I point straight down, fire level 3 and destroy the roof we stand on.

We drop through flaming debris back into Ellery's office. Before we hit the ground I shoot the guard on my right, forgetting I'm still on level 3. He is vaporised and half the great cylindrical window bursts into a sparkling plume over Centria.

I land well. A gruesome wet snap to my left indicates the last guard did not. He screams and rolls from side to side as beneath him I see the shadow of Ellery healing in the Basis.

The roof begins to collapse. One cruiser drops past the window outside; another noses over the crumbling edge of the roof to crush the remaining guard. As the cruiser rolls towards me I scramble up and sprint out. An alarm begins to shriek.

A solid block of diamond now fills the entire floor below and the elevator stays locked above me. I dash up the stairs beside it and out onto the remains of the roof. I edge along to the last cruiser and jump on board.

I try to access the cruiser's in-Aer controls but they're blocked so I head for the seat with the backup controls. Before I can reach it I'm flung against the transparent side of the cruiser as my weight tips it over the tower's broken rim.

I panic as I'm pressed against a surface I can't see. Below me is the dreadful height; I try and scrabble away from it but the cruiser turns slowly as it falls. One moment the ground approaches, the next I tumble back and see the wrecked top of Ellery's tower recede.

The spinning makes controlled movement almost impossible; when I pull myself to the seat it's like lifting a terrific weight. I cling to the armrest and finally manage to activate the manual control.

The cruiser slows, rights itself and I thump to the floor. For a moment I lie there shuddering as if trying to throw off tension and fear. It doesn't work. I climb shakily onto the control seat and stare numbly out. Centria hangs before me.

I want to go away, curl up and deal with everything slowly over time. However, I need to find Ursula before something happens to her, to get Mum out of that coma, to stop the Velossin murdering Dad-

I scream and pound stupidly against the armrests until the meat aches on the side of each hand. As I stop I slump forward as if unable to support my weight. My mind... slows.

Distantly, I realise I may be in shock. I wish Harlan was here, holding me. He's probably sent me a message. I should check but I can't even work the Aerac. I want my mum.

The Comms Tower begins to sink into the floor. No, wait – it's the cruiser that is rising, higher and with increasing speed as someone else takes remote control of it. I clutch furiously at the manual controls but they no longer work for me. As usual anger is no use at all.

Why does it have to be me? I'm no saviour; I'm just a girl.

The cruiser gets higher and turns out over Centria. I think about calling Keris to tell her what I've found but I haven't really found anything. So Zero isn't a person. What is Zero then?

Maybe Zero is just zero.

The little voice in my head is the only urgent thing about me. Even my blood has slowed. Zero. Nothing. What would Centria have run out of for them to be so worried? Patents? Hardly; Ursula was never short of work advertising them. What then?

Oh. Of course. How on earth could it have happened? Kilos. Centria has run out of kilos. I remember Harlan's description of Diamond City as a free-market utopia. The greatest sin here is to have no money. Centria clearly has something to operate with but not for much longer. I imagine Security Control being deposited to settle debt, maintain appearances, keep the story going...

If this information becomes known the rest of Diamond City will tear Centria apart. The enclave might keep people out for a while but not indefinitely. Those inside would want to escape because who would tolerate living in Centria without its wealth and power? No wonder the merger with a tenth rate outfit like Loren's was so urgent. She discovered the secret and used Fulcrus to ensure her offer would be impossible to refuse.

The cruiser seems to drift but when I look at the controls I see I've sped up. My surroundings begin to look familiar. Unease rises through my lethargy.

The attack on Mum and Dad finally makes sense. The New

Form Enterprise spied on Centria to get the kilos Jaeger thinks Keris is hiding. Instead the NFE learned things they couldn't understand; weird accounts, tolerance of toxic relationships, nothing literally adding up. Mum and Dad were able to partly decipher what was going on using Centria's database, which Jaeger no longer had access to. Unfortunately for my family, that information was meant to stay hidden.

In the distance a little island floats in the air. My blood thickens with surging adrenaline and I start to come out of shock. I'm no expert but I know such a quick recovery is unusual...

My plan to get more power after Ursula's wedding endangered us both. Ursula was too popular to kill so we had to be discredited. Centria's brutal rules were engaged and Diamond City was meant to have taken care of the rest.

The cruiser begins to whine as the island races at me. I recognise it finally; I've just never seen it from this angle. I'm heading like a missile for Mum and Dad's house. At this speed even the diamond walls won't keep the cruiser out. Behind those walls lies Mum, unconscious and helpless.

I gif a top-range flybike and picture it grow from the floor. Slow, so slow. The flybike controls finally appear over my view of the enlarging island. I focus my weary mind and instruct the bike to rendezvous with my coordinates. I set the n-gun to level 3 and blast a big hole in the side of the cruiser. Wind lashes hair in my eyes so I press an elbow crook to the top of my head and dispense cool gel. There's an odd tickle as it slicks my hair flat and winds the blonde fall into a tight braid.

Mum and Dad's house gets closer and I get up to wait nervously by the rushing hole. The assembly sequence the Basis has followed to make the flybike is fixed. My speed is fixed too, as is the time the flybike will take to reach the cruiser and the remaining distance to impact. These elements are a little universe of horror, its terrible perfection like a machine whose purity of function will expel all humanity without even knowing. The Crystal Mind could not have designed this scenario better.

Finally the flybike appears two metres off the side of the cruiser and I jump. My flight between the vehicles lasts less than a second, just long enough for the flybike to get slightly ahead. My hands skitter along the seat and for a long moment it doesn't look like I'll find a purchase but I just manage to grab the back end.

Immediately I'm yanked forward; my legs flail behind and air booms into my lungs. I get a good grip on the seat with my left hand, turn my eyes from the blistering wind and aim the n-gun at the cruiser's pyramidal pads. The target sight settles. I fire.

The bolt destroys the nearest pad and the one on the far side. The cruiser wobbles and spins; I fire twice more and shred the vehicle into fiery streaks.

I grip the flybike with both hands and use the Aer controls to slow it down. The front hits the roof nonetheless and my legs are slung forward, almost jerking me loose. Debris whizzes past. One chunk hits my arm and knocks me off the bike onto the protective diamond covering the house.

I slide down the roof with my left arm on fire as heat forms a bracelet of agony around my exposed wrist. I try and get the arm underneath me to smother the flames but quickly run out of roof. Grabbing the edge before I go over, I hang as my boots swing above the garden. My burning arm convulses and I let go without thinking.

There's a second of suspension, then jaw-snapping impact as I hit the grass. Dull pain jolts up my legs and I sprawl on my side. Two fizzing halves of a Basis interaction pad come right at me. I blast one into tiny stinging fragments and roll aside. The other smashes itself to pieces on the protective layer.

Flames crackle up my arm as the last fragments of the cruiser plink off the house and plough into the garden. I get up and stumble to one of the pools. Something clunks into the side of my head and I topple in headfirst, stunned but aware enough to hear the flames hiss out.

After that I become far less concerned. I relax into the cool depths of the water and its comforting darkness echoes the promise of oblivion. It is so calm here, so quiet. Distant submerged clunks have an inevitable quality, while the silence that follows does not bother me at all. Why in the world did I worry?

I feel tingling throughout, a curious lightness. I am dissolving. It is such hard work being Charity, being anyone. This slow dissolution is better.

The last frantic bubbles rush out of my mouth. Their multiple spheres are like all the layers of Diamond City, adrift and flowing away. Will struggling make any difference in the end? I imagine the house as it was, the garden, the surface of the pool as it ripples with my final breath…

No.

Good seduction is Harlan. Bad seduction is drowning in a decorative garden feature. I rise, rise… The surface breaks around me; there is no spluttering, just calm re-engagement. My boots find the pool bottom and the surface comes to my chest. The sweet air is reassuring, unremarkable. I take my bearings.

Above the deserted garden the flybike angles off the roof as if protruding from it. No guards approach and the air is empty of ships. Something glints in the depths of the pool and I see the cruiser fragment that knocked me out. I put my hand to the side of my head; the hand comes away bloody.

My hair is still slicked back despite the water that trickles past my eyes. I run my hands slowly over it and grip the thick wet braid as water laps gently under my breasts. Everything feels good. I begin to drift again.

I should deposit the flybike; I should… I should probably get out of the pool but I realise I barely have the strength to move my legs.

Fear of another attack gets me going. I haul myself out of the water and stagger dripping to the house. I open a doorway and stumble into the living room, where I turn and watch the diamond wall rise behind me. Before it reaches the top I'm unconscious…

34

I wake up on my back shrouded in dull pain. The time doesn't mean anything; it's mere numbers amid a glaze of ache and confusion. I get to my knees and retch wearily but nothing comes up.

After a while I crawl to the sofa. Leaning against the hard surface that covers it I access the house recs to look outside but there's nobody in any direction.

I slowly get up and support myself against the wall as I climb the stairs. Mum is still unconscious in her room. I lie next to her and pull her arm around my waist as if she's cuddling me but it flops away. I decide not to call Harlan because I don't know who is listening. Instead I call Keris.

My call is blocked. I try Ellery. The same. Gethen. Blocked. They are all on the ifarm, which is monitored by Security, who are now controlled by Bal.

I sit up angrily, ignore the nausea and swing my legs over the side of the bed. When the room steadies, I slip down to sit on the floor. I access a med package for 30 kilos, press my burned hand into the Basis and use the other to apply cream to the wound in my scalp. As the healing tingle begins I grow four multicakes and a large glass of water. I drink it in one go and almost hear my shrivelled cells gasp in relief. I grow another glass of water, drink that as well and then munch purposefully through the multicakes.

When I finish them I withdraw my hand from the floor and get up. I deposit the damaged jumpsuit and gif a new one straight on, then grow a dental block and bite into it until my mouth feels fresh and the droning ache in my teeth subsides. Pulling my hair clean, I apply a generous coat of makeup to hide the exhaustion that tightens my face then drop the dental block and stand away from Mum to hide her.

I call Balatar Descarreaux. He appears before me as a hologram wearing a newly designed, rather menacing uniform. Although his eyes glitter his face is without expression as I toss my hair and flash him a big smile.

"Bal!" I say brightly, "how are you?"

"Oh, you know," he says. "Better when you're fucking dead."

"To think you were going to be my brother-in-law."

"It's a good thing I'm not," he says. "Your sister is a stupid whore and you are an abomination."

My smile freezes. Bal laughs.

"Keris Veitch thinks no one can listen to her," he says. "However, since I arranged that encounter between Anton Jelka and the Sons of the Crystal Mind I've been able to put eyes and ears wherever I want. I heard everything Keris told you about the Guidance. I know who you are. I know *what* you are. You're not smiling any more Charity."

"Why are you doing this?" I whisper.

"Because Centria is old and greedy and pathetic. I'm not surprised Keris and those other creatures lost their grip; all we need do is hasten the inevitable."

"I'm still alive," I say, more pedantic than defiant.

"For now. Ellery is unconscious and after your little drama the Comms Tower Keris will know if I do anything else. I shall wait until after the merger; you're not going anywhere."

Be subtle.

"You support the Sons of the Crystal Mind," I say eventually.

"Yes," he says.

"What did the Blanks ever do to you?"

"Nothing."

"Then why hate them? Us?"

"Because I can, Charity! Every economic system needs its pariahs. If it wasn't you it would be the subs or some other garbage. Besides, it's just…" he shudders, "…disgusting. Have you even got a soul?"

His words hurt because I've wondered that myself.

"If you had any decency," Balatar Descarreaux says, "you'd kill yourself."

"You're so incompetent I'd have to."

We cut the call simultaneously and I sit back on the bed, drained.

35

When I approach Keris's assembly on the flybike, three red warships descend to cut me off. For a while I hover, regarding the implicit violence in their ridged faces. I could destroy at least one warship but remember then the proximity to Keris; how a stray beam could cut through her assembly, through her…

A better idea presents itself; I pull back the joystick and the flybike arcs up. The warships move closer, twitching their mighty guns but I ignore them and loop over towards Centria's great doorway. I fly under the rotating circular assembly and pass the Comms Tower, which is whole again as if no damage had ever been done to it. I picture Ellery there, unconscious in the floor as the tiny machines of the Basis heal her.

Centria's door is open to admit a stream of people. I soar over them and out through the huge doorway, descending to a couple of metres above the diamond road. Speeding into the train terminal, I rise to weave through the pulsing tubes and glance back but no one is following me. Soon I leave terminal behind and fly the same route I took when I flew Ursula to the golden saucer.

When I reach VIA Holdings I slow down and look around. Two warships drift with slow, calm menace. Their design is unfamiliar; square and bright blue, they sport unusually prominent cannons. There are white-uniformed guards everywhere: some stand to attention while others march in formation around the charmless architecture. Bal has learned his new trade quickly but he's no Anton; unchallenged, I join the flow of airborne vehicles to blend in and scan the structures around me.

Soon I'm back where I started, increasingly nervous. I circle VIA Holdings again but the other vehicles dissipate and I feel exposed, as if I'm ten times my actual size. The warships are nearby so I move out of their line of sight around an oblong assembly mounted on the ceiling. That's when I spot her.

Loren Descarreaux strides along a twenty-metre enclosed catwalk linking one of her ugly square buildings to another. The catwalk is high above the floor, the tiny figures inside a dramatic contrast to their bulky surroundings. Loren is escorted by four guards, two in front of her and two behind.

I wait for them to pass. My grip on the joystick is slippery, while my heart races like it wants to speed up time. Loren takes another step, another, another. Go on Loren, don't look down.

And then they are where I want them. I fly up behind Loren's party and use level 3 to demolish a third of the catwalk. The bolt shears through so efficiently there is little sound and only one of the guards turns. He shouts and snaps his rifle to his shoulder; I reset the n-gun to level 1, fire twice and stun both of the nearest guards. The others spin around and Loren throws herself back in panic. The remaining guards try to wrestle her out of the way; as they struggle I stun all three.

I fly into the open end of the catwalk, setting the bike down beside Loren who sprawls in a shiny green dress and purple heels across her unconscious guards. Even in sleep there is something decadent about Loren, as if I've arrived at the end of an orgy when everyone has passed out.

I get my hands into her smooth armpits and lift, hefting her onto the flybike which wraps restraints around her dainty ankles. Jumping onto the saddle in front of her I glance back to see more guards bunched on the broken stub of catwalk behind me. They shout but their words are lost as I vaporise the catwalk roof, rise through the hole and accelerate away.

The two warships change direction towards me. I bank left and speed into a tangle of VIA structures built too close together for the warships to follow. Through windows either side I see panicked soldiers run after us but nobody shoots in case they hit Loren. I rake the buildings in both directions with white n-gun fire, carving great jagged lines through the tedious facades as my pursuers dive out of the way. Cold air rushes against the inside of my lips and I realise my teeth are bared in a snarling grin. Some of the soldiers gif flybikes but I'm out of VIA Holdings before anyone gets airborne.

My protection slumps against my back, her chest pressed against me. Ahead, a huge wall begins to grow in the archway to the next chamber so I slow and swerve into a vertical shaft. I start to descend but it's too slow so I cut the flybike's power. We drop at once; down, down, wind streaming my hair and Loren's together, copper and gold, linked as we have been all along.

Aerac coordinates tell me we are near the train terminal so I reactivate the flybike and soar through a portal into the blue light of the terminal sphere. Landing on the nearest platform, I deposit the flybike and catch Loren as the vehicle subsides beneath her. I buy two tickets for the Outer Spheres and drag Loren towards the train.

Four people wait to board. I pull Loren past them and her shoes judder lightly on the platform surface. Unease emanates from the queue and I set the n-gun to level 1 as one of the men clears his throat loudly.

"You can't just push in like that," he says.

Behind him I see the first VIA warship squeeze into the chamber. A siren blares from it like the mournful cry of some great, mechanised beast. Everyone on the boarding platform turns, sees the warship and runs. As it begins to descend I haul Loren onto the train and drop her on the carriage floor. The doors close and shut off the electronic wail.

I am safe; train tubes are part of the Diamond City superstructure so the warship cannons won't work against them. As the carriage begins to move I look back, smiling at the large blue shape that hovers uselessly above. A moment later the train picks up speed and quickly carries us far away.

36

Loren lies face up on a couch at the back of a small ship, her arms and legs tied. Harlan looks down at her.

"Did anyone see you?" he says to me.

"I don't think so," I say. "After the train I giffed a ship and flew around for a while. I dumped the ship at an empty station, got another train, repeated the whole thing and picked you up."

"We should be all right," Harlan says. "Centria only looks at Centria and VIA Holdings isn't organised enough to have eyes everywhere." He frowns. "Mind you, she could be sending Bal our coordinates."

"How long are people usually unconscious for?" I ask him.

"I've never stayed around long enough to find out."

I look out of the ship's window at MidZone and then back at Loren.

"It's been two hours. What does Dodge say?"

"Dodge rarely takes calls and I can rarely stand being around him so I don't know," Harlan says.

I should get the Basis to run a diagnostic on Loren but that will mean untying her. What if she's got a hidden weapon like an n-gun? I go in-Aer to research unconscious states, cross-referenced with the effects of known stun weapons.

Harlan sits on the couch next to Loren, pulls one of her eyelids open and gently runs a fingertip across the exposed eyeball.

"Aarggh! Get off!" Loren screams.

Harlan laughs. I quietly abandon my complex research and hope he didn't intuit what I was doing.

"Find anything good out?" he asks.

"No," I say.

"What am I doing here you fucking bastard animals?" Loren yells.

"Good point," Harlan says and turns to me. "What is she doing here?"

"She needs to answer some questions," I say.

Loren must hear the uncertainty in my voice. She laughs.

"You ask me questions? You are a stupid little secretary who does a small bit of training with her spoiled, fat Centria friends and thinks she knows the way of Diamond City. Fuck your questions and fuck you."

"Not very ladylike is she?" Harlan says to me. "Nice accent though."

"My son will kill you you fucking savage," Loren says.

Harlan is unmoved.

"Would this be your son who uses women as shields and runs away from the big kids?" he says.

"He controls Centria Security now. He has a whole army! He is on his way here."

"We're on a random flight path," Harlan says. "He won't be able to predict where we're going."

"He will if I keep telling him my location," Loren says.

"I thought of that," Harlan says.

Harlan rips the bindings off Loren and picks her up as if she weighs nothing. She struggles and claws but her nails seem unable to connect and her blows ricochet weakly. Her wide eyes stare at the floor but the ship is mine so she can't gif a weapon. The hatch opens. Harlan plucks Loren off him, turns her towards the hatch and starts to push her out.

"No!" she screams.

"Stop broadcasting our coordinates."

"All right, all right, I will do it."

"I don't believe you," Harlan says.

He pushes Loren again and I watch her closely. Her terror looks genuine; I don't think growing a crash pad has even occurred to her.

"Stop!" she cries.

"Understand this Loren," Harlan says, "if I see any ships I don't like the look of I will kill you. Do you understand?"

"Yes! I will stop! Please!"

Harlan lets go of Loren and she scrambles across the ship to press her back against the side furthest from the hatch, which closes. She breathes heavily as she tries to calm down, looking so pathetic I almost feel sorry for her.

"I cannot die," she says, almost to herself, "I am too valuable."

"We're all valuable," Harlan says.

"No! Some are more so. Some people don't matter at all. I matter. I must not die. I am precious."

I laugh at her.

"What do you want?" she says.

"Tell me about Centria," I say.

"Centria is broke," she spits with a slightly crazy smile.

"I know," I say.

They both look at me, Loren warily and Harlan with new interest. His beauty is distracting; I try to block him out and focus on Loren.

"You're using Fulcrus to blackmail Centria so the merger can take place entirely on your terms," I say.

Loren seems to look into herself.

"It is not money," she says. "It is something more powerful."

I remember the last part of Mum's message.

"Loren, what does VIA stand for?"

"Vengeance!" she screams, her eyes bright. "Vengeance Is All! VIA. See?"

"Vengeance for what?"

"I was in Centria before. They-they threw me out," she says.

There is an unlikely moment of understanding between the three of us.

"Me too," Harlan says finally.

"And me," I say. "It was your fault Loren."

Loren ignores that.

"In Diamond City are many ex Centria people with a big, big axe to grind but no one can do anything about it," she says. "I am doing something about it because to be thrown out is the worst thing, yes?"

"No," I say. "The worst thing is your family being decimated.

The worst thing is being shot while you watch your sister burn. The worst thing is morons trying to rape you."

Terrific energy surges through me.

"THE WORST THING IS KILLING PEOPLE," I roar and I don't recognise my voice. "YOU. MADE. ALL. OF. THAT. HAPPEN!"

I'm not quite in control; I could do anything. Loren looks more scared of me than she did of Harlan.

"Technically," Harlan says, "that's four worst things. You can really only have one."

I giggle.

"Things like that happened to me," Loren says.

I look at her but she stares at the floor and talks as if we aren't here.

"Being thrown out was still the worst because it caused everything that came afterwards," she says.

She looks lost as I cross the ship and stand over her. When I move, she flinches and light ripples over the shiny green dress. I slowly sit and she stares into my face.

"Tell me," I say.

"I was in love with Gethen Karkarridan," Loren says.

My surprise must show.

"I know," Loren says. "A man like that you think how could anyone love him? He is ruthless; like a machine. But a machine with such passion, and so incredibly clever. He makes money as if it flows from his hands, thousands of kilos, millions. Patents, terms, all of it like magic implements to him. Even now it amazes me what he could do.

"Everyone does what he says; they do not even question him, while Ellery in her silence she makes it all beautiful you know? And Keris is the leader we adore. They work so well together, like a family, as if they do not need words. But strange; not… normal.

"And me, this young girl, there in the middle of it. I learned to do what Gethen could do; he was my inspiration. Other people they faded away when I compared them, then I did not think about them at all. Only him, as if he possessed me.

"I was like a part of him. He knew as well. He told me I was special: I was the first person he had met who could make money like he did. He said maybe one day I would have the power he had, but I didn't want that. I just wanted him.

"That love you know it was so strong, like it was burning me up but I did not care. I could not sleep or think or do anything except love him and do my work for him. And when finally we did make love it was like…"

She stares back through the years, a shaky hand pressed to her brow. Her eyes are wide but her expression vague.

"Only the one time as it turned out, because Ellery Quinn loved him too and she was more powerful than me. One silly girl, what does she matter? I did nothing wrong, made no mistakes, unless you say loving him was a mistake. I don't think so though, not even now.

"But Ellery, she… she turned all her power on me. Such horrible words; I never knew words could hurt so much. How she had been Gethen's lover for a hundred years and would be his lover for a thousand more and I was nothing, nothing.

"When she had finished talking the guards came and took me to the door and walked me out. They put me on a train straight to the Outer Spheres with only two thousand kilos. Two thousand. After all the money I had made."

She looks sick. I wonder who else she has told, whether even Bal knows.

"I ran," she says. "They came after me: the subs, the nasty people. I knew nothing about how to survive out there; all my life was in Centria, which is so different. I had no preparation, no understanding.

"I made it to MidZone, but what could I do? By then I had no kilos. My skills they were in big business not practical things. I had to eat. What does a pretty girl do in MidZone when she has no money? I try not to think of it now but…

"The people they come and fuck me and-and other things and they go and… They all blur into one person with no face and the same smell. I get the money. I survive. Then others give me drugs to control me and I lose years. I don't remember a lot, only in nightmares.

"And one day life comes back into me. I am pregnant. I do not know who by. It does not matter. I have a reason other than myself to survive. I have a short time to do something for me and for the baby.

"I get off drugs. I just… one day just do it. My body is changing and that helps. But my will, I find my will. And all that has happened makes me stronger; furious and raging and powerful now.

"I do things for money but not like before. I seduce people and drug them into giving their kilos to me. Some I kill. The kilos come quick and many. I am bad bad bad. I do not care. My soul is gone but my life is on her long journey back to the light, back to Centria."

Harlan stares impassively at Loren who talks on, her lips wet.

"Because I blame them you know," she says, "for what happened to me. I was punished and did nothing wrong. But that is not all.

"I see Centria from out in Diamond City: there like a person at the heart of it making these decisions that affect everybody. And I realise… these decisions are not good.

"It was strange, this learning, to know that Gethen who I admired was wrong in so many things. Because I see his hand in it, and Ellery's. There was a pattern there and in that pattern I saw an opportunity.

"Most exes they just become nothing or die because they are weak from being in Centria. Not me. I am strong now and I know Centria. I see how to tempt Gethen with his greed and his arrogance.

"I set a trap for him. He does not know it is me. I am rich now, using my bad money to make good money. I use other people to approach Gethen.

"He is tired you see. Ellery is tired. They want to stop but they do not know how to do anything different. That is why they seek the big score.

"So I give them the big score: a whole patent system that will change itself every year so people must buy the same thing over and over, even more than now. The Basis it would never allow this but I convince Gethen a way has been found, out here in Diamond City where we do not respect his rules.

"Gethen he buys it. He does not even tell Keris, not Ellery. He buys it. And it has no worth Charity; he spends all your money on something that has no worth. Stupid no?

"Soon he realises. I tell Fulcrus to call him and make him start to pay so they shut up and stay shut up. Because if anyone were to find out the truth Diamond City would fall on Centria and all their clever guns would not keep the people out.

"Centria has always fooled us into thinking we need it more than we do. Gethen he will take me back so the secret can be kept. And so I will go home."

She looks at us, eyes wide and smile wider, as if she has forgotten why she is here.

"Why did you attack my parents?" I ask.

Loren blinks and then blinks again.

"They were going to find the truth," she says.

"But Bal destroyed the merger," I say.

"Bal destroyed the wedding; the merger will still go ahead. You and your sister had become a problem because we feared what your parents might have told you."

"My sister was burned."

"Your sister was burned, I was burned," Loren points at Harlan, "he was burned. Grow the fuck up."

Be subtle.

"What did Bal use on my mother?"

"Oh that was easy. Once we knew she was spying on us we embedded a one-time disguised file. Anyone looking at it after would just see accounts."

I smile as if at her cleverness. She seems relieved, as if we have connected.

"What was really on the file?" I say.

"A looped vix link!"

"Of…?"

"Sleep! Me asleep!"

She laughs hugely. I laugh too but halfway through I hear my laugh become a weird howl.

Level 3 – side of her head – fire-

Part of the hull bursts outwards. Loren screams and then her screams choke off. I was not aware my hands were around her slender throat until Harlan prises them loose. Loren makes odd mewling noises and crawls away as my limbs thrash with delirious abandon and utter viciousness. Only Harlan's greater physical weight enables him to restrain me and even then I nearly break free. I cannot blink; my eyes feel like they blaze white fire. Loren screeches from the ship's far wall and slowly her screeches become words.

"You cannot kill me, I am too precious; you cannot or all my horror will have been for nothing," she cries.

It is pity that calms me; pity for this wreck of a woman, this used up scrap of desiccated humanity. I kick for a while longer to wring the madness out and then let myself relax. Harlan strokes my hair.

"We need her," Harlan whispers as he kisses my neck.

"I know," I whisper back, too quietly for Loren to hear.

Harlan slowly lets go and I walk over to Loren, who cowers.

"How do we make my mother better?" I say.

Loren peers up at me.

"A virus sent to the file will corrupt it," she says. "I-I will send it now. When the loop finishes she will wake up."

Loren blinks a few times and then nods nervously. I watch her for a while. She swallows.

"You will sell VIA Holdings to me for one kilo," I tell her.

"Wha-? No, it's not possible Charity; it is not just me who owns it. We guard against the very possibility of me or Bal or any of us being taken like this-"

"Fulcrus then, sell me Fulcrus. That's smaller and there won't be as many stakeholders because you need to keep it secret."

"I cannot do that-"

"Yes you can," I say. "You don't need Fulcrus now anyway. If you want to merge with Centria go right ahead but tell Bal to step down as Director of Security."

Loren shakes with fear and reluctance but after a moment an option appears in my Aerac:

Fulcrus: 1 kilo – BUY?

I accept and a sub-routine opens showing Fulcrus operating patents and revenue calculations. I file them for now and call Keris. When she appears in a window on my eye screen I hear myself gasp with relief and triumph.

"Charity," Keris says. "Are you all right?"

"Yes thanks. Balatar Descarreaux has stepped down as Director of Security. Please accept his resignation and get him out of Centria immediately."

Keris's lovely violet eyes go out of focus for a moment and then fix on me again. I like the most powerful woman in the world doing what I say.

"Done," Keris says. "I never liked him anyway."

I go to tell her about Loren and stop. Before any conflict between VIA Holdings and Centria breaks out I need to make sure my sister is all right.

"I'll be back soon," I say, "but I'd like Ursula home as well."

"I agree," Keris says, "although she'll have to keep a low profile. Do you think she can manage that?"

"If I have to anaesthetise her," I say.

Keris smiles and ends the call.

I send Mum a message that says:

CALL ME NOW!

I look at Loren as if I've just remembered her. She shakes and cries as I slowly raise my gun arm.

"No!" Loren screams, "nooo-!"

I cut her off with a level 1 stun bolt. She slumps disappointingly against the side of the ship. I let out a long sigh and turn to Harlan, who grins.

"You really are surprisingly awful," he says.

"Your influence," I say.

"I wonder," he says but looks pleased.

I call Ursula but she still won't answer so I send her a message:

Get back to Centria, they will let you in

My Aerac begins to accumulate profit from Fulcrus. The kilos seem dirty, as if they pollute those Keris and Anton gave me out of love. I try to decide what to do about Fulcrus and Loren but I'm too jumpy, too exhausted.

Mum calls.

"Charity?" she says, sounding irritable.

There is no way I can explain it all now. I just laugh at her cross-looking face as tears make my eyes feel nice.

"I love you," I say to her. "You are the best and I love you I love you I love you."

"What-?"

"Ursula will be back soon. I'll be in touch."

I end the call and stand there smiling, head cocked to one side. Harlan steps forward and grips my shoulders, working away at the knotty tension that soon drains to pulse between my legs. They tremble and I clench myself to ease the lovely torment but only succeed in making it worse. I remember how Harlan restrained me, the weight of him, the physical power...

Very aware of the friction between my jumpsuit and skin, each breath becomes a sigh. Harlan strokes my hair again and every strand carries pleasure straight to the core of my mind, which lights up. He pulls my head back, kisses me and keeps kissing until my lips feel deliciously bruised.

At some point I deposit the jumpsuit but don't realise it's gone until I feel the shiny roughness of Harlan's clothes all down my shivering front. Through the open wall of the ship assemblies and buildings drift by. I don't care whether their occupants can see us or not.

Harlan inhales the scent of my neck, right where it ends and curves into my shoulder. As he bites me there my body undulates in response along patterns of delight like music. Harlan pinches my nipples and makes me gasp, then pinches harder and harder again until I'm astonished at the pain and joy of it. As his hands move down my belly I turn away and bend over Loren to spread my palms against the wall. I look back at the beautiful man whose face is almost a snarl with lust for me and push my bottom towards him.

"Mr Akintan," I say, "if you wouldn't mind."

My hair tumbles over one shoulder and tickles my breasts. Simply breathing now seems joyously hard work. When Harlan takes hold of my hips I actually shout with desire! He pulls me towards him but I keep my hands against the wall so I'm arched over Loren. Harlan leaves his clothes on, knowing it will make me wild. However, he has slipped one part out and begins to ease it into me. I squeeze my eyes shut. Millimetre by millimetre he penetrates me and millimetre by millimetre I engulf him.

It's like being deeply tickled and soothed at the same time. Soon the gorgeous tension spreads through me until I don't know if I'm fainting or waking. Pleasure dulls every concern until I'm bright and super-aware. I feel like the world! I start to fuck, hard and sweet and long over the sleeping body of my enemy.

37

Lovely, relaxing sleep. The drug-induced comas I put myself into weren't as good as this. Something, however, is wrong. I should be...

Awake-

I snort into full consciousness. The gentle weight pressed against me is Harlan, whose arms and legs tangled with mine. Everything is deliciously cramped and aching, which gives me a naughty sense of achievement. I look through the punched-out hole in the side of the ship, where the terrible glory of Diamond City moves past as if for my inspection. Increasingly uneasy, my dopy gaze takes in the rest of the cabin.

It's empty.

I try and jump up as if speed and efficiency now will make any difference. My caught limbs are reluctant; instead I roll onto scuffed knees and climb to my feet. Harlan doesn't wake so I prod him with a toe. His eyes open as he stands, alert at once and looking around.

"Shit," he says.

I scan behind us for pursuit but there's nothing. Part of me is relieved Loren has gone; she served her purpose. I gif the red and yellow jumpsuit and feel it clean off the dried sweat. Sitting down in the pilot's seat I absently rub my neck and face to freshen them before pulling my hair through. It rustles comfortably down my back.

"When you do that I can't concentrate," Harlan says.

I wriggle on the seat, which feels very good.

"Hmm," I say.

"How did she escape?" Harlan says.

I get the ship recs up and run the footage backwards. It's slightly nauseating because one eye registers the ship in reverse while the other, in real time, sees us go forward. Fortunately, Loren appears about three minutes before we awoke. She gifs a cushion up ahead, waits until she is over it and then leaps through the hole. I don't see her land because the ship flies around the corner of a large building.

"Jumped," I say.

"We should get off this ship," Harlan says.

Nervously, I guide us towards the nearest train station as Harlan pulls on his clothes. We land and I jump out with Harlan close behind. As we walk I deposit the ship and get us tickets for the other side of Diamond City.

We get on the empty train and sit down next to each other. Harlan takes my hand, which is now slippery with sweat. I grip him tight and glance out, picturing blue warships, soldiers in white… The carriage doors close. As the train fires itself down the tube I call Keris.

The call is blocked.

"No," I whisper.

I call Mum. That call is blocked too. I call Ellery. Blocked.

Bal still controls security in Centria. Loren must have sent a message when she was free telling him to stay. What will happen if Keris tries to get rid of him and he won't go? What will happen to Mum?

Guilt sears me. I had everything under control and let it go, almost wilfully. I stare numbly through the train at the blurred landscape outside. Everything goes at a speed the human brain can no longer cope with. Great forces do their own thing and the view is impossible to make out.

Ursula will be able to get a message to Mum however so I call my sister again. There is still no reply and I get angry. Why won't Ursula answer? I scan my waiting messages and find one from her sent while I was asleep, thirty minutes ago. It says:

please call thom3 hobb please please

I go from guilt to horror. Why does Ursula want me to call Hobb? If only I'd stayed awake. If only I hadn't make love with Harlan. If only if only. I pull my hand away from his as self-disgust sours the memory of our lovemaking. Harlan watches me.

"What is it lovely?" he says.

I just shake my head.

"You're very good you know," Harlan says.

I don't deserve to look at him.

"You are," he says, "you're all right."

"I'm not," I say.

"Look at what you've coped with. I don't know anyone else who could do that."

"You did."

"It took me longer. You're exceptional Charity. I… I've known a lot of women…"

"Don't…"

"I have, but none like you. When Dodge showed me your golden threads I was surprised and yet… not.

"I know it was a mistake to let Loren to get away but people make mistakes. We aren't meant to be perfect. If humanity ever did manage it we'd die out. Besides, you wanting sex over that loopy bitch was inspired. Wrong, but inspired."

Despite myself I laugh.

"Everything is beautiful with you," I say.

He strokes my face.

"Charity, you're not alone. A lot of people love you; you just have to let them."

"Okay."

"That's better," he says. "So what's wrong?"

"Bal is still in charge of Security."

"I didn't think he'd go that easily."

"What if he's got Keris and Mum hostage?"

"Unlikely. VIA Holdings still wants to merge with Centria don't forget."

I start to feel a bit better.

"What else?" Harlan says.

"There's a message from Ursula to call Thom3 Hobb."

"Sons of the Crystal Mind Hobb?"

"Yes."

I wait for Harlan to say something encouraging.

"Oh dear," he says.

We travel in silence for a while.

Whatever Hobb has to say will not be beyond my comprehension. There will be an answer. I may not like it but I've been involved in a lot of things I don't like recently and have survived them all.

I call Hobb. For a while he doesn't respond and my certainty wavers. Eventually he appears on my eye screen, his craggy face beatific with rage and the shiny burn scars reflecting an unseen light source nearby.

"Well," he says, "the Golden Princess."

I feel dizzy. How can he know that?

"My friend Balatar Descarreaux told me some interesting things about you, Charity Freestone," Hobb continues.

I stare at him and keep my face very, very blank.

"You have spread lies," Hobb says. "You have cost us money. You have killed my Sons. You have HURT ME!"

His breath comes in jumpy starts for a while and then he gets it under control.

"And yet," he continues, "I could respect that. You see, the Sons of the Crystal Mind value women. We need them to breed, to create proper humans not floor-spewed filth.

"I wanted to mate you with every one of the brothers. I thought children by you would be worthy Sons and worthy breeders with strong wombs. But no. You are- You are… a…"

He almost can't say it, like the word is vomit. He shakes his head as if working up the strength to speak.

"You are a Blank, Charity Freestone. How can you dare to even breathe?"

"What do you want?" I ask.

"I want you here with us, so we can do what must be done."

"Well that's just not going to happen," I say.

Hobb stares at me, his eyes suddenly mournful.

"I think it is," he says.

The picture changes. I see Hobb in real time rather than the usual eye screen image created by muscle readouts and subtle animation. He must be in front of a rec, which shows him seated on a bench. The surrounding landscape is unpleasantly familiar: a high, dark ceiling, nondescript buildings, a swinging sign…

Hobb smiles as he sees my reaction.

"Yes," he says, "we'll always have New Runcton. And look! Your sister is here."

The view recedes and my mind goes with it. Next to Hobb on the bench sits Ursula, her hair cropped short and her eyes glazed. She doesn't look at the rec, or at Hobb. Hobb strokes Ursula's head. There is no tenderness or even desire in it. Ursula does not react.

"She must be a Blank too," Hobb says.

"No," I say. "She… she's not my real sister."

"The same way you're not real you disgusting freak?"

"Ursula's family brought me up," I say. "I'm not their biological daughter."

"So Ursula and her family have not only cavorted with a Blank but taken it in as one of their own!"

"They didn't know who I was. I didn't know myself until recently. You have no reason to hurt Ursula. Let her go."

"You think you can order me around? Look how many followers I have!"

The rec opens the view further to reveal a huge crowd of black-clad men, covering New Runcton like some revolting Old World fungus. Hobb laughs and Ursula finally notices him. She laughs too but clearly has no idea why. Love and concern tighten in my chest. The strain must show because Hobb smiles again.

"Your sister hasn't been harmed, hasn't even been touched other than to clean her. But that could change. I may conclude you are lying and she is a Blank after all, which will force me to cleanse her from this world with fire. Do you want me to do that Charity Freestone?"

"No, please! Don't, not her. Take me."

"That's the spirit! Oh, Charity, Charity, I hate you more than anyone or anything but I admire you. Why did you have to be a monster? Why? WHY?"

"I don't know. I didn't ask to be who I am. It's just the place I found myself in."

The madness goes out of his face as we look at each other, two lost children whose world refuses to make sense to us. Is there a solution here…?

"Don't try your mind games on me you cunt," Hobb snarls.

His eyes betray fury at having to destroy me, which will make him even harder to deal with. His hand skitters over Ursula's cropped hair and grabs her ear, which he twists. She doesn't notice at first, but eventually she starts to cry.

"Where are you?" Hobb asks me.

"On a train," I say. "I can be with you in thirty minutes."

"You've got twenty."

He cuts the connection and I sit here, sick and helpless. Ursula's death is more unthinkable than mine. In whatever way I love my sister, I love her totally. Centria might have rejected Ursula but she is still my Princess.

"What?" Harlan says.

I don't know how to explain any of it to him; I just wait for the train to stop so I can go in the other direction. Harlan puts his arm around me but I'm not entitled to comfort. My stupid decisions put us here.

"What is it you think you've done this time?" Harlan says, faintly annoyed.

"Hobb has got Ursula," I say. "He'll kill her if I don't go to him."

"What happens then?"

"What do you think?"

"Why? You're not a Blank."

"What if I was a Blank Harlan?" I say.

"Are you?"

"Yes."

The pause is like that galaxy above me in Keris's assembly, huge with endless possibility and dread.

"You've got a navel," Harlan says eventually.

"It's not real, apparently."

"Oh," he says.

There's another pause.

"Is that it?" I say.

"Charity, I don't care if you're a Blank. I'm not some racist; I mean look at me…"

I hug him, so relieved and grateful that tears of humility burn my eyes.

We arrive at the station. I let go of Harlan, take his hand and lead him off the train. Hobb gave me twenty minutes; there are eighteen left.

"What are you going to do?" Harlan says.

"I can't ask Centria for help. Bal controls the army and he's blocked all communication anyway. Maybe Ashel 5…"

I call her but there's no reply so I scan the Aer for news. Weather on the other side of MidZone shows the Blanks fighting the Sons. I watch Wrath Umbilica take a barrage of shots and crash into a building. I think of Ashel 6 and shout in panic.

"What?" Harlan says.

"Ashel 6, a little girl; she might be on that ship…"

"You can't save everyone Charity. Concentrate on what you *can* do."

Harlan watches patiently. His faith in me helps. I shut off the weather and think for a moment. Presently, an idea rises like the sun over the Old World.

I call Jaeger Darwin.

"Jaeger," I say before he can speak, "I need the New Form Enterprise."

Jaeger's face gives nothing away.

"Really," he says.

"Ursula is being held by the Sons of the Crystal Mind in some hole called New Runcton. There are thousands of them there. She needs to get out alive and unharmed."

"I think you misunderstand our mission Charity," Jaeger says.

"I've got something you want."

"Which is?"

"Help me now," I say, "and I will let you into Centria."

38

I walk alone towards New Runcton. Hobb calls.

"Where are you?" he says.

"Near," I say.

"Why didn't you get off at the station?"

"I-I'm scared."

I hear Ursula scream in the background.

"Do you want me to hurt Ursula again?"

"No! I'm coming. Please."

"You've got two minutes before I start cutting," Hobb says.

He ends the call. I walk faster through the unnamed community beside New Runcton. There's no street; I just weave through narrow buildings positioned almost at random.

I hear someone behind me and turn. A chubby man in a black cloak stops and stares, his expression suspended uncomfortably between loathing and lust. I scan him.

"Oh please," I say. "Am I really going to be hounded to death by someone called %jAmted3?"

%jAmted3 giggles nervously.

"We're going to kill you and fuck you," he says, his voice strangulated as if forced out by conflicting frustrations.

"I'd prefer it in that order."

He goes red as I turn my back on him and start to walk again. More black-clad men creep around buildings and appear on roofs to stare at me; I know if I turn I will see a trail of them like a ragged cloak. I fix my gaze ahead and listen to my boots hit the road, one steady step at a time.

When I reach the outskirts of New Runcton something trips me. The floor is covered by a diamond layer, which I scan. It belongs to Hobb on closed protocol, so I can't gif cannons, a flybike to escape on...

I'm shoved from behind and walk onto the layer. I only manage a few steps before I'm pushed from the right. I hear sneering laughter.

Now I'm pushed hard from the left and stumble. I turn but my attacker is safely anonymous in the crowd. Someone slaps the side of my head; the stinging blow is startling, outrageous.

I raise my gun arm but they seize me so my finger points at my side and the n-gun goes offline. One of the Sons touches a metal pad to my right index fingertip and agony crackles up my arm as if my nerves have been electrified. I manage not to scream but when I try to access the n-gun nothing happens.

The Sons of the Crystal Mind close in and I'm borne along by a black tide. Their hate makes everything hyper-tense and magnifies sound: the men as they breathe, the great patter of all our feet, the murmur of abuse and prayer.

I wish I could convince them they are... not wrong exactly but that there is so much more than the tiny world they have sealed themselves into. I think of what I found with Harlan, the still-untapped world of the Guidance, Anton Jelka's mysterious last words.

Each of these wonders is a universe in itself. Some wait for me while others are lost forever although their echoes affect everything. The Sons of the Crystal Mind will never know such frightening glories. Release for them is another sacrifice, another burned body gone into the floor. Don't they get bored?

Sons watch from every vantage point as we flow across New Runcton. There are so many, each one looking my way. A mad, delighted little voice in my head says, "All this... for me?"

Hobb sits on his bench with an air of cultivated humility that doesn't suit him. Beside the bench is a pyre with a diamond post and tied to the post is Ursula. She looks more conscious now.

I'm sent sprawling by a hard shove from behind, smacking my hands and knees on the unyielding floor.

"Charity!" Ursula cries.

I look from side to side and see a variety of large, clunky weapons pointing at me. The n-gun is still offline.

"It's all right baby," I say to Ursula.

"It's not all right baby," Hobb says.

For once Ursula keeps her mouth shut. Hobb looks calm and happy: a man who is exactly where he wants to be. He gazes around his followers and as they stare silently back Hobb seems to absorb strength from their vast, lumpen presence.

I start to get up. Something hits me between the shoulders and I'm clubbed back down. Winded, I look at Hobb, who ignores me. Ursula whimpers, loud in the silence.

Hobb climbs slowly onto the bench. It rises on a growing block of diamond and stops when Hobb reaches sufficient height to be seen by everyone present. He spreads his hands and stares towards his god in the floor.

"Brothers," he says, "I thank you for the sweet gift of your faith."

His awestruck voice is hushed but amplification makes it sound like he is in the very air.

"Today, we have with us two women. They were friends to us once, when they blessed our last sacrifice here. Since then however, they have fallen into vice and betrayal."

Hobb points at me.

"This one has murdered many of our brothers," he says.

The Sons murmur, a sound rich with menace. I stare at the floor, too frightened to look anywhere else. I'm suddenly very conscious of the delicate organic processes that make my body work and the flimsiness of the skin containing them. Ursula sobs quietly.

"She has spread lies about us," Hobb says. "Lies about the Crystal Mind."

Their eyes snap back to look at me as I cower on the floor. There is a dreadful moment and then they lunge like a single vicious creature. Hard fingers dig into my shaky flesh and I hear myself scream as they hurl me up into the air. For a moment I'm free, then fists thud into my back and the jumpsuit armour is useless against them. I writhe and buck onto more blows, afloat on a black sea of cloaks and agony. I try and shield my head with my arms but they are wrenched away to reveal a fine red spray of my blood in the air.

Punches batter my face and now I can't see. The sound of

hitting is an awful dull staccato, almost too fast for my stunned nerves to match. Pain comes in astonishing waves; I can't move because of it but it keeps on and on.

"Enough," Hobb says.

I smash to the floor and the impact cuts through all other agonies. Dazed, I lie on my back and shake. My body jolts excruciating little puffs of air into what's left of my lungs and each breath is like another blow. I don't know whether my eyes are open or not.

"She cannot help what she does," Hobb whispers. "She is evil."

My hair is stuck to my face, which feels like it's full of extra blood and flesh.

"This evil comes from an unexpected source: Centria."

Sight blurs its way back. My feet point towards Hobb and the pyre. I look at the barricade of black-clad figures, who glare down at me with uniform cold contempt.

"The heart of our realm has revealed itself to be unworthy of our regard. In its arrogance, Centria has bred monsters."

Hobb closes his eyes. When he opens them again he looks stricken with grief, as if he has been betrayed.

"She is one."

The Sons emit a euphoric sigh. Hobb tenses and the crowd leans forward as one.

"Centria tinkers with the works of God as if those mighty endeavours are playthings for stupid pampered children. No wonder the outcome is abomination!"

"ABOMINATION!" the Sons of the Crystal Mind roar.

The deafening word strikes my trembling core like all their punches in one.

"We must teach her the meaning of love my brothers. We must burn away distractions that keep her from seeing the Crystal Mind."

He points at Ursula.

"Distractions like this false sister of hers."

Hobb aims his hateful little device at the pyre. Dumfounded, I watch the wood begin to smoke. Ursula looks at it dully and passes out.

"You said you would let her go if I came here," I croak at Hobb.

He looks theatrically bemused.

"No," he says, "I didn't. You have contaminated her, but her cleansing will be quick. Yours alas will take years."

Hobb nods at the Son nearest to Ursula.

"Wake her."

The Son jabs something into Ursula's arm. She inhales sharply and her head comes up. She sees the fire around her and strains to escape but can barely move. Flames chew through the wood towards her. She screams.

I try to stand. A boot that seems almost disembodied flies in from the left and kicks me back down. Ursula's screams go up a pitch.

"Get up," Hobb says.

I try. They beat me down again.

"Get up!" Hobb shouts.

He sounds confused and I slowly angle my head so I can see him. He isn't talking to me.

The flames reach Ursula and smoke gags her screams. She becomes senseless with choked hysteria as her trouser legs blacken horribly and-and then they catch fire.

Suddenly, water pours onto her from above. Flames hiss out and the pyre spreads in a fan of blackened wood. I look up. Above Ursula hangs a ship, smaller than a warship but heavily armoured. Water drips from its hatch and I glimpse Harlan in a black cloak as he ducks back inside.

"No!" Hobb screams, "nooooo!"

Painfully I clamber to my feet. No one looks at me; Hobb hasn't even noticed that Ursula's fire is out. Instead he stares into the crowd and I follow his gaze.

There is a civil war among the Sons of the Crystal Mind. Great swathes of them lie motionless on the floor. Elsewhere, their black-clad brethren methodically cut them down and Hobb's floor cover stops the Basis absorbing the bodies.

I see Jaeger under a black hood, his expression eerily calm. His troops respond to the tiniest indication from him as he whirls untouched through knives and weapon beams to fling Sons of the Crystal Mind into their own fields of fire.

One of the Sons flies back and knocks me flat, his weight crushing my injuries. I gasp and inhale the smell of his sour body and musty clothes; then grab his rifle and struggle out from under him.

The Sons who surrounded me have all dispersed. They've got no idea who to kill; they don't know it's the New Form Enterprise dressed in identical black robes.

Two of the genuine Sons fight their attackers. One of the two then shoots the other. The NFE have got an identifier I can't see to ensure they don't make the same mistake.

"Stop," Hobb shouts.

One of the Sons turns and sees me. He raises his fuze but I blow him apart with the rifle. Behind him I see the pyre. Ursula is gone.

"Charity!"

Harlan's voice. I turn; his ship has landed nearby. I limp towards it.

The ground in front of me erupts! I stumble back, stunned. I look around and then up. Hobb points a rifle at me from the top of his diamond block. He laughs and shoots again; he wants me to know it's him.

As I lift the rifle I notice a number on the side: 3, which becomes 2, which becomes 1… The rifle dissolves in my hands. It must have been a cheap model, only made to last a short time.

Another blast from Hobb explodes in front of me and the shock wave throws me back. I struggle up and a shot smashes down behind, hurling me forward to land on the jagged edges. Hobb fires again and again, his shots churning up the floor. Although I cover my head and throw myself out of the way bright fragments still cut through.

I writhe and scream in a storm of bloody diamond but all of a sudden it stops. I look up to see Hobb fire at Harlan's ship and then my head nods forward involuntarily. My entire being is agony but in the terrible heart of it I notice… Hobb has blasted away a large patch of his floor cover.

Harlan fires a white n-gun bolt that shatters part of Hobb's block. A few of the remaining Sons notice and shoot at Harlan. Harlan ducks into his ship, which rocks under the impact of gunfire.

I shelter against the base of Hobb's block and gif a fuze in the patch of revealed floor. As I watch the gun form and grow, hot blood drips off my face like tears. Finally, my fuze rests on the floor and I reach over to pick the weapon up. Pushing myself to my feet I limp backwards until I can see Hobb.

"Hey handsome," I say.

He turns, his expression a mix of surprise and guilty delight at my words. He notices the fuze and looks too confused to raise his rifle. His eyes flick to the exposed floor patch and as realisation softens his features I shoot him in the stomach. An impressive red spray jets out behind him; he doubles over and the rifle falls from his hands. For a moment he kneels and then slowly somersaults forward to land on his back with a dull thud.

I point the gun at his face. He blinks slowly and tries to speak as the noise of battle around us gradually fades. I let the fuze fall to my side, drop it and kneel next to Hobb. Ignoring the pain I grip his shoulders and pull him up until he sits with his back against my front.

"Look," I say.

We face the remains of the crowd. Amid a horrible layer of black-clad bodies, the disguised New Form Enterprise pick off the last of the Sons and then disperse across Diamond City.

If anyone cares enough to investigate, it's unlikely the NFE will be suspects. There's no historical animosity or even link between the two groups. Hobb scared everyone out of New Runcton and none of the Sons are left alive to pass on scanned IDs.

"I don't... understand," Hobb says.

"Perhaps the Crystal Mind had other plans," I say.

"Was... I... wrong?"

"I think you might have been."

A strange sob escapes him and he seems to become lighter.

"I did... terrible things," he says.

"Yes," I say. "So did I."

"No," he says.

With effort, he turns until his horrified eyes look into mine.

"If only…" he says, "if only…"

His hand grips my fingers and then it slowly lets go.

New Runcton is silent. Hobb's block slides down my back into the ground and I slowly descend as the floor cover sinks too. The bodies in their black cloaks are absorbed with Hobb the last to go, slipping down me as the Basis claims him.

I look out over a field of shadows under a bright surface. They blur, shiver and are gone as the Sons of the Crystal Mind go to meet their maker. Or, rather, mine.

39

Harlan helps me up the ramp into his ship; the hatch closes behind us and a slight jolt indicates take-off. Ursula sits trembling against the far wall, her glassy eyes bright and her breath rapid. Great scarlet burns weep on her beautiful legs, which are covered with a glowing anaesthetic sheath. I sit beside her and Harlan sits across from us. There's a very peculiar pause.

"I-I'm sorry," Ursula says.

Her voice has none of its usual confidence.

"You've got nothing to be sorry for," I say.

I reach out to stroke her brutally cropped hair but she moves her head away.

"I wanted to stop you getting hurt," she says, "and I had to watch those bastards beat you to pulp."

"They didn't quite do that," I say.

"Charity, your face…"

My face does feel odd. At the moment, shock and adrenaline keep the pain at bay.

"At least we got out," I say.

"How many people died?" she asks.

I look at Harlan.

"Three thousand, two hundred and sixty-two," he says.

I didn't ask Jaeger to kill everyone but I knew he would do something drastic and horribly efficient. That Hobb seemed to absolve me of it at the end changes nothing; he had no idea what really happened to his followers. As far as he knew they turned on themselves, an event as mysterious and terrifying as a genuine miracle.

Ursula groans.

"How did they find you anyway?" I ask her.

She looks down.

"They didn't find me," she says.

Harlan makes a funny noise in his throat. His expression is strange.

"She found them," he says.

His words echo through me and get louder until the pressure seems to crack my chest. Ursula looks devastated, worse than from the pain. She hasn't let the Basis heal her because she wants to punish herself for-for… joining the Sons of the Crystal Mind.

"I'm sorry," she whispers. "It's just… the fucking bastard Blanks. They shot you and burned me and left us in that stupid craphouse to get raped and killed. I hate them. I-I didn't think it would end like this."

Her words hurt more than the injuries to my body. I would need to multiply that pain by a hundred, even a thousand to come close. The one I love most has wounded me right in my soul, the secret part of me that keeps the rest together.

The little voice in my head just goes

very

quiet

Out of the silence comes hatred for this vain, stupid woman. My rage has a voice now; not a roar but something cold and quiet. It sounds like Ellery's brutal truth, Keris's implacable will, Jaeger's ruthlessness and Gethen's utter disregard.

"Ursula, I found out who I really am. Part of my heritage is that I'm a Blank."

Her eyes go very wide.

I continue, remorseless. I am the Guidance.

"There is more to know," I say, "but I am not going to tell you because I no longer trust you."

"Stop," she whispers, "Charity, please…"

"The vix link the Blanks used was a recording of an atrocity that happened right in front of you," I say. "Perhaps you could have saved 88 Rabian, perhaps not. We will never know now because you are unable to think for yourself.

"To save you I have caused the deaths of over three thousand men. I've made a deal with the New Form Enterprise and I don't know how that will turn out for me. I did all this for you.

"And you are not worth it."

She puts her nails to her face and starts to claw it. I pull her hands away.

"No," I say, "none of that for you Ursula. I want you to think about what you've done. Eventually you'll arrive at an understanding. When that happens tell me and I will work out how I am going to forgive you."

Her eyes are stretched so wide no part of their lids is visible. She gives a tiny nod. After a moment I let go of her hands.

"We're going to land. Harlan and I will get off. You go back to Centria and make sure Mum is okay. After…" I look at my wrecked body, "three days tell Gethen Karkarridan to call me via Aerac, not ifarm. Tell him I now own Fulcrus. He will know what that means. Do you understand?"

She nods, mute, terrified.

The ship bumps slightly as it lands. I get up and stride out of the cabin, giving no indication I'm in any pain. The hatch opens to reveal a MidZone day, the same day it was ten minutes and another life ago.

I walk down the ramp and across the broad roof of a triangular building. Harlan runs to catch up as I keep going and don't look back. There is something in my eyes; tears, blood, both. I blink it away.

"I think," Harlan says gently, "it's as well you love her a little less."

I nod. He is very wise. The armoured ship passes over us and heads for Centria.

"You're not just any Blank are you?" Harlan says.

"No," I whisper.

40

A tickling crosses my naked body as if I have surfaced through water yet remain dry. The tender contact reassures, like Harlan's caress. Light is low and comfortable. Support structures under my neck and back recede and I settle onto a cool, hard surface.

My mind feels calmer than it has for a long time. I remember gentle, whispered conversations but not their content, as if they were healing dreams. I open my eyes.

It takes a while to see properly. A dark friendly shape shifts nearby and a large hand takes mine as a streak of white above me becomes Harlan's smile. Outlines resembling giant letters sharpen into Old World-style furniture: loops of ornate wood border rich purple fabric whose designs hint at lost kings and their imminent return…

I go to speak but I'm too dizzy. It doesn't matter; I'm in no hurry. I yawn, a great lung stretcher that wakes my injuries although their clamour is an echo of what it was. I arch my back against the floor and extend my arms and legs carefully to push the sleep out. I feel latent, readied, the distant pain less an obstacle than a reminder of what I have survived.

"You've been out for three days," Harlan whispers. "Here…"

A new pressure applies itself to my back, soft but also firm. The room seems to sink away as Harlan gifs a bed under me, a construction of mahogany swirls and rich pink drapery in keeping with the decor. I relax onto it as he runs his hands over my front. Warmth in my body rises sweetly in response and my breathing deepens.

"Easy now princess," Harlan says. "You're still healing."

"I just need you to kiss it better," I whisper.

He leans over and kisses my neck.

"Oww…" I drone, sleepy.

He leans back with a laugh.

"You'll be all right," he says.

"Gethen will call soon," I say. "I don't want him to see me like this."

Harlan helps me upright until I sit on the edge of the bed, slightly short of breath. I look down at myself. Two thirds of my body are covered with red marks in a variety of shapes and sizes.

I get a diagnostic up. It describes external wounds including lacerations that will heal without scars in a few days, ripped muscles in my arms and legs, a twice-broken nose, eight cracked ribs and damage to one of my eyes that I didn't even notice. Six teeth were loose and four were knocked out. The Basis has grown me new ones and I tongue them dubiously. They feel the same as the originals.

"Did you pay for all this?" I ask Harlan.

"Of course."

"You really can't keep doing that."

"There's nothing I'd rather spend my money on than you Charity Freestone."

"Awww. Thank you though."

He smiles and I feel a tug of loss.

"They broke my n-gun," I say.

"You can't break an n-gun. You can neutralise it but it just grows back. Try."

The little target sight appears.

"Oooo!" I say, delighted. "I'd like to go and shoot something."

"Soon baby, soon."

"What are these 'Other Therapies'?"

Harlan looks slightly uncomfortable.

"I took the liberty of running some psych programs on you," he says.

"Oh."

"They work while you sleep, like a mind massage. I was worried you'd have a breakdown."

I look at the psych readouts. They are closed protocol so no one except me has access to them. I flick through the findings and notice the words 'hypersensitive', 'resourceful' and 'unquantifiable'. 'Unquantifiable?' Typical.

"Did you speak to Jaeger?" I ask.

"He said to talk to you."

"He and I exchanged terms."

Harlan sighs.

"What terms?" he says.

"To rescue Ursula from the Sons of the Crystal Mind, I agreed to get Jaeger and five hundred of the New Form Enterprise to a set of coordinates one hundred metres inside Centria."

"By when?"

"11am today," I say.

"So you've only got five hours. How are you going to do it?"

"I've got a plan."

"All right," Harlan says, "what then?"

"Once the NFE are there, my terms are automatically discharged and I'm released from all obligations."

"And if not?" Harlan says.

"The Basis will automatically assign operation of my Aerac to Jaeger."

"That would give Jaeger control over everything you do," Harlan says.

"At the time it seemed better to be enslaved by Jaeger than burned alive by Hobb," I say.

"And now?"

"Ursula willingly joined the Sons of the Crystal Mind, who have since all been killed."

The Basis may have fixed my body but it can't do anything about the ambiguous, shifting bruise of guilt.

"You didn't do that," Harlan says.

"I caused it."

"Jaeger made the tactical decision, not you."

"Maybe."

I want to look at him but instead keep my gaze fixed on the floor as I stand and grow the jumpsuit straight onto me. Dressed, I feel no less awkward.

"Harlan, Centria fought a horrible war to keep the New Form Enterprise out. I'm going to blow that victory."

"'That victory' wasn't as straightforward as you thought though was it?"

"I suppose not. I just don't know what will happen."

"Have faith," Harlan says.

The Basis has cleaned and conditioned me so I don't need to pull my hair through, which is a relief. Harlan likes it and intimacy seems wrong now.

"Jaeger thinks Keris has unlimited kilos," I say. "Keris says she hasn't. Given that Centria is bankrupt I'm inclined to believe Keris. What will Jaeger do when he finds out?"

"If it's true then there isn't anything he can do."

"I still don't know what the NFE ultimately want. All I've got is vague hints about 'new humanity', whatever that is."

Harlan isn't smiling anymore.

"You've agreed terms so it doesn't matter," he says. "You haven't got a choice."

The room seems chilly as we sit in silence.

For something to do I touch my face, which feels unfamiliar. I get a holo up but hardly recognise the hard-faced young woman who stares coldly back. My eyes... my eyes are scary. The Guidance glare out of them from a grey and purple bar of bruising. There is a bolshy pride in the mottling on my jaw while more pronounced cheekbones make me seem functional, uncluttered. My chest rises and falls; other than that I am still, more so than I used to be. The soft blonde flow of my hair seems deceptive, like decoration on a weapon.

Gethen calls.

"I need to take this alone," I tell Harlan.

"Can't do that," he says.

I tut at him. He doesn't move or react so I cancel the holo and turn. Gethen appears in front of me as a hologram, looking angry and worried. From this angle he can't see Harlan.

I watch Gethen calmly. His higher status dictates that I should speak first. I don't blink.

"You have Fulcrus," he says finally.

I nod.

"What do you want to do?" he says.

"I want to listen Gethen, while you explain to me what is going on."

"I don't understand."

"No? My parents were going to find out about you and VIA Holdings. You couldn't let that happen. By your own rules you'd have to become an ex."

Gethen looks at me impassively.

"I don't think you'd have got far though," I say, "what with all the Centrian exes out in Diamond City."

Gethen shakes his head, as if he can't believe how his valuable time is being wasted.

"You ordered Centrian soldiers to kill my dad in MidZone," I say. "Loren knew you'd fail so she and Balatar hired a Velossin to do the job properly."

"Nonsense," Gethen says.

"Keris didn't want me and Ursula to become exes and neither did Anton Jelka. You made sure of it though didn't you?"

He licks his lips.

"Have you got any idea what happened to me because you did that?" I say.

He tries to stare me out but his gaze flickers away.

"Look at me Gethen. Look at my *face*."

I see him register the damage as if trying to pass the time until I forget what I wanted and move on.

"Tell me about the Ruby War," I say.

His eyes and nostrils both flare.

"We won," he says.

"No thanks to you."

Gethen is flustered now. He is too used to people doing what he wants and his experience is turning against him.

"I don't know what you're talking about," he says.

"It was never supposed to happen was it?" I say. "Someone was meant to let the New Form Enterprise into Centria. That someone was you."

"No!"

"Keris wouldn't have done it," I say. "She fought them off, and to physically let an enemy in wouldn't even occur to Ellery.

"Neither of them had any motive Gethen. You did though didn't you? You were going to let the NFE in to cover the fact that you lost all of Centria's kilos to a lunatic like Loren Descarreaux."

Gethen jolts as if I've shot him with an Old World projectile weapon.

"Were you hoping Jaeger's story about unlimited kilos was true so you could rebuild the finances before anyone found out?"

He looks at me, frozen and then bites his lips nervously and swallows.

"Anton was too good though wasn't he?" I say. "He knew the instant Jaeger was near. What a shame Anton's dead. You're less safe now."

Gethen opens his mouth but no words come and he shuts it again, slowly, with effort.

"Who else knew that Centria was bankrupt?" I say.

Gethen groans. His appearance is the same but he looks different, as if all the things that hold him together have begun to collapse.

"Ellery," he says finally.

"No one else?"

"No."

"Not Keris?"

Gethen looks surprised.

"Of course not," he says. "Keris would never have sent your parents after the New Form Enterprise if she'd known. She authorised the mission when Anton Jelka told her he'd found the NFE. A one-man investigation was nothing out of the ordinary or I would have heard about it and stopped it."

"Did Ellery know you were going to betray us?" I say.

He clutches at his jacket, stares at me and then shakes his head. Without his ruthless exterior he is a sad-eyed, desperate man.

"Gethen," I say, "I want you to do something for me."

"What?" he says.

"Balatar Descarreaux is still in charge of Centria Security despite Keris authorising his removal. Get rid of him and shut

Security Control Surveillance down for forty-eight hours. No one else in Centria is to know, so leave the army functioning. Do you understand?"

"I-I don't know how to-"

"Find a way."

"It's impossible…"

"Do it or I will tell Keris and Ellery."

"I want to help but-"

"And Jaeger and Sol and Louis and-"

"All right!" Gethen shouts.

His hands tremble.

"How do you know about… them?" he says.

"Just accept that I do."

Gethen runs his palms back over his head, a mannerism I now realise we share. After a while he looks up.

"Like anything, Security requires a budget," he says, his voice shaky. "I shall divert certain funds…" He thinks for a moment. "When do you want it shut down?"

I look past the projection at Harlan, who smiles.

"Now," I tell Gethen.

41

Makeup covers the bruising on my face as I stand outside Mum and Dad's house, which is no longer shielded. Through a downstairs window I see a corner of the sofa and some cupboards against a wall. At the end of the garden our little island hangs in the air, unchanged and sweet as a childhood memory.

Around me, Centria goes about its business. Jaeger and the New Form Enterprise arrived six hours ago in time for the 11am deadline. They came silently, in small groups without their orange uniforms. There have been no battles, no pronouncements; no soldiers imposing a new order.

I should enter the house but hesitate. Ursula will have told Mum everything. What if my Blankness repulses her, however much she might not want it to? What if she thinks I was too harsh with Ursula?

Harlan remains a source of profound confusion; I don't know if I really mean anything to him or not. After we walked into Centria we reached a junction where Mum and Dad's was in one direction and Harlan's unknown destination was in another. After an awkward pause he smiled sadly as if he wanted to kiss me and then we walked away from each other although he moved first. I told myself I was fine.

I go to knock on the door, then just push it open and walk in. Mum and Ursula sit beside each other on the sofa. Mum jumps up when she sees me while Ursula's gaze drops to the floor. She stays where she is, hands folded in her lap. Part-healed burns redden her neck and arms.

Mum was unconscious for so long I forgot how fast she can move. She is on me in a second, her expression weird and intense as she lifts me off the floor. I get my arms around her and grip tight as she makes a keening sound into my hair.

"My baby, my little girl," Mum says, over and over.

Oh, to feel her move again! Her coma and our banishment are like an eerie alternative world now, its presence like the aches in my flesh, resonant but growing weaker. Eventually, I'm lowered to the ground as Mum unhooks herself from my shoulder and looks into my eyes. She has always been so controlled but now her face is wet with tears and almost hysterical. I touch her cheek.

"I missed you," I manage to say.

I feel another presence beside me. Without looking I grab Ursula around the waist and pull the three of us together. I bury my head between the two of them and lose myself in a strange triumphant grief that rocks me on my feet. My mother and sister hold me firmly as gravity seems to recede. No one moves except me and even then I can't be sure.

Finally, they guide me to the sofa and my legs buckle as I sit, drained and breathless. I close my eyes and feel their gaze on me. More time passes, during which they stroke my arms and hands and hair. Eventually I open my eyes again and look up at Mum.

"You know, then?"

"Yes," she says, "Ursula told me a lot of it and the rest I've gleaned from the Aer. What you've achieved is incredible."

"I killed people Mum."

"They were trying to kill you Charity. It was self-defence."

"It doesn't feel right."

"I'm glad it doesn't darling. It's never felt right to me or your father either, but that is the nature of this place."

"Have you heard from Dad?"

"No," she says sadly, "and I don't expect to. Any contact could be enough for the Velossin to trace him."

"We have to deal with that Velossin," I say.

"Yes," Ursula says.

"We'll think of a way," Mum says.

There is a pause. Mum and I smile again. Ursula doesn't.

"Charity," she says.

"Yes Ursula?"

"I'm sorry," she says. "I'm sorry I did that stupid thing. I was so angry and in so much pain and… still am but that's no excuse.

Sometimes though you do something and it's wrong but when you realise you see… you see a bigger world."

I watch her.

"Thank you for saving me," she says. "And thank you for saying what you did; it would have been worse if you hadn't said it. I know how much you loved me; it's enormous, your love. I've never told you what that meant, how it's helped."

Her voice is clear and her face almost without expression as tears trickle down it.

"You've always had my back, but things have changed, forever I think. I've got your back now; whatever you need. I hope you love me still."

I take her beautiful, ridiculous face in my hands and kiss her. The softness of her lips is a world that blossoms and then sweetly fades. We part like a gentle exhalation.

"Of course I love you," I say. "You're my sister."

"Really? Even now?"

"Always."

"Oh," Mum says, her voice catching.

"Don't you start," Ursula says.

The three of us sit and hold hands for a while.

"What was the deal you did with the New Form Enterprise?" Mum says.

"I let them in," I say.

Mum goes white.

"Eh?" Ursula says.

"There have been five hundred of them in Centria for the past six hours," I say.

Mum looks out of the window.

"What are they doing?" she whispers.

"Looking for a mythical kilo source," I say. "It's what caused the Ruby War."

Mum turns back to me, her face set in its usual reserve.

"I lost friends in that war Charity."

"Should I have let Ursula die Mum?" I say.

Mum looks at Ursula and then looks at me.

"No," she says.

"That's good then," Ursula says to Mum pointedly.

"There's something else," I say. "I own a horrible company called Fulcrus, which has been blackmailing Centria for the past year."

"Blackmailing Centria about what?" Mum says.

"Centria is bankrupt."

"How?" Mum and Ursula say simultaneously.

"Loren Descarreaux tricked Gethen into gambling all our kilos away."

"Loren?" Mum says.

"Loren is an ex. She was in love with Gethen but Ellery made him throw her out. VIA stands for 'Vengeance Is All'. You were about to find out so she put you in a coma and sent the Velossin after Dad."

Mum looks sick.

"If we'd worked it out sooner..." she says.

"It wouldn't have made any difference," I say.

"At least you didn't put her gimp son in charge of Security," Ursula tells Mum.

"Balatar's role just became vacant," I say. "It's yours Mum. Anton would have wanted that."

Mum frowns as she thinks about every aspect of the proposal.

"All right," she says.

"Better give Ursula a job," I say. "She likes thumping people."

"I do actually," Ursula says. "That and-"

"Not now darling," Mum says.

I send Gethen a message:

Make Julie Freestone Director of Security

There is a pause.

"Huh!" Mum says.

"Got it?" I say.

"Yes. I've accepted."

Mum looks at me, impressed.

"I don't know how you did it but thank you," she says. "And well done."

This is my best ever moment. If only Dad was here it would be perfect-

Gethen Karkarridan appears in holographic form, looking scared.

"You need to come to Security Control," he says.

42

The elevator is a stubby cylinder on its side whose floor stays level as we rise up the enclave's curved inner wall. We pass the last buildings jutting away from us towards the scintillating hoop assembly and for a while we are in clear air. I gaze down at Centria, whose diamond buildings resemble the frozen beams of a restless, flashing star.

We pass into soothing clouds but the coloured light pulses here too like a mysterious visual language. We emerge from the whiteness to spend a few moments sandwiched between its puffy upper surface and the ceiling, where the menacing dark slots thin to indistinct lines as we ascend. A second later we pass through the structural layer and see its interior: a silent, apparently motionless piece of technology whose only miracle is its existence.

We emerge at the flat base of the broad shallow dome and travel up the side of it. Our height reveals training camps and ships spread across the floor, which looks like a strangely decorated plate that slowly angles towards us. The central pillar with its bright upper band enlarges as we approach.

Soon we join it, sliding down the outside to a stop. I tap my gun finger on my thigh as the doors open and we walk out side by side. In the middle, Mum strides with natural authority. On her left, Ursula is all poise and coiled anger. As for me, I will kill anyone who tries to hurt either of them.

We reach the central surveillance chamber and walk in, staring around at the huge, empty space. Centria is unwatched, possibly for the first time.

The chamber is occupied, however. As the floor moves us towards them I see Jaeger and Harlan, Gethen and Ellery and Balatar Descarreaux.

Bal's back is pressed against a central column and Harlan leans casually beside him. Although they are the same height, Bal seems much smaller. He tries not to cower as blood from a wound in his forehead trickles down his face.

Jaeger stands further towards the far wall with his arms crossed, his unnerving gaze fixed on us. He and Harlan share an energy that makes them a potent double force.

Ellery stands further back again. As we approach she starts to walk towards us and then stops, uncertain. She rubs at the spot between her chest and left shoulder where the squad leader shot her.

Gethen paces and looks at the floor, his fearsome energy directed inwards now. He shakes his head, mutters and glances at Ellery, who ignores him. The love of a hundred years looks like it has come to an end.

The floor stops at the centre of the group. I meet Harlan's gaze briefly and then look at Bal. The wound is between his eyes; someone has ripped out his seed so he can't send any messages. He straightens to glare at me haughtily but swallows and looks down when he sees Ursula at my side.

"Jaeger," Mum says.

I turn away from Bal.

"Julie," Jaeger says.

"Why are you here?"

"There is something in Centria I must have," Jaeger says.

"What is that?"

"Keris Veitch," Jaeger says.

Gethen stops pacing and looks at Jaeger. Gethen's expression is strange. It's more than fear or even awe and I wonder how much of our current dilemma is the result of Gethen's unconscious desire just to see Jaeger again.

"You did have her," Ellery mutters to Jaeger. "You left."

"I had to go," Jaeger says. "I had to find a path. But I can't do it without her, not without what she knows."

"Why are we here Jaeger?" I ask.

"Julie is now Director of Security," Jaeger says. "She is infinitely more capable than Balatar here."

"Fuck you," Bal says.

Harlan looks at Bal, who cringes.

"Keris is somewhere in Centria," Jaeger says. "Julie will help me find her."

"No," Mum says, "I won't."

"I think you will Julie," Jaeger says. "There are five hundred of my people in Centria now, enough to cause significant damage should I wish it. I don't wish it but I must have Keris. Find her please."

"Keris is our leader Jaeger," Mum says. "You of all people should know-"

"Is she your leader Julie?" Jaeger says. "Are her decisions the right ones?"

His quiet, soft voice sounds as dangerous as the Sons of the Crystal Mind in their rage, perhaps more so.

"Who are you to question decisions Jaeger?" I ask. "You're a soldier."

Something deadly flickers in his eyes. Mum notices too.

"All right Jaeger," Mum says, "I'll check."

Mum closes her eyes, which makes her too vulnerable for my liking. I glance at Harlan, who looks worried. Gethen seems ill, as if the strain he's been carrying has finally bloomed in his flesh like a bruise. Beside him, Ellery generates a field of skittish, neurotic energy I can feel from here.

Mum opens her eyes.

"Keris is not in Centria," she says. "There is also no word from any of our associates."

"I fucking told you," Bal says.

"She must be here," Jaeger says. "She would never leave Centria."

"Look for yourself," Mum says. "I can give you access for up to five minutes."

"Do it please," Jaeger says, his politeness far more terrifying than Bal's aggression.

He shuts his eyes. Unlike Mum Jaeger doesn't look vulnerable, as if he can still see us. Frustration emanates from him; after less than a minute his eyes open and rage makes them impossible to meet.

"To complete our mission we need Keris Veitch," he says, his voice even quieter. "Why is she not here?" He turns to Bal. "Did you tell her?"

"No!" Bal says. He tries to slither away with his back still pressed against the column. "I-I didn't. I wouldn't. I mean, maybe, before Gethen came in and sold everything from under me one of the guards might have noticed something but not me, not me."

Bal is lying. He would have done as much damage as he could before they threw him out. Jaeger walks towards him.

"Now listen," Bal says, "I-I may have sent a small message, to-to see if there was something she could do about- Oh, look, I didn't know you were after her. I just wanted to do a good job, to serve her, to serve you, anyone really-"

He falls and Jaeger looms over him. I don't see Jaeger's expression but Bal does; he screams and gibbers and then suddenly calms down.

"I know how you can find Keris!" he says.

He points at me.

"Charity," he says.

I get my gun up to shoot Bal on level 1 but before I can fire Jaeger sees, turns and darts behind me almost too fast to see. He pins my arms against my sides in a grip that is part restraint, part embrace. His body feels like hot diamond. Mum and Ursula step forward but their movements compared to Jaeger's are ponderous and slow.

"I'm not going to hurt Charity," Jaeger says to Mum. "I just want to stop her shooting Bal. Stay where you are."

Mum stops but Ursula doesn't so Mum puts her arms around Ursula and yanks her back. Ursula gasps at the pressure on her tender skin as Bal scrambles to his feet.

"You," he says to Jaeger, "you," he points at Gethen, "you" he looks at Ellery, "Keris and eight others are a super race called the Guidance. You were meant to save us but you failed and we all ended up down here two hundred years ago.

"You can't breed but the scientist found a way to-to combine you, your DNA or something to make Charity in the floor. She's a Blank you see, which is why the Sons of the Crystal Mind wanted to burn the interfering little bitch."

Mum and Ursula stare at me open-mouthed, which makes them look almost identical. I feel my cheek twitch up in an embarrassed little smile.

Gethen falls to his knees, hands extended as if to reach for me and ward me off at the same time. Ellery turns on him.

"You threw her out," she screams and starts to hit Gethen. "You would have let her die!"

Gethen makes no move to defend himself and when blood soaks the shoulders of his grey jacket Ellery stops. For a moment Gethen stares at nothing and then he puts his battered face in his hands and sobs.

Jaeger gently turns me.

"Oh," he says, "oh…"

He looks down at me in wonder and runs his hands over my arms, shoulders and face. Tenderness is strange in him.

Harlan stares at me too, but he smiles. Not just any Blank indeed Mr Akintan.

Suddenly, Jaeger holds a fuze; I see it fire and hear Bal fall. When I look over, his dead body is already in the floor.

"Best we keep this to ourselves," Jaeger says.

I stare at him in shock. Loren will unleash all her forces to avenge Bal. VIA Holdings encircles Centria almost completely now…

"Keris," Jaeger says almost to himself.

I turn and Keris is there. Her hologram is slightly brighter in the dim light but otherwise she could be standing before us. She wears rich robes of scarlet and gold and her hair is a glimmering cascade.

"Hello Jaeger," she says. "You've got our girl I see."

"Mine," Mum says.

Keris and Jaeger ignore her. I notice then that Harlan is very tense and Gethen has stopped sobbing to stare at us. Ellery edges closer.

Jaeger's arms are back around me.

"Tell me what I want to know," he says.

"You know I won't do that."

"Not even now?" Jaeger says.

"There is so much more at stake than you and me or even Charity," Keris says.

"Quite," Jaeger says.

"I know you won't hurt her Jaeger."

"Won't I?"

Jaeger's hands are light on me but I know I wouldn't be able to struggle free before he snapped my neck.

Keris smiles.

"Jaeger, at the end of the Ruby War I stood in front of you and put a gun to my head," she says. "I told you I would pull the trigger unless you retreated and you went because you know we cannot destroy each other."

"Things have changed since then," Jaeger says.

"They haven't," Keris says.

"That's the problem Keris," Jaeger says, his voice rising. "You always stay the same! Despite everything, you will not let us evolve out of this!"

"Let Charity go Jaeger," Keris says.

I feel Jaeger's fuze at my head.

"Tell me," he says to Keris.

LIGHT-! Blinding

Burns- N-gunfire…

I am still alive. The pressures of Jaeger's arms and Jaeger's fuze have gone. I'm thrown sideways and land on my side.

"Run Charity!" Harlan's voice.

So I do. I don't think about anything except getting my legs to go as fast as they can, stretching my stride to make every push off the floor count. I remember Mum and Ursula and stop to look back just in time to see Jaeger rip Harlan's n-gun finger clean off. Harlan head butts Jaeger; Jaeger staggers back and Harlan jumps on top of him.

Behind them, Mum and Ursula run in the opposite direction and disappear through a door into an elevator. The hologram of Keris looks at me and then she is gone.

Jaeger kicks Harlan away despite Harlan's greater size. Gethen throws himself at Jaeger and clings to him. Jaeger, unfazed by the additional weight, pulls Gethen off and punches him in the mouth. Gethen staggers back. Harlan attacks from the other side and knocks Jaeger over. As Jaeger skids across the floor, Gethen rushes forward and stamps on his head.

Harlan looks up and sees me.

"RUN!" he roars.

I turn and sprint away from them.

Reaching the lobby I rush into the elevator and nearly hit the wall as I spin around. The doors close; I shiver as the elevator starts and imagine Jaeger scrabbling up behind me in pursuit. Soon Security Control is just a band of light in the distance again although I keep my wary gaze fixed on it until I'm down through the floor and into the main body of Centria.

43

The elevator opens onto a beautiful park, which seems abnormally peaceful after Security Control. I run out over the grass past tall spirals of plump white blossom and boulevards of precision-cut hedges studded with dark red roses like flung blood. As the park gives way to a sinuous diamond road I try not to think about Harlan fighting Jaeger.

My limbs are heavy; I wish I could rest for a moment or a year. Instead I pump more energy into my legs and gif a flybike ahead. As it comes to rest on the road surface I vault onto the saddle and key up. I fly behind the nearest building and rise towards the rotating assembly.

As I close in on one of the great hoops I see a square opening in the side. I fly through it, down a slope and into a hanger where I hover for a moment and then set down between a sleek plane and a rectangular sky bus.

My legs feel even heavier but I force myself off the flybike. I walk slowly through an arch to a deck in the out-facing wall. In front of the broad window is a semicircle of chairs; I sink into one and gaze numbly at the view. From in here the movement is less violent than I expected and the enclave seems to rotate with smooth, easy elegance. When I look up though I see the great shadowy slots in the ceiling and picture Jaeger dropping through towards me…

Mum calls and I jump. I accept and watch her on my eye screen.

"Charity! Where are you?"

"In the… swirly thing. Who else is there?"

"Ursula and Harlan," she says.

"Harlan? Is he all right?"

"Not really."

I call Harlan so I can talk to them both simultaneously. He accepts voice only.

"Thank you for saving me," I say.

"I couldn't risk him hurting you."

Harlan's voice sounds higher and thicker than usual. I recognise the sound of damage.

"Mum?"

"He'll be okay Charity."

"Harlan, why aren't you healing in the Basis?" I say.

"I can't," Harlan says. "My kilos are all gone."

"But you're richer than Centria!"

"I agreed my own terms with Jaeger a long time ago. He would teach me everything he knew but if I ever rebelled he would automatically get my wealth."

I shut my eyes tightly.

"You gave up everything to save me?"

"Yes. I love you, you see."

There is a very long pause. I go to speak but notice the call is terminated from Harlan's end.

"Harlan?" I say softly.

"He's passed out," Mum says.

"Can't you help him?"

"Yes, but he wanted to talk to you first."

"Where are you?" I say.

"At home. Ellery and Gethen are here too."

"What about the NFE?"

"They've all gone," Mum says.

"After everything Jaeger did to get in?"

"What he wants isn't here Charity."

"Has Keris come back?"

"No."

"Where is she?"

"We don't know," Mum says. "That Security Control transmission was the last we've heard from her."

"If only she and Dad were there."

"Come home sweetheart."

I end the call and new energy surges through me. I jump up, run to the hangar and climb onto the flybike. When the corridor faces Mum and Dad's house I squeeze the accelerator and the flybike leaps up the ramp and out.

I soar laughing over the glittering landscape as the bright cloud catches my flight in a beam of gold so powerful it seems to light my soul.

I found out what is wrong with Centria. I know who I am. Harlan loves me.

Ahead is the little island with Mum and Dad's house behind it. I swoop down to land in the garden, climb off the flybike and run inside.

Mum is halfway to the door; she grabs me and swings me around. Nearby, Ursula's smile is touched with sadness and when Mum lets go I walk up to my sister and put my arms around her waist. Unexpectedly she seizes me to her and I feel the strange warm pat of her tears on my hair.

Ursula holds me for a long time. I lock against her with my eyes closed but can still almost see her emotions as they swirl around me like magnetic fields. For the first time she feels like my sister rather than an embodiment of impossible beauty through whom I vicariously live my life. I feel her awkwardness and her confusion, her anger and her grief. She reminds me suddenly of Diamond City itself, with which I have such a confused and powerful relationship.

Ursula slowly lets go.

"Stay in reality," she whispers.

"Be subtle," I whisper back.

She strokes my hair as I wipe the tears from her face. Eventually, she looks down to her left at a large shadow in the floor. I let go of Ursula and kneel over Harlan.

"He'll be in there for a while," says a voice that seems strange in these surroundings.

I look at Gethen Karkarridan, who sits on the sofa next to Ellery. Gethen's left ear is half pulled off and one eye is obscured by swollen purple flesh. His right hand is at an odd angle and he holds it away from his body with the elbow resting awkwardly on one knee. Ellery says nothing, her eyes huge as they gaze at me with a potent mixture of wonder and fear.

I get up.

"So Gethen," I say. "What are you going to do now?"

He takes a deep, slightly rattling breath.

"I don't know," he says. "What do you think?"

"It depends," I say. "By rights you should be an ex by now."

There is a long pause.

"Unless of course we did away with that policy," I say. "Perhaps we could re-engage with exes out in Diamond City and make the best of their experience. Call it a new business model. Harlan could help."

Gethen looks at Harlan in the floor.

"Yes," he says, "Of course…"

"Hn," Ellery says.

Suddenly I need to be on my own. This new way of being mustn't be rushed.

"Can you all give me a minute?" I say.

I leave without waiting for a reply and cross the garden. The day lights dim and suffuse the air with soft amber light, which plays gorgeously over the plants as I gif a diamond bridge to the little island. Walking across I look over the side. The view is different to when I was a teenager but I get the same thrill imagining what would happen if I hung there by a fingertip, a hair, a thought…

I shiver with nervous pleasure and step over the little stream. The springy grass is a welcome change to the roads I've walked and I seem to drift across the island to the pool. I slowly sit and watch Centria's night lights begin to wink on, their luminescence rippling through the water like stars.

Another glow lights the pool surface. I smile when I see it and turn to a hologram of Keris. She smiles too, down past the soft curtains of her hair.

"Hello Charity," she says.

"Hello Keris."

"Are you all right?"

"Yes. Everything's fine. Everything's… better."

"Good."

I look at Keris and she regards me calmly, waiting.

"Keris, would you have let Jaeger shoot me?"

"He wasn't going to shoot you."

"I'm not so sure."

Keris looks out over Centria.

"I want you to have all of this one day Charity."

"All of…?"

"Centria. And everything that goes with it. When that happens you will understand."

"Understand what Keris?"

She thinks for a moment.

"The scale of everything," she says.

"I wish you were here."

"So do I. But it's too dangerous and not just for me."

"When will I see you again?"

"I don't know. Is that all right?"

"Yes. I really want to talk to you again soon though."

"You will my Golden Princess. Good night."

"Good night Keris."

Her hologram fades and I'm alone over Centria.

Perfection is possible because I feel it now: a fleeting, unexpected thing, tiny and vital like one of the microscopic machines that built this place; that built me. It can't last though; try and someone 'imperfect' gets pushed out. Instead it is a little milestone, like a girl on an island in the air with a strange journey behind her and a stranger one ahead, by a house full of loved ones and others with potential.

Whatever else happens I will always have this moment, when everything made sense. It takes my fear and changes it in a hidden flash to strength and certainty. I feel radiant with a joy and sureness I have never known. It will be my own source of cloud light amid the ever-moving fabric of my life, throwing brightness and shadow in equal measure on the astonishing landscape around me.

A breath catches in my throat. The darkening view blurs so I hear rather than see my first tear splash into the little pond. I start to cry but laugh as well because the tears are not born of grief but of love.

44

I head back across the bridge to Mum and Dad's garden. It's nearly full night and the lights in the house are on. I no longer want to be alone. I want to be with Mum and Ursula as we wait for Harlan to come out of the floor; I even want to see Gethen and Ellery.

Jaeger Darwin calls. I consider ignoring him because of the battering he gave Harlan; however, Jaeger is as much a part of me as Keris so I stop walking and accept the call. Jaeger appears as an image in the corner of my vision, superimposed over the almost unbearably alluring house. I wait for him to speak.

"Keris was right," he says eventually. "It seems I can't kill you any more than I could kill her or Gethen."

"You nearly murdered Harlan."

"He knew what would happen."

"What are you going to spend his money on?"

"Secrets," Jaeger says.

"What can I do for you?"

"Meet me outside Centria. There's something you must see."

"Must?"

"Yes."

"When?"

"Now."

"I'm…"

"You're not busy Charity and it won't take long."

I look past him at the house. I could just peek in, see everyone and then meet Jaeger but if I do I won't leave.

"All right," I say. "Where?"

"Just outside the main door."

I end the call and climb onto my flybike. The weariness has returned, as if I move through a narrowing tunnel of awareness. I'm going to need a long, slow rest after all this.

I key up and fly towards the main doorway. This evening seems particularly warm. I fly smooth and even, not too far off the ground but above the heads of people as they stroll below. Voices and laughter mix with the soft rush of air across my face.

Soon I leave the pathways behind and weave through great diamond buildings, their lit facades sheets and patchworks of thrilling colour. The buildings thin out as I head for the great door, which slowly opens for me.

Jaeger waits alone on the diamond road that leads to the train terminal and I slow down to land beside him. He wears his orange NFE uniform again and has no visible injuries despite Harlan's terrific assault.

"Thank you for coming," he says, his expression quietly quizzical as I get off the flybike.

"That's all right. We are… linked Jaeger. There's no reason we can't make the most of that."

"I agree Charity. I regret what happened with Harlan because his potential will never be realised, but terms are terms."

"I'm sorry you didn't find what you were looking for."

"Not yet," Jaeger says.

"Jaeger, Centria was bankrupt," I say. "There was no unlimited kilo supply."

"We'll see," Jaeger says.

"You're so obstinate."

"As are you."

I smile but Jaeger continues to regard me with that strange expression. I think about home, about Harlan and wonder why I never let myself have what I want; why there is always some other thing that must be done before I deserve it. If I just solve the mystery, if I just rescue Ursula, if I just prove that Harlan loves me before I will admit to myself that I love him and acquiesce in that roaring bright cascade…

"What was it you wanted to show me?" I say.

Jaeger looks over my shoulder and indicates with his chin. I turn and see the five hundred New Form Enterprise soldiers walk from behind Centria, dressed like Jaeger in their orange uniforms. As the NFE close in to surround me I look at Jaeger and then at the flybike.

It sinks into the floor without any decision from me and I watch stupidly as the Basis takes the vehicle apart. I try to go in-Aer for an explanation.

Nothing happens. My Aerac fades and the world is naked, as if I've lost part of my ability to see. I feel my head whip from side to side in uncontrolled panic.

"What…?" I stutter.

"Your terms are not discharged," Jaeger says.

"They are!"

"I was serious when I said I wanted you to join us. Now I know who you are there is no question."

"Jaeger, I got you and five hundred of the NFE into Centria at the place and time we agreed," I say, my voice rising to a shout.

"No," Jaeger says. "I sent one of the team back to MidZone."

And my heart feels like a vast empty diamond sphere.

"But…" I say.

No other words come because there are no other words.

"So Charity, you got me and four hundred and ninety-nine of the New Form Enterprise into Centria. You therefore broke the terms of our agreement."

I stare at the floor where the flybike was absorbed as if doing so will gif it again.

"I have had control of your Aerac since eleven o'clock this morning," Jaeger says.

I watch helplessly as my red and yellow jumpsuit dissolves off me into the floor. For a moment I am naked among these strangers and then a new suit grows up over me. It's orange.

Jaeger smiles.

"You are mine, Charity Freestone," he says.

The end
of
Sons of the Crystal Mind

Charity Freestone will return
in
The Outer Spheres

For more details please email aerac@diamondroads.com

Acknowledgements

Thanks to Mark Edwards for the kindling, Stewart McCure for the economics, Gary Smailes for the big bag of editing jewels and Debs Joyce for the beautiful cover.

Thanks also to Dad for a galaxy far far away, Mum for putting up with it and Emma for everything else.

Finally, thanks to Vicky for a fabulous today and Lana for all our tomorrows.

Printed in Great Britain
by Amazon.co.uk, Ltd.,
Marston Gate.